THE BODYGUARD

NORCROSS SECURITY #4

ANNA HACKETT

The Bodyguard

Published by Anna Hackett

Cover by Lana Pecherczyk

Cover image by Wander Aguiar

Edits by Tanya Saari

ISBN (ebook): 978-1-922414-25-0

ISBN (paperback): 978-1-922414-26-7

WHAT READERS ARE SAYING ABOUT ANNA'S ACTION ROMANCE

Heart of Eon - Romantic Book of the Year (Ruby) winner 2020

Cyborg - PRISM Award Winner 2019

Edge of Eon and Mission: Her Protection - Romantic Book of the Year (Ruby) finalists 2019

Unfathomed and Unmapped - Romantic Book of the Year (Ruby) finalists 2018

Unexplored – Romantic Book of the Year (Ruby) Novella Winner 2017

Return to Dark Earth – One of Library Journal's Best E-Original Books for 2015 and two-time SFR Galaxy Awards winner

At Star's End – One of Library Journal's Best E-Original Romances for 2014

The Phoenix Adventures – SFR Galaxy Award Winner for Most Fun New Series and "Why Isn't This a Movie?" Series

Beneath a Trojan Moon – SFR Galaxy Award Winner and RWAus Ella Award Winner

Hell Squad – SFR Galaxy Award for best Post-Apocalypse for Readers who don't like Post-Apocalypse

"Like Indiana Jones meets Star Wars. A treasure hunt with a steamy romance." – SFF Dragon, review of *Among Galactic Ruins*

"Action, danger, aliens, romance – yup, it's another great book from Anna Hackett!" – Book Gannet Reviews, review of *Hell Squad: Marcus*

Sign up for my VIP mailing list and get your *free box set* containing three action-packed romances.

Visit here to get started: www.annahackett.com

CHAPTER ONE

I can't wait to wrap my hands around your neck and squeeze. To watch you struggle, and see the fear in your eyes.

With a sniff, Princess Sofia of Caldova crumpled the note in her hands.

Her stalker wasn't particularly creative.

She leaned back in the plush seat of the private jet and threw the ball of paper like a mini basketball. It hit the rim of her empty water glass, bounced off the table, and rolled to the floor.

She looked out the window. San Francisco lay in the distance. They'd be landing soon. It had been a long flight from Caldova, with a stopover in New York to refuel. She'd be happy to get off the jet and stretch her legs.

She'd hoped to escape her stalker for the week and a half that she'd be in San Francisco. Unfortunately, the bastard had slipped a note into her bag. He was proving very industrious, and extremely annoying.

She rubbed her temple. She'd been born royal. She'd

grown up in the spotlight and was used to people being interested in her life, talking about her, and prying into her private affairs. But her stalker was starting to give her the creeps.

Her parents were worried, so they'd saddled her with extra security for this trip. She eyed the two Palace security guards at the front of the jet. It was their job to deliver her to her new bodyguard—Rome Nash.

Sofia's belly did a fluttering, sickening roll. Why, of all the men on the planet, did it have to be him?

Embarrassment filled her like hot, sticky goo. She'd first met Rome four months before, when he'd provided her security for a ball she'd attended in New York with her parents. He was former military, and worked for a private security firm in San Francisco.

The moment she'd first laid eyes on him, her body had malfunctioned. Even now, she remembered the hot ripple that had passed through her when he'd introduced himself.

She pressed her head back against the headrest. It took no effort to remember what he looked like, probably because she'd thought of him every day since. He was big. Tall, broad shoulders, long, powerful legs.

His dark hair was shaved close to his scalp, and his skin was a beautiful dark brown. Strong brows sat low over eyes that were a startling pale green.

He'd been with her the entire night, and when a crazed gunman had stormed the ballroom, Rome had carried her out, locked them in an office, and kept her safe.

Then she'd ruined it all by kissing him.

Embarrassment was a hot rope around her throat.

He hadn't kissed her back.

Sofia closed her eyes. After that, the police had arrived and she'd been swept away by her father's security team. She'd flown back to Caldova the next day. She remembered acutely the impassive, cool look on Rome's handsome face when she'd kissed him.

Not a flicker of interest.

So, he wasn't attracted to her. She got it. She wasn't attracted to every handsome man she saw.

She swallowed a groan. She hated that she'd humiliated herself, and no doubt embarrassed him.

Well, she was a princess, and pretty used to dealing with uncomfortable situations. She'd survive spending almost two weeks with Rome. She just needed to be professional and polite.

Besides, she had a very important job to do in San Francisco. She wasn't about to let anything, or anyone, distract her from it.

Her laptop resting on the table in front of her chimed. She opened it.

Her best friend's face filled the screen.

"Caroline!"

Her friend smiled and waved. Caro's golden hair was pulled up in a messy bun, and she looked tired. They'd met at university years ago, and after a spilled latte in the campus coffee shop, become fast friends.

"Sofie, you look wonderful," Caro said.

"As do you."

"Liar," Caro replied with a laugh.

"Are my godsons asleep?" Sofie asked.

"You mean your god-monsters? Hans is getting them settled. No doubt they're asking him to read story number ten."

Caro had adorable, energetic, two-year-old sons. Sofie spent as much time with them as she could.

"I'd prefer to be with you." Caro waved her hand in the air. "Wearing glamorous dresses, attending galas to celebrate exquisite jewelry collections, and having hot flings with sexy Americans."

Rome's rugged face filled Sofie's mind before she squashed the image. She smiled. She'd give her favorite tiara to have Caro's life. Hans was often away on business, but he loved his wife and sons. They had a gorgeous, sprawling home on the outskirts of the Caldovan capital.

And freedom. To be who they were, act as they pleased, and show their love.

Sofie shook off the burn in her stomach. She was healthy, wealthy, and privileged. She had nothing to be sad about.

She also had purpose.

Their other best friend from university, Victoria, had none of those options anymore.

Sofie's jaw tightened. Three years ago, after a vicious robbery and attack, Victoria had committed suicide. In the blink of an eye, a bright, wonderful woman had been gone.

"You're thinking of Tori."

At Caro's comment, Sofie blinked at the screen. Her friend was staring at her intently. Caro had always had the uncanny ability to read Sofie, even when she had on her best, expressionless, "princess" face.

"I miss her."

"Me, too," Caro said quietly.

Tori had been the outgoing, funny, life of the party in their trio.

Then, a gang of ruthless international thieves had targeted her. She was from a wealthy, aristocratic family, and Tori had owned an impressive collection of family jewels. The thieves had taken the gems, and two of them had brutally raped her.

Tori had been...shattered.

On top of that, her family had blamed her for the loss of the family heirlooms. Despite her boyfriend's support, she'd sunk into a dark depression, and Caroline and Sofie hadn't been able to pull her out of it. Several months after the attack, Tori had swallowed an entire bottle of sleeping pills.

"I wish..." Sofie wished a lot of things were different. Tori's absence had left a gnawing ache in Sofie's chest.

"I know," Caro said. "But Sofie, to honor her, we have to live."

Sofie nodded.

"I'm going to go hug my babies. And I want you to find a hot, American Hollywood star to have a fling with."

Sofie laughed.

"You're attending a star-studded gala, and of course, wearing some of my best jewelry designs. I'm sure you'll find a square-jawed hunk to give you wonderful orgasms."

Caro was a successful, highly-sought-after jewelry

designer all across Europe. Sofie's collection of jewelry was arriving separately under heavy guard.

"For a happily married woman, you sure have sex on the brain," Sofie noted dryly.

"When was the last time you had sex?" Caro demanded.

"Quit obsessing over my sex life. You know it's...difficult."

She had constant security, and the eyes of the press on her. The last time she'd had a man in her bed was when she'd dated a German diplomat. Martin had been... handsome, with impeccable manners. And very boring in bed.

Before that was her almost-fiancé, Prince Not-So-Charming. The self-absorbed, spoiled ass had cheated on her. Multiple times.

"Darling, I have twin toddlers," Caro said. "My sex life is nonexistent, so I'm hoping to live vicariously through yours."

Sofie rolled her eyes.

"Have a good time, that's all," Caro continued. "You're stalker-free for the next week and a half."

Sofie wrinkled her nose. "He slipped a note into my things."

Caro cursed.

"Don't fret, my parents organized additional security." Sofie wrinkled her nose again. "I'm picking up a big, stoic local bodyguard here in San Francisco."

"Good." Caro pressed her fingers to the screen. "Stay safe, look gorgeous, and have some hot sex."

"Off you go, you sex fiend."

Laughing, they ended the call.

The plane started descending and Sofie looked out the window. She had a perfect view of the city of San Francisco, the waters of the Bay, and the Golden Gate Bridge.

She had almost two weeks of interviews and photo shoots to help promote the Glittering Court: A Royal Jewelry Exhibition and Gala starting in just over a week. The exhibition would donate a large sum to her charity. She was also fitting in some work to support her charity.

In just a few moments, she'd have to put on her "princess" face. She'd smile, be polite, gracious.

The copilot appeared from the cockpit. "Your Highness, we'll be landing momentarily."

She nodded. "Thank you."

With a sigh, Sofie picked up the note she'd tossed on the floor earlier and stuck it in her bag. No doubt someone would want to see it.

She clicked her belt on, and focused herself to be ready for the onslaught. For the most part, she liked it. When little girls handed her flowers and asked about being a princess, it was fun. When she got the chance to talk about her charity and the work they did, she appreciated the attention.

But the paparazzi, hoping for topless shots of her, or catching her in a clinch, made her shudder. She sighed.

She had fairly thick skin. The tabloid stories could get pretty ridiculous. She was pretty sure that over the last year alone, she'd been secretly married to a sixty-eight-year-old Italian count, had a famous model's love child, and had been in a secret conspiracy with aliens.

She leaned back in her seat. What no one knew was her real reason for being in San Francisco.

She'd gotten information that the same jewelry gang—known to Interpol as the Black Fox gang—responsible for stealing Victoria's jewelry and raping her was planning to target the exhibition.

Or more specifically, they were planning to steal the Sapphire Wave Tiara. A long-lost tiara that had recently resurfaced, and had once belonged to the Romanovs of Russia. Sofie would be wearing it to the gala.

She tapped her nails on the armrests.

They wouldn't get the tiara. She planned to stop them.

Along with some help from the international jewel thief known as Robin Hood.

She smiled.

So, she'd do her royal duties, and when required, slip out from under the watchful eye of Rome Nash to get her real objective achieved.

The jet landed. Sofie pulled out a mirror and checked that her strawberry-blonde hair was tucked neatly into its French roll. She freshened her makeup, running some pink gloss across her lips. She flew so much that she knew all the tricks for looking fresh, even after a long flight.

Outside the window, she saw a crowd waiting for the plane. There were people with cameras, others holding flowers and signs.

Welcome to San Francisco, Princess Sofia.

There were also some giant, black SUVs, along with a long, black limo, and several men in suits. Rome would be there, somewhere.

A tiny tingle ran through her.

Stop it, Sofie.

The jet pulled to a stop. She rose and nodded at her father's security men.

"I'll see you back in Caldova."

They nodded. "Your Highness."

Sofia pulled her coat around her and fastened it. She pasted on her "princess" smile.

She heard the thud of heavy footsteps up the jet's stairs, and her belly contracted.

A man stepped into the jet.

Her heart stopped.

It seemed like he took up all the space.

Suddenly, the jet was gone, the guards were gone, the crowd outside was gone.

There was only *him*.

Rome wore a dark suit and he wore it well. It fitted him so that she could see the muscles in those strong thighs. She licked her lips and tasted her gloss. His white shirt strained over his chest.

He lifted his head and those gorgeous, pale-green eyes focused on her. She already knew that he was a man who missed nothing, not the smallest detail. He'd know how many people were in the crowd outside, all the vehicle registrations, and the quickest routes out of the airport.

"Princess Sofia." His voice was a deep rumble that she felt along every nerve, before sensation curled low in her belly.

The air rushed back into her lungs.

"Mr. Nash, a pleasure to see you again." She slung

her sleek bag with her laptop in it over her shoulder, not quite meeting his gaze. She kept her tone cool and professional. "Thank you for your assistance on my trip." She stepped closer, willing him to move.

"I wanted—"

"I'm sure we can discuss security issues once we get to where I'm staying." She shot him a cool, polite smile.

See, totally unaffected by you, and ignoring the fact that I threw myself at you and you didn't respond.

Her gaze met his for a second, and she forgot how to breathe.

Rome had a sense of strength. He was sure of himself, rock-solid. And he was devastating to a woman's senses.

She managed to shove past him and step into the sunshine.

Thank goodness. She could breathe again. The sun was shining, but the air was cool, and she was glad for her matching blue coat over her blue sheath dress.

Lifting a hand, she waved. She heard shouts and cheers from the crowd as she descended the steps.

She was careful to hold the railing. It paid to avoid the chance of an embarrassing tumble down the stairs.

Sofie had had more than enough self-induced embarrassment for one day.

ROME NASH FOLLOWED Princess Sofia of Caldova off the jet.

She stopped halfway down the steps, waving regally to the crowd.

She was doing a damn good job of pretending he didn't exist.

He ground his teeth together. She was beautiful, but he'd already known that. Her creamy, golden skin glowed, and her brown eyes glittered with an inner light. The sunshine lit her hair, turning it a unique shade of pink-gold.

She had perfect bone structure. She was elegant and refined, except for the fact that she had full lips that looked like they were made for sin. She wore a blue dress and coat that outlined a slender frame that had just the right amount of gentle curves in the right places.

She was a shock to the senses.

When he'd first met her in New York, he'd thought her beautiful but cool, a little icy, and boring. The press loved to call her the Ice Princess. But he'd spent nine hours and thirty-seven minutes with her that night, and he'd soon learned that while she had her public "princess" mode, there was a woman under the gloss. He'd caught glimpses of the real Sofia when she'd let her guard down.

When she wasn't all cool smiles, elegant glides, and polite chitchat, there was a smiling, friendly, energetic woman under it all. He'd heard her laugh, mutter sarcastic comments, and roll her eyes. He'd also caught her sneaking a hamburger before the ball.

No, Princess Sofia hadn't been what he'd expected.

And when she'd kissed him...

Rome's fingers curled into his palm. *Fuck.* That night, he'd come close to breaking all the rules a bodyguard had to follow.

In front of them, reporters and fans were shouting, cameras clicking. Rome was used to that. He'd provided security for lots of famous people.

The princess continued down the stairs. At the bottom step, her heel caught.

Rome shot forward and grabbed her arm.

It pushed his body up against hers. He heard her suck in a breath and his damn fingers tingled from touching her.

She steadied herself. "Thank you, Mr. Nash." She had a slight, crisp accent, her tone slick like glass. The princess talking to the peasant.

She waved to the crowd again. She had long, delicate fingers, and wore two rings. One was a large diamond, and the other was a twisted, complicated design. Funkier than he'd imagined would suit royalty.

Rome nodded and let her go. "If you'll come with me, I'll take you to your accommodation."

"Thank you, but I'd like to greet my fans first." She stepped onto the tarmac.

"Princess, you are going to follow my orders over the next week and a half. I'm in charge of your safety."

She stiffened. "I follow no one's orders, Mr. Nash." Big, brown eyes locked with his. Her gaze was firm, with a faint spark in the depths of it. "I will, of course, consider all your expert opinions on security matters."

Hmm, there was the real woman.

"I assume you can stand behind me, looking hulking and intimidating, and keep me safe from those little girls who have flowers to give me?"

He narrowed his gaze. Her tone was still polite, but

he was pretty sure that there was sarcasm hiding in there somewhere.

"Five minutes," he said.

She smiled. "There. A compromise. We'll work fine together, Mr. Nash."

Rome blinked. *Shit*. Her smile, her real one, was gorgeous. It brought her to life.

It wasn't the careful, polite smile she gave to the crowd. It was real, lighting up her beautiful face.

She walked ahead of him and he followed. His gaze traveled down her body.

Hell. She was slender, but she had a shapely ass. She wasn't tall, but she wasn't short, either, and a lot of her height was all leg.

The princess walked along the temporary barrier holding the crowd back. She waved and smiled, sharing a few words and accepting posies of flowers.

Rome followed silently behind her. He eyed the crowd. They weren't all kids or giggling teenagers. There were hard-eyed paparazzi, and several adults, as well.

"Princess Sofia!"

"You're so beautiful, Princess."

"Here, Princess. I love you!"

Sofia waved and smiled.

Rome dragged in some breaths. So, she was beautiful. He'd guarded beautiful women before.

But in the four months since he'd met her, he hadn't forgotten the feel of her pressed against him, the sensation of her lips on his, or the faint, tantalizing taste of her that she'd given him.

And since that night, he also hadn't been with

another woman. A fact he'd deliberately not examined too closely.

Princess Sofia of Caldova was strictly off-limits.

For the next two weeks, he would keep her safe. That was it.

Rome loved his job at Norcross Security. He loved the challenge of keeping his charges safe. Vander Norcross, his former Ghost Ops commander, was a good boss. Vander let Rome do his job and provided everything he needed. He also paid well.

After several years as a Navy SEAL, and then two years in Ghost Ops, doing the toughest missions of his career, Rome had been ready to stop being shot at. When Vander had offered him a job, Rome had jumped at it.

And he liked San Francisco. The only downside was that his mother and sister were on the other side of the country, but he kept an eye on them, visited them in Atlanta when he could, and they regularly visited him.

It had just been him, his mom, and his sisters since his dad took off when Rome was eight. It'd been rough, his mom working two jobs to support them. She'd depended on Rome to look out for his younger sisters.

Except he'd failed spectacularly. It'd been rough when they'd lost Lola.

Remembering his sister's death, an ugly sensation moved through him. He ground his teeth together.

Head in the game, Nash.

He needed to keep his new charge safe. Not rehash his worst failure.

He hadn't kept Lola safe, but he'd made a career out of protecting others.

Teenagers were pushing against the barrier, chanting the princess' name. Sofia smiled, but he saw it dim the more they shouted.

The fence scraped on the ground, pushing forward.

Rome looked up and saw a sweating man with a ball cap staring at the princess. Beside him were two middle-aged women, recording with their phones. Everyone was shoving forward.

Two little girls, maybe seven or eight, were handing the princess some flowers.

Rome took a step closer, and waved at some of the security guards.

Then the fence gave way.

The crowd surged forward. Princess Sofia's mouth moved, and he was pretty sure she'd cursed.

And the man in the ball cap lunged at Sofia, sunlight glinting off the knife in his hand.

Fuck. Rome charged into the fray.

CHAPTER TWO

"Get back!" Rome roared.

He shoved people out of his path. He had to get to Sofia.

Some assholes were still taking pictures. Rome pushed through. The princess had her arms around the two little girls, shielding them from the man with the knife.

The man slashed out, and Sofia shoved the girls back.

With a growl, Rome lunged. He rammed his arm down, hitting the man's forearm. There was a sharp crack, and the man let out a high-pitched yelp. The knife hit the ground.

Rome kicked the blade away, grabbed the man, and shoved him facedown on the tarmac. "Move and I'll break your neck."

The man went still.

Security guards rushed in, some controlling the crowd, while two sprinted toward Rome.

"Secure him and call the police," Rome ordered, spinning back to Sofia.

She was trying to console the crying girls. Her pink-gold hair had tumbled free, spilling around her shoulders.

"It's okay now. You're safe."

Not worried about her own safety. Two frightened women ran to the little girls.

"Thank you," one cried. "My baby."

As the mothers grabbed their daughters. Rome moved to Sofia, he saw her face was pale, her breathing fast. Not stopping to think, he scooped her into his arms. He pulled her tight against his chest and felt her burrow into him, one arm sliding across his shoulders. He heard her quick, shaky intakes of breath.

He jerked his head at the other guards. The men fell in behind him, blocking them off from the crowd.

Ahead, a limousine was waiting, the driver watching with a shocked expression. A worried assistant stood beside him, wringing her hands.

"Meet us at the house," Rome barked.

He bypassed the limo and strode to the black Norcross Security BMW X6 he'd driven.

He maneuvered her so he could open the back door of the SUV.

Sofia shook her head. "I want to sit in the front."

Her face was sheet-white, but she met his gaze. She was getting herself together.

Made of sterner stuff than he'd guessed.

"I hate sitting alone in the back like a self-important idiot," she said.

He nodded and circled the car. He put her in the passenger seat before heading for the driver's seat.

Once in, he gunned the engine and pulled out. He drove out of the airport, and once they were heading north to the city, he glanced her way.

Her hands were twisted in her lap. Her hair was falling in waves of pink-gold around her shoulders.

"You okay?" he asked.

She nodded. "Yes, thanks to you." She dragged in a deep breath. "I've grown up with this, and sometimes I forget the insanity of obsession." Her voice lowered. "They don't see me as a living, breathing person."

"Hey." He reached out and grabbed her hand.

He immediately regretted it.

She sucked in a sharp breath, and her fingers squeezed his. Rome felt a jolt through his body. Sofia must have felt it too, because she froze.

At least she had some color back in her cheeks now.

"I'm going to keep you safe, Princess. I promise."

She swallowed, then let his hand go. "Thank you, Mr. Nash."

"Rome. It'll be a long, few days if you keep calling me Mr. Nash."

She hesitated. "Rome."

She rolled it around, saying it with her slight accent. He liked hearing her use it.

Shit. His hands flexed on the wheel.

There was a smudge of red on his hand. He looked down at his shirt and saw a bigger smear. Every muscle in his body stretched tight.

"Princess, I have blood on me, and I'm not cut."

A shaky breath. "I think it's just a nick."

Rome cursed. She was *hurt*. Bleeding.

He yanked the wheel and took an exit. He sped down several streets before pulling off to park on a residential street lined with neat houses. He scanned around. At this time of day, it was quiet.

He climbed out, circled the SUV, and yanked open her door. His heart was hammering in his chest.

"Rome, really, it can wait until—"

He saw the blood stain on her dress, like an ugly flower. "Let me see."

"Um—"

He pressed a finger to her chin and tilted her face up. "Let me take care of you."

Sofia bit her lip and nodded. She waved at her side.

Rome pushed her coat open. He saw the slash in her dress on her right side. He probed it gently, even though his damn pulse was pounding hard.

"I can't see well enough." *Shit*. He eyed her dress. He didn't have a better option. He grabbed the hem and started pushing it up.

She sucked in a breath. "What are you doing? You can't—"

"I need to check how deep it is. I'm not letting you bleed out because you're shy."

Sofia looked out the windshield. "Fine."

He dragged the fabric up, revealing slim, toned legs. Heat ignited in his gut. *Shit*. He struggled to get a lock on it.

Asshole. She's hurt. Next, tiny panties the same blue shade as her dress made his breath catch in his throat. He moved on. Then, he finally had her hip uncovered.

The cut wasn't bad. Air whistled through his teeth. He carefully touched it and watched the muscles in her belly clench. Such delicious golden skin under her clothes. "Cut isn't bad. Won't need stiches."

"See, I told you."

"Here." He opened the glove box and pulled out a small first aid kit. He pulled out some gauze and pressed it to her side. "Hold that. When we get to the house, we'll need to clean it. No telling what germs were on that guy's knife."

She shuddered and pulled her dress back down.

Carefully, he pulled her belt back on.

Brown eyes met his. "Thanks, Rome."

He wanted to cup her cheek, but he made himself step back and nod. As he headed back to the driver's seat, he paused for a second to pull in some steadying breaths.

She was okay. And his unruly cock was going to have to learn that the princess was way out of his league, and way off-limits.

SOFIE WATCHED the buildings of San Francisco stream past. She was still a little shaky, but already felt better.

She'd be *fine*. The cut didn't need stitches. She'd learned very young to dust herself off and get on with things, thanks to her mother. Princess Emily was the most practical woman in the world, and Sofie adored her. And her father, Prince Nicholas, was a very proper prince, who'd taught her to focus on what she could control.

She glanced over at Rome.

His delicious cologne filled the vehicle. It had a woody undertone, with a hint of something that made her think of incense. She drank in his strong profile, and watched as he held the wheel in an easy, firm grip.

There was something sexy about watching a man drive with obvious skill.

She felt a lick of desire.

God, the man had just seen her underwear. Sofie quickly looked away. It wasn't done to be attracted to one's bodyguard, not at all. It definitely wasn't done to outrageously lust after the gorgeous man who'd scooped her up like she weighed nothing, and held her against his strong, hard body. A man who'd protected her.

She mentally rolled her eyes. *He was just doing his job, Sofie. And remember the last time you gave into this attraction.*

Shaking it off, she dragged in a breath. She didn't let too many people close. Rome Nash didn't know her, and she wouldn't get the chance to know him well. Her stomach clenched.

Finally, she spotted the familiar rotunda of the Palace of Fine Arts ahead. It was one of her favorite places to visit in the city.

Rome pulled the vehicle to a stop, and she looked up at the Marina-style house. She'd combed through rental listings and selected this one to be her home-away-from-home for her trip.

She loved it. It was painted a pale gray, with lots of

windows and Art Deco-like curves. She threw open the car door.

Rome joined her, lifting a hand to acknowledge several security guards near the house. He slipped his keys into his pocket, then slid an arm around her. “How’s your side?”

“It’s okay. Stings a little, but it’s tolerable.”

His scowl deepened. “We’ll take care of it inside. The team from Norcross came earlier. They’ve upgraded the security system, and I’ve planned out schedules for the exterior guards, who’ll patrol the grounds.”

She walked toward the door, trying to hide her grimace. Walking actually hurt a bit. “You sound unhappy, Rome.” She raised a brow. “Or do you always sound like that?”

He grunted. “I figured you’d be staying at a hotel, or a fancy penthouse.”

“Ah. Somewhere easy for you to secure.” She shrugged. “I like a place to feel like home.”

Suddenly, he stepped close and lifted her into his arms.

“I can walk!”

“I can see it hurts.” He opened the front door and strode in.

The man was way too observant. She felt a little spike of worry. How hard would it be to slip out when she needed to?

The house was gorgeous. The floors were a warm wood that instantly felt homey and welcoming. Out the main windows, there was a perfect view of the Palace of

Fine Arts rotunda. She felt like she could open the window and touch it.

He carried her straight into a stylishly decorated guest bedroom and set her on the bed. "I'll grab a first aid kit. You strip."

Sofie jolted. "Strip?"

He strode to the closet and pulled out a fluffy robe. "This will have to do until the limo arrives with your luggage. I'll be right back."

Well. Sofie straightened and winced. She quickly slipped her coat and dress off. She thumbed the slash in the dress before tossing it over a chair. She'd just wrapped herself in the robe when Rome reappeared.

Sofie's pulse did a crazy dance. He took up so much space, and somehow, that made her excruciatingly conscious of the fact that she was only wearing her bra and panties under the robe.

Perched on the edge of the bed, she watched him fish around in the big first aid box. He ripped open some antiseptic wipes and gestured.

Swallowing, she lay back and opened the bottom of the robe. The first touch of his hand made her jump.

"Sorry," he rumbled.

"No, I'm sorry. This must be...uncomfortable for you." Having to see her half naked.

She felt his gaze on her but didn't look. He kept wiping and she glanced at the mirror on the wall. Her belly tightened. All she could see was his dark head bent over her body.

Don't lust after your bodyguard. Don't lust after the man who isn't interested.

"I've seen injuries before," he said. "This doesn't bother me. I'm just pissed you got hurt. I shouldn't have let it happen."

"Rome, it wasn't your fault. I asked to greet the crowd, and we couldn't have guessed an unhinged, knife-wielding maniac would be there." She stilled and wondered if that guy was her stalker? No, she doubted it.

"It's my job to anticipate that." Rome cleaned her wound, fingers brushing her skin, making her stifle a moan.

His job. Of course. She was sitting here, breathing in his scent, weaving silly fantasies, but to him, she was just a job.

"Thank you again, Rome. I know this is beyond your job description."

"Hey." He gripped her chin. "I'm here, whatever you need."

If only. *Be an adult, Sofia.* "I want you to know that what happened in..." Goodness, this was much harder than she'd thought. "That what happened in New York won't happen again. I know you...are a professional, and it's clear you don't think of me that way. I'm sorry I ever put you in that situation."

Rome cocked his head. "What?"

Was he going to make her spell it out?

"I..." Ugh, this was horrible. "I won't make the mistake of letting things get personal. I get that I'm...not your type, and you aren't interested."

Rome carefully pressed a bandage on her wound. "Are you serious?"

She blinked. "Yes. I'm trying to clear the air, after

New York." Then the horrible thought hit her. God, what if he'd forgotten? Hadn't even thought about it or her? Nausea washed through her and she felt her cheeks burn. Sofie prayed for an earthquake, or maybe a crashing meteor, to hit and save her. "Just forget I said anything."

"You think I'm not attracted to you?" Rome said slowly.

She managed what she hoped looked like a smile. "You probably haven't given me a thought. Let's just... pretend I didn't say anything."

He gripped her chin again, forcing her to meet his gaze. A dark, intense look crossed his face, like he was fighting something. "Have you looked in the mirror?"

She made an annoyed sound. "I know what I look like."

Then his thumb stroked along her cheekbone. It ignited a whole slew of sensation inside her.

"Thought of you a lot, Princess Sofia. Especially wearing that sexy column of green silk you wore to the ball."

Her chest hitched. *Oh, God.*

She shifted and her robe gaped. It displayed the secret she kept well hidden—her navel piercing. Rome's gaze fell on her belly and the purple amethyst in her piercing, and he froze.

Oh. Her cheeks caught fire. She fumbled for the robe. What if he thought she was displaying herself on purpose?

He reached out as well, but when she moved, his hand fell on her skin, right above her piercing.

They both froze.

His fingers moved over her skin and she felt the sensation right between her legs. She stifled a moan. His big hand practically spanned her belly. She looked up and she saw heat in his green eyes.

She blinked. Terrified that she was imagining the desire.

"I'm not allowed to think of you that way." His voice was deep, harsh.

Her belly clenched. "Rome—"

"But I have."

Her mouth dropped open.

"Doesn't change the fact that I'm your bodyguard." He stepped back. "I have to be focused on your safety."

She tried to breathe, tried to talk. She managed a nod.

"I don't sleep with my charges. Ever." He straightened. "Air clear now?"

Sofie swallowed. "Um, no, I don't think it is."

His lips twitched, and his gaze roamed over her face. "You should take some painkillers."

She nodded. Her side stung, so she wasn't going to fight that. She closed the robe and tightened the belt firmly. She tried to ignore the heat in her belly.

"If it gets infected, let me know," he said.

She nodded again. She really needed a minute by herself, away from his overwhelming presence, to gather her thoughts.

Rome wanted her. Her heart did a giddy dance. But he wouldn't cross the line because he was her bodyguard. *Boo.*

"If you aren't too tired, I'd like to go over your schedule," he said.

Schedule? The man was giving her mental whiplash. "Okay."

"Get dressed, Princess. I'll meet you in the kitchen."

He strode out, and Sofie let out a huge, shaky breath. *What the hell had just happened?*

CHAPTER THREE

What the fuck was he doing?

Grinding his teeth together, he headed downstairs. He shoved his hands on his hips, then closed his eyes, and instantly he saw her, naked except for dark-blue panties, all slender limbs and golden skin.

Fuck.

And who would have guessed that Princess Sofia of Caldova had a belly button piercing? A sexy little gem that had begged him to touch it.

He growled. When she'd made that stumbling apology, cheeks pink, and eyes miserable, he hadn't been able to sit there and stay silent.

He should have. He should have kept his mouth shut and his hands off her.

He had no business imagining her naked, writhing under his hands. His jaw tightened. He had no business fantasizing about a princess destined to marry some wealthy, aristocratic prince, or duke.

No business wondering how she'd taste. What

sounds she'd make with his mouth on her skin. How tight she'd be when he sank his cock inside her.

Fuck, he wanted her.

Then Rome looked down and spotted the bloodstain on his shirt. *Sofia's blood*. She'd been under his charge for only minutes before she'd been hurt.

He knew better than anyone that taking your eyes off the situation for even just a second meant people could die.

He wasn't going to let anyone hurt Sofia.

Rome made his way to the guest room where he'd stashed his duffel bag earlier. He washed the blood off his hands and changed into a fresh shirt.

As he headed to the open-plan kitchen, his cell phone vibrated and he yanked it out. "Nash."

"Rome." Vander's deep voice. "Heard there was a problem at the airport."

"One attacker. Had a knife."

Vander cursed.

"Princess got nicked, but it isn't bad."

"Need a doctor?"

"She didn't want one. I cleaned it up. Police took the guy. I was about to call Hunt for an update."

Hunt was Detective Hunter Morgan. He was former Army, but when an injury had ended his military career, he'd joined the San Francisco PD. He was Norcross Security's main police contact, although Hunt spent a lot of time cursing them for making messes and giving him a headache.

"You need more support?" Vander asked.

"No. We're safe at her rental house now, and the

exterior guards are in place, along with the increased security system." Rome huffed out a breath. "But shit, I should never have let her get that close to the crowd."

"Let me guess, she talked you into it?"

"Yeah."

"She's fine, Rome, that's the main thing." Vander paused. "You read the brief from Prince Nicholas' head of security?"

Rome's gut tightened. "She has a stalker."

"So far, it's just threatening notes, but the guy knows her schedule. Let's hope he hasn't followed her Stateside."

Rome narrowed his gaze. Let the asshole come, and Rome would be happy to teach him a lesson.

"Stay sharp, Rome. Keep me updated."

"Yeah. Later, Vander."

A quick call to Hunt confirmed the man with a knife was just a local crazy with a deep hatred of anything royal. He claimed he was the long-lost love child of some British royal. He'd been arrested twice for causing problems when various royals had visited.

Rome needed to keep his head in the game...and not on a certain princess' sexy body and beautiful face.

He made a quick trip outside to organize for her suitcases to be brought in. Someone had retrieved her handbag as well. He also checked in with the team of exterior guards. He'd hand-picked them all himself, and set up their rotating schedule.

Back inside, he heard footsteps, and turned.

With a smile, Sofia walked into the bright, airy kitchen and living area. "Oh, this is even nicer than the photos." Her smile widened. "I'd love a house like this one."

She was still wrapped in the robe, but she'd tied her hair up in a messy knot on top of her head. No one looking at her right now would think she was a princess.

"What's your place like back in Caldova?" he asked.

"I live in the palace. I have my own apartment in one wing." A look crossed her face. "But I dream of a house like this, all of my own. Not big and palatial, not too small. Just right."

Rome eyed her. Funny that most people with normal houses would probably kill to live in a palace.

"My bag!" She took it from him. "Thank you." She set it on the coffee table.

"Your luggage is in the master bedroom upstairs. And I wanted to go over your schedule so I can ensure all your event security is arranged."

"A few things have been added to the itinerary since it was sent to you."

Rome grunted. He hated surprises.

She sat on the couch and wiggled into the soft cushions. She curled her legs under her and pulled out a sleek, silver laptop. He'd noticed that about her—outside, she was all polished and elegant, but behind closed doors she relaxed and enjoyed being comfortable.

"Here." She turned the screen to face him.

He sat beside her and her scent hit him—a subtle, floral fragrance that teased the senses. Ignoring it—or trying to—he focused on the screen.

He grunted. "You have a lot of interviews."

"To increase awareness of the Royal Jewelry Exhibition and Gala, which in turn, raises money for my charity."

"Charity?"

She nodded. "The Victoria Foundation. It supports domestic-violence victims. Mainly women, and often children, escaping terrible situations."

He eyed her for a second before he turned back to the screen. He kept reading, his scowl deepening. "Photo shoot?"

She nodded. "With the jewels. It's part of the promotion."

He released a breath. "Okay. Email me a copy, and I'll start working on the security logistics."

Nodding, she tapped the screen. "Done. I have some jewelry pieces with me, but the main pieces are arriving tomorrow with an escort."

He nodded. "That's all been arranged. We had a safe installed here. It's a new prototype from Rivera Tech that hasn't hit the market yet. A Riv3000."

"My father swears by Rivera safes."

"Any other surprises?" Rome asked.

She arched a blonde brow. "Did you expect me to just sit around, having baths and going to the spa?"

He crossed his arms, watching her with a narrow stare. "How about we talk about your stalker?"

Her nose wrinkled. "Not a pleasant subject to discuss on an empty stomach. I'm hungry." She rose and strode into the kitchen. "Let's eat, then you can pepper me with questions about crazy stalkers."

SOFIE LOVED the dark-gray granite countertops. Everything in the kitchen gleamed—the granite, the white cabinets, the appliances. It wasn't too sleek and modern, but it wasn't lacking anything, either. It was the kind of kitchen where hungry kids would sit at the island with their homework, and tired parents could share a glass of wine at the end of the day. She wanted one just like it.

"I can order you something," Rome said.

She opened the refrigerator. No, that was a cupboard. The next door was the built-in refrigerator. It was fully stocked, as she'd requested.

"No, I'll cook. Are you hungry? It's a little early for lunch, but I need to eat. It helps beat the jet lag."

"You cook?" he asked dubiously.

She arched a brow, pulling out the makings of a salad. She also pulled out some chicken to pan sear. "Yes, I can cook. Am I ruining all your fantasies about royalty?"

His green gaze met hers.

The word *fantasies* seemed to hang in the air between them, and she felt her skin flush.

Oh boy, how would she survive two weeks in close proximity with this man? Her insides were alive, like they were filled with butterflies. *No, Sofia Helena Elizabeth Marguerite, no lusting after your bodyguard.*

But he'd admitted that he was attracted to her, that he'd thought of her. Fantasized about her. She fought the urge to rub her thighs together.

"You don't need to cook for me," he said.

She shrugged and started fixing the salad.

"I was told you'd received some threatening notes," Rome said.

Sofie pulled a face. "Unfortunately, yes. It goes with the territory."

"Your Caldovan security team seemed concerned. I'd like to see the notes."

"I'll get palace security to send you copies." She dumped lettuce and other fixings in a bowl. She searched the large pot drawers and found a pan. Next, she poured in some olive oil into the pan, and started frying the chicken.

She turned and found Rome staring at her hand holding the wooden spoon.

"There's a note in my bag," she said.

His face changed, turning a little scary. He strode to her bag and yanked it open.

"Hey, you can't just dive into a woman's handbag uninvited."

He ignored her and pulled out the note.

He smoothed it out, read it, and unsurprisingly, scowled. His grumpy vibe filled the room, and she hid her smile. My goodness, he was a big, grumpy hunk of deliciousness. Why did she find that even more attractive?

He looked up at her. "This is more than just some threatening letters."

She scooped the cooked chicken out onto a plate to cool. Next, she pulled out a small bowl, and cracked an egg in, followed by more oil. She started whisking up the makings of a salad dressing from scratch. She hated store-bought dressings.

Besides, cooking calmed her.

"Yes, I have a weird stalker."

"Who wants to kill you."

Her heart skipped a beat. "You aren't going to let that happen, are you, Rome?"

His full lips flattened. "I'm taking this." He slipped the note into his pocket. "Your security back home get any prints off the notes?"

She shook her head. "They were unable to identify anything that narrowed down who the notes might come from."

"I'll see what my guys can do."

She served up two bowls of salad and eyed Rome's big frame. She put an extra serving of chicken on his. She pushed the bowl his way, then sat on a stool.

Rome eyed the salad like it was a live grenade.

"I promise I'm a decent cook. My mother taught me."

He still looked skeptical, but sat. "Your mother's a princess and she cooks, too?"

"She wasn't born a princess. She's Australian, and a commoner. You haven't heard the grand love story?"

He shook his head.

"My father was on a tour of Australia and met my mother at a local pub. Their gazes met across the room, and the rest is history. My mother is an open, friendly, gorgeous woman, and she helped my very proper, slightly stuffy father unbend. They love each other."

"And your mother gave up her life in Australia to move to Europe with your father?"

"Yes. She learned several languages, learned royal etiquette, and became beloved by the Caldovan people.

She's wonderful." Sofie ate some more salad. "Oh, I have one other thing to tell you."

Rome's shoulders stiffened.

"No more stalkers, murderers, or thieves, I promise." Well, that wasn't exactly the truth, but she wasn't going into that with him. "I have some visitors arriving after lunch."

Rome leaned back. "I figured you'd rest after your flight."

"And lie around like princesses do?" Her tone was sharp. "Maybe order some servants around, or get a massage?"

"I didn't say that."

Sofie sniffed. "I know. Sorry. I'm used to people making lots of assumptions about princesses." She chewed her chicken and swallowed. "It's a mother and daughter. My charity organized it. They won an afternoon tea with a princess. They're domestic-violence survivors." Sadness moved through her. "The woman lost her son. The father beat him to death. He was nine."

Rome's fingers clenched into a fist.

"The man's in jail, and the woman and her six-year-old daughter are safe now."

"With the help of your charity?"

She lifted her chin. "Yes."

He stayed silent, that x-ray gaze boring into her. "I'll sort out security for their visit."

"Thank you."

He tried his salad and grunted.

"What?" she asked.

"Guess I didn't think princesses could cook. This is good."

Sofie felt a flush of pride. "Thank you." She reached out to grab the salt shaker, just as Rome did the same thing. They ended up face to face, their mouths inches apart.

She sucked in a breath, sensation rippling through her.

Rome's gaze dropped to her lips.

"Rome—"

"Can't happen."

She swallowed. "Are you sure?"

He groaned. "Don't make this harder than it already is."

"You mean the situation...?"

"I mean the situation, but it applies to other things as well." His tone was dry.

Her gaze dropped to his lap and her eyes widened. There was a very distinct bulge in the front of his trousers. She licked her lips, heat coiling through her.

He groaned. "Sofia, if you don't stop staring at my cock, we're going to have a problem."

She gasped. She wanted a problem. She really, *really* wanted it.

His cell phone rang. Muttering a curse, he yanked it out. "Nash?" Pause. "Okay, I'll let her know." He ended the call. "Your guests are five minutes away, so you'd better get dressed."

She nodded and pulled in a shaky breath. *Duty called.*

ROME CHECKED HIS WATCH. Princess Sofia's guests were coming up the front path.

He glanced up the stairs. She'd gone up to change.

He was concerned about the stalker business. His instincts were itching. He planned to send the note, now in a Ziploc bag, to the Norcross Office to get analyzed. Vander used an outside lab that was brilliant.

Rome liked to consider all angles, and cross all his Ts and dot all his Is.

He heard the click of heels.

He turned and his gut clenched.

Sofia came down the stairs. Slim, black pants fitted her like a glove, and ended at her slender ankles. Her white shirt had a ruffle at the neck, and a narrow, black belt cinched around her waist.

She gave him one of those polite princess smiles, and was holding a box in her hands.

She didn't look like the same woman who'd easily moved around the kitchen in a robe. Or who had a naval piercing.

His phone pinged. It was a message from the outside guard. "Your guests are here."

The doorbell rang, and Sofia moved past him and pulled the door open.

A thin woman stood on the doorstep, her brown hair neatly tied back, and a nervous smile on her face. A small, blonde girl was clinging to her leg, wearing a pink dress.

"Hello," Sofia said. "You must be Ellen and Amanda."

"Oh, um, hi," the woman swallowed. "We've never met a princess before."

Sofia smiled and held out her hand. "I'm Princess Sofia of Caldova. I'm *so* pleased to meet you. Come in."

Both the woman and girl shot nervous glances at Rome. He was used to people looking at him. He was big, he was black, and he didn't have an easygoing, overly friendly countenance.

But he realized that this was something more than that.

"Oh, don't mind Rome," Sofia said. "He's a big teddy bear, and he protects people. He's my bodyguard."

Ellen and her daughter looked at him, eyes wide.

He pulled back in the doorway so he didn't make them nervous. He had no idea exactly what they'd been through, what they'd survived, but he guessed they'd been taught to be wary of big guys.

They settled in the living room. Sofia ducked out to the kitchen and came back with a tray of pink cupcakes.

"I had these especially ordered for us. Princesses love cupcakes."

"I love them too," the little girl said.

"Excellent. I've heard that you've both been very brave. I really wanted to meet you."

The girl's smile trembled and her mother managed a smile. Sofia grabbed Ellen's hand and she shared a look with the woman.

"I thought princesses wore tiaras," little Amanda whispered quietly.

"Well—" Sofia leaned forward. "You're right, but I

usually only wear them for special occasions. I have a very large collection."

The girl gasped. "Really?"

"Really." Sofia grabbed the box she'd brought down with her, set it in the center of the coffee table, and flicked open the lid.

Amanda's mouth dropped open.

Rome watched as Sofia lifted a gleaming tiara out of the box.

"This is one of my favorites. My grandfather gave it to my grandmother on their wedding day."

"It's so pretty." The girl reached a hand out.

"Amanda, no touching," her mother said quickly.

Sofia smiled. "I have a better idea. How about you wear it for your visit?" She gently settled it on the girl's head.

Amanda just giggled.

"Oh, it's too—" Ellen leaned forward.

"It's fine." Sofia adjusted the tiara. "It looks beautiful on you." She gestured to Ellen. "How about some photos?"

Ellen pulled a phone out of her handbag.

As they laughed together, and took some selfies, Sofia asked Amanda about school. Rome leaned against the wall and watched them.

He listened to Sofia laugh—a bright sound, unfeigned.

Who the hell was this woman? Once, he'd help guard some Spanish royalty. The woman hadn't spoken directly to him once, and there had been plenty of orders. No one was to touch her, or her things.

Sofia was letting a six-year-old wear a priceless, family heirloom with a ruby the size of an egg in the center.

Rome pulled out his phone and messaged Ace Olivera, the tech guru at Norcross Security.

You got the princess' itinerary?

Yes. Already putting together security briefs on location and players.

Thanks.

Heard your princess is a looker.

Yeah. They call her the Ice Princess.

But Rome knew that didn't apply. Not at all.

Ice melts, Rome.

He rolled his eyes.

She has a stalker.

Fuck.

I've got a note the asshole slipped into her bag. Can you send someone over to collect it? See if we can get anything off it.

On it.

Checking back into the living room, he saw Sofia had

Amanda in her lap. The little girl had tears glimmering in her eyes.

"I miss Jack. I don't know why daddy had to hurt him."

"I know, baby. Your daddy is very, very sick. And Jack will always be in your heart, no matter what."

It was like a kick to Rome's gut. He thought of Lola. His sister who would never grow any older.

"I lost my best friend Tori, only three years ago," Sofia said.

"She died?" the girl asked.

"Yes. Some bad men hurt her. But at night, when I look at the stars, if I see a bright one twinkle at me, I know it's Tori looking down."

"Mom, can we look at the stars? Can we see if we can spot Jack?"

"Sure thing, baby girl," Ellen said, voice thick.

Rome moved away from the living room, careful not to make any sound. He did a lap of the house and checked in with the exterior guards.

Who is this friend that Sofia had lost? He guessed even he had the stupid idea that princesses were shielded from life's worst hardships. But even royalty were just people.

When he returned, there was a knock at the front door. A security guard ready to show Ellen and Amanda out.

"It was so great to meet you." Sofia knelt to eye level with the girl. "You keep trying hard, and being brave. Remember on sad days, hug your mom. She gets sad, too. We all do."

"Thank you, Princess Sofia." Amanda gave Sofia a tight hug.

"Thank you so much." Ellen smiled. The woman was far more relaxed than when she'd first arrived. "Your charity saved our lives."

"No, *you* saved your lives," Sofia said. "But I am glad my charity could help ease the way."

Ellen smiled down at her beaming daughter. "She hasn't been this happy in a long time. Thank you again."

Sofia closed the door. Rome watched her slump against the wall.

"You all right?"

She jumped, pressing a hand to her chest. "Oh my gosh, Rome, make some more noise. No sneaking up on me."

He just watched her.

"I'm fine. Or I will be. It's just so sad, knowing what they've been through."

A cell phone rang.

"That's mine!" She ran past him.

In the kitchen, she was talking on the phone.

"Luis, you're an *angel*. I can't wait to see what you've put together for me." She placed a hand over the phone. "My local designer has dresses to bring over for my interviews and for the gala. I need to try them on. He's going to come over tomorrow morning."

"I have to check him out."

"He was on the original list."

"Name?" Rome pulled out his phone and opened the list.

"Luis Medrano."

Rome checked the list. Ace had run background checks on everyone. The man checked out. "Okay."

She sniffed. "Thank you. Luis wouldn't hurt a fly. He's likely to either cower at the sight of you…or ask you out."

Rome scowled, and Sofia smiled.

CHAPTER FOUR

Sofie stretched up, elongating her body, balancing in tree pose. There was nothing like morning yoga on a rooftop to get the blood flowing.

Her gaze rested on the Palace of Fine Arts and the man-made lagoon that enclosed it. *Stunning*. The sun was shining, the air was crisp. To the left she had a wonderful view of the city as well.

She loved San Francisco. She also loved Caldova, but it had much cooler, and often grayer weather. They had very short summers.

Winter was coming here in San Francisco, yet the sunshine was glorious.

She'd had a busy night researching all the gems and jewelry that would be on display at the exhibition. Families and museums from around the world were contributing. Everything would be on display at the Bently Reserve building in San Francisco's Financial District. The imposing structure had once been the Federal

Reserve Bank of San Francisco, but was now rented out for events and conferences.

Her mind was already whirling, making plans. The Black Fox gang had plenty of targets to choose from.

The biggest prize would be her Sapphire Wave tiara. She stretched a little more and smiled. But she wasn't letting them get that.

Sofie set her foot down, then leaned down into downward facing dog. Then she turned her head, and almost lost her balance.

Rome stood in the doorway to the terrace, staring at her.

Or more specifically, her ass.

For a fleeting second, what she saw on his face made her chest lock. Then he blinked, and his face was back to a rugged, impassive mask.

Sofie straightened.

"Good morning, Your Highness," he said. "I hope you slept well."

"I did, Rome. I thought I'd start my day with a little yoga."

His gaze dropped to her leggings before flicking back to meet hers.

"You're exposed out here. It would be better if you'd stand on this part of the roof." He pointed to another part of the terrace. "It's more protected."

With no view. "Protected from what? We're three stories up."

"Sniper."

She blinked. "I think my stalker's been pretty clear about being up close and personal to strangle the life out of me." She shivered. "I can't see him taking up sniping." Suddenly feeling a chill, she wrapped her arms around her middle

Rome moved closer. "Are you okay?"

She nodded. "I am taking the situation seriously. The notes creep me out."

Rome touched the end of her pony tail, before pulling his hand away. "It's sensible to feel some fear."

"I bet you're never afraid."

"Be stupid not to feel fear in some situations. I do feel it, but I use it. I'm trained to deal with it."

"From your time in the military?" She knew he'd been in some covert special forces team.

He nodded.

Sofie sucked in a breath and got a hit of his scent. He'd recently showered and she smelled fresh skin and soap. Along with that tantalizing cologne. She stepped closer.

"Sofia." His voice held a tight edge. "Don't look at me like that."

She swallowed. "I'm trying."

"Try harder."

"Then you shouldn't look so good, or smell so good."

He growled, his hand gripping her hip. "And you shouldn't wear leggings and a tiny top that leaves your belly bare. And that damn piercing."

Like magnets, they moved closer and she pressed her hands to his chest. God, the look in his eyes...it was a mix of anger and something else that took her breath away.

A shiver went through her, and he spun her so her back was pressed against the wall. She loved the way his big, strong body made her feel so small. Her pulse fluttered madly.

"Fuck," he muttered, his head lowering.

Then the distant squawk of a radio interrupted. They both froze. Down below, the murmur of some guards talking echoed in the morning air.

Sofie blinked and watched Rome morph back into her cool, protective bodyguard. He stepped away from her.

No. She heard the word echo in her head.

"We should head inside," he said.

"Are we just going to ignore what almost happened?" she asked.

"Yes."

She saw his hand flex, and for some reason that made her feel better.

"You do yoga every day?" he asked.

"Most days. I have a bag full of tips and tricks to avoid jet lag." She waved a hand. "That includes yoga."

"Next time, do it over there." He nodded to the protected spot on the terrace.

"Yes, sir." She saluted.

"That's a terrible salute."

She leaned down and rolled up her yoga mat. He held the door open for her.

"Your designer arrives in an hour."

She nodded as they descended the stairs. "I'm going to shower and change."

"I'll be in the living room. I want to work on the security for your upcoming interviews."

"Thanks, Rome."

Suddenly, Sofie missed a step and, with a cry, she fell.

Strong arms caught her, and she found herself yanked against a rock-hard chest. Everything in her flared to life. He was so big and hard, and smelled so good.

"Sorry, I'm not usually clumsy." Damn, her voice was breathless.

His arm flexed against her, then he quickly released her. She almost lost her balance again, and he reached out to steady her on the step.

"Go and shower. I'll let your designer in when he arrives."

Sofie stayed on the stairs, watching Rome walk away, and bit her lip.

It was official. She was totally in lust with her bodyguard. She hadn't known Rome Nash long, but she knew he was a professional who took his job seriously.

He'd fight this attraction between them. She sighed. She didn't think she'd get the chance to explore that big, intriguing body anytime soon.

She was surprised by the depth of the ache that thought generated.

She shook her head. She had a jewelry gala to attend, and jewelry thieves to outsmart.

Her plate was full. She had no time for a sexy, brooding bodyguard.

She continued down the stairs and headed to her bedroom. She was just finishing blow drying her hair when there was a knock at the bedroom door.

She turned her hair dryer off. "Come in."

Rome opened the door, scanned the room, then stepped back.

A short, slim, elegant man in fitted, white pants and a blue shirt rushed in.

Luis Medrano was lean, dark-haired, and handsome as sin. He was always filled with energy, looked stylish, and was quick to smile, or frown, depending on his mood. She never knew if he'd have a boyfriend, or girlfriend, or both when she visited him.

He held out his arms. "Darling, you look gorgeous, as always."

"As do you, Luis."

He kissed both her cheeks.

Rome reappeared, directing a man and woman pushing racks filled with clothes, mostly dresses.

"Over here, over here." Luis directed traffic.

Arms crossed, Rome watched from the doorway.

The assistants disappeared, then brought several bags in, dumping them on the bed. Rome even carried a few in himself.

"Thank you, big man," Luis said.

Behind Rome's back, Luis caught Sofie's gaze and pressed a hand to his chest and rolled his eyes to the ceiling.

She smiled. She couldn't blame Luis for his obvious appreciation one little bit.

Finally, the assistants finished arranging everything.

"Out." Luis shooed them. He looked at Rome. "Thanks again, big man." Luis paused. "I don't suppose you're gay or bisexual?"

"No," Rome said.

"Shame. Now go, I have a princess to make look beautiful."

Rome glanced at her and her toes curled. Then he strode out, closing the door behind him.

"Sofie, darling, that man is *fine*. He's fantasy-inducing, belly-clenching fine."

"I know."

Luis cocked a dark brow. "Do I detect some repressed burning desire?"

She couldn't help but smile. "He's rugged, big, and sexy, not to mention scowly and moody. Of course, I'm attracted."

"Did you see the size of his biceps?" Luis shivered.

"I did." And she'd felt them around her. They'd made her feel safe. "But he's my bodyguard."

Luis released a dramatic sigh. "So, off-limits?"

Her belly twisted and she nodded.

"Well, then, let's do something that's sure to cheer you up." He clasped his hands together. "Try on fabulous outfits that will achieve the impossible, and make you look even more beautiful than you already do."

Sofie smiled. "I like the sound of that idea."

"And..." Luis rushed over and dug through the bags. "I brought a very special something that you requested."

She smelled a delicious aroma, and saliva pooled in her mouth. "You are a wonderful, wonderful man."

Luis held up a Burger King bag. Sofie snatched it and tore the paper open, then pulled out the container of fries. Beneath them, she spotted the neatly wrapped Whopper.

"Don't get grease on me, darling."

"I'll save the Whopper for later. Let's try on some clothes. I need you to make me look like a million bucks."

"I'll make you look like *ten* million."

And maybe she could make a stoic, serious body-guard's mouth water a little bit.

ROME WAS SITTING at the kitchen island working on his laptop when the designer finally reappeared, two hours later.

How long did it take to try on dresses?

"Finished?" he asked.

Medrano jumped and slammed a hand to his chest. "For a big man, you are awfully quiet. Yes, we're finished, and she looks even more ravishing than she did before."

Rome didn't think that was possible, and he wasn't going anywhere near the word *ravishing* in relation to Sofia.

He followed Medrano to the front door.

The man spun. "Big man, do me a favor and take care of my girl. She deserves a little laughter."

Rome scowled. "I'm here to keep her safe."

"Keeping someone safe requires more than just guarding the body. You need to understand them, their light and shadows. All their hopes and secrets."

Secrets? What secrets did Sofia have?

The designer gave Rome another thorough once-over, sighed, then sailed out the door.

Rome wandered back, glancing at the stairs.

Sofia had a few phone interviews throughout the afternoon. Another hour passed, and she still hadn't appeared.

Their first off-site interview was tomorrow at the television station. He had everything prepped for security. She also had a photo shoot at City Hall, where she was going to pose with some of the jewels for the promotion of the gala. Sorting out security in such a public place had been a headache, but he'd finally gotten it all arranged.

When she still didn't come down, he went up to check on her.

Dead silence.

Rome felt a brush of sensation across the back of his neck. Was she napping?

"Princess Sofia?" No answer. He stopped at her bedroom door and knocked. "Princess?"

No answer.

But as he leaned closer, he heard noise. Movement.

He pulled the Glock from his holster and shoved through the door.

Then he froze.

Sofia froze as well—right in the middle of jumping on her giant bed.

She was in her yoga gear again, earbuds in her ears, and a half-eaten Whopper in one hand.

She eyed the gun, then pulled her earphone out of her ear. "Rome..." Pink flushed her cheeks. "I was just... um..." She pushed at some hair that had escaped the messy knot on the top of her head. "I guess you can't pretend you never saw this?"

He cocked a brow and slid his weapon away.

With a sigh, she bounced and dropped to sit on the edge of the bed.

"Well, I'll have you know that this giant bed has been

begging me to jump on it, and I love Whoppers. Luis snuck it in for me."

"Why didn't you just order it?"

"It's just not done. It doesn't fit with what everyone believes a princess should do, or eat." She smoothed her hand over the covers. "Nor does jumping on the bed."

"Like an excited kid." She was nothing like he'd expected.

"Can we keep it between us?" she asked, hopefully.

Rome nodded. "Princess, I'm here to keep you safe. I don't judge."

She nodded. "Just to keep me safe. Right."

He saw the faint flash of something in her eyes before she looked down.

He followed her gaze, and noticed her feet were bare. Damn, even her feet were beautiful. Her toenails were painted a soft pink.

No one looking at her now would think that the cool, haughty, ice princess who'd arrived off the jet yesterday was this woman. She looked like a college student.

"But if you want a Whopper," he said, "just say so. I'll order it and say it's for me."

Her head snapped up and she shot him a bright smile. "Thanks, Rome." She leaped up and hugged him.

He stiffened, his brain telling him to step back.

But she felt so good. Smelled so good. He slid an arm around her. There were so many contradicting pieces to Sofia of Caldova, and they were all too damn attractive.

She hugged him tighter and beamed up at him. "I also think it's time you call me Sofie. All my friends do."

Sofie. That suited her much, much better.

"I'm not sure it's appropriate," he forced himself to say. He also forced himself to let her go and step back.

Her smile dimmed, but she rolled her eyes. "People are always so worried about what's correct—" she did air quotes "—but I prefer to do what's right. How about Sofie behind closed doors, and Princess Sofia out there?" She jerked her head toward the window.

"Deal. I'm guessing you don't need lunch."

She patted her belly. "No."

"Then I want to go over the gala."

She wrinkled her nose. "Do you go over everything with a fine-tooth comb?"

"Yes."

They settled in at the kitchen island. She made them coffee.

"The gala's being held at Bently Reserve," he said.

"Yes. They're going to do up the grand Banking Hall to be dazzling. The space sounds incredible. Twenty-five-foot-tall Doric columns flank the room, and there's hand-painted travertine walls and Italian-marble floor tiles. Not to mention two stunning chandeliers. The jewelry will be displayed on the main floor and on the mezzanine level. Under bulletproof glass, of course. The jewelry pieces all have royal connections, and they'll have one real princess on hand."

Her smile dimmed a little. Rome guessed that being on display wasn't always appealing to her.

"Security for the gala will be tight," he said, "but I'm not taking any chances. I'll be by your side the entire time."

Sofia tilted her head. "You'll have to wear a tux."

"I have a tux."

She got a faraway look in her eyes. "Figures."

"Your first off-site interviews are tomorrow."

"Yes, a daytime TV talk show is first up. They sent a list of questions."

"I'll take you there in the morning." He looked down at the sheet. "And the jewelry shoot is in the afternoon at City Hall."

She nodded again.

"Okay. I think everything is set."

"Rome, can I ask a favor?"

He looked into those pretty, brown eyes. They could pull him in, and make him promise anything, if he wasn't careful. "Sure."

She leaned forward and made a praying gesture with her hands. "I *really* need some ice cream."

He wondered how she stayed so slim, packing away burgers and ice cream. "Isn't there some in the freezer?"

"Yes, but I really, really need ice cream from Mitchell's."

Mitchell's was a San Francisco institution. Rome stiffened. "No."

"*Please*."

"I need time to prepare. To scout the area—"

"We'll go incognito. I'll...wear a ball cap."

He was certain no one would expect Princess Sofia to be in yoga gear and a ball cap at an ice cream shop. Still...

"I don't think this is a good idea."

"Come on. You'll be with me, no one expects us to visit an ice cream shop. Plus, my stalker is far, far away."

Rome scowled. He'd prefer to keep her safe inside these walls.

She widened her eyes, stopping short of fluttering her lashes.

Fuck. He couldn't say no. "Fine."

"Yay." She leaped up.

"You'll stay by my side the entire time, and follow my orders."

"I'll do *anything* you ask."

As those words tipped off her lips, he froze. Their gazes meshed and Rome felt heat hit his gut.

He imagined being able to ask this woman to do anything he wanted.

Shit. "Get your shoes."

She nodded and hurried out. As she did, his gaze dropped to her perfect ass cupped by pale pink Lycra. He was sure those sweet curves would fit exactly in his palms.

Dammit to hell. He had to get a lock on this desire, or he was going to have to talk to Vander about getting reassigned.

His gut revolted at the thought. There was no one else he'd trust to keep her safe.

Dragging in a breath, he grabbed his keys and followed her.

CHAPTER FIVE

Sofie climbed out of Rome's SUV and smiled.

Mitchell's Ice Cream shop had a bright, striped awning, and a short line of people waiting to go in. The place was well known, and had been around since the 50s.

"Come on." She jogged toward the door.

"Slow down." He grabbed her arm. "We're undercover, remember?"

She nodded. She preferred going out without the fanfare. In her leggings and her light, zip-up sweater, no one would recognize her. She also had a ball cap pulled low over her face, with her hair tucked up inside.

She looked like any other California girl. The thought made her ridiculously happy.

Some young men walked past, jostling her. Rome pulled her close and wrapped an arm around her shoulders.

Her pulse tripped. It was like they were just a normal

couple. Sofia had never just wandered the streets with a man.

"Relax," he rumbled.

She swallowed. "I'm relaxed." She wrapped an arm around his waist.

"I'm not sure you know the meaning of the word."

"I'm going to get the avocado ice cream."

Rome's nose twitched. "Avocado ice cream?"

With a smile, she leaned into him. "Rome, it's *delicious*. You have to try it."

His lips quirked.

She grinned. "Oh, my God. You do smile."

His smile widened. "Yeah."

She felt like she'd won a prize. "It's a nice smile."

His gaze traced her face.

Her pulse sped up, and she struggled for some control. Then the line moved, and they stepped into the store.

Sofie looked at all the flavors, then ordered her avocado in a cone. Rome ordered Mexican chocolate.

"Chocolate." She shook her head.

"I'm traditional."

She licked her ice cream and moaned. When she opened her eyes, he was staring at her lips.

She sucked in a breath, and then his gaze moved to her eyes.

Heat pooled in her belly. "Rome—"

"You want any chocolate?" His voice was gruff.

She shook her head. "No, but you have to try the avocado." She swiped her finger through it and held up her hand.

She was sure he'd shake his head, but instead, his fingers wrapped around her wrist and pulled her hand to his mouth.

Oh. *God*. The flutters in her belly went wild.

He licked the ice cream off, his tongue touching the tip of her finger.

She felt that between her legs. "*Rome*." Her voice was a husky whisper.

"You're right. It's good." Flames danced in his eyes.

"Rome, I—" She dragged in a breath. "I really want to kiss you."

Her words broke the spell and his face shuttered. He stepped back, leaving her feeling bereft.

"This isn't happening. It *can't* happen."

All the fizzy feelings in her crashed to her feet. "I know."

"Sofia, I'm in charge of your safety. I can't afford to be distracted, or focused on other things."

"Right." She hated that her voice was shaky.

She heard him bite out a curse. "You're a beautiful woman..."

She winced.

He released a breath. "I mean it."

"I get it, Rome." She pulled all her embarrassment and disappointment into a tight ball in her belly. "Let's go, and just enjoy our ice cream."

She shoved out the door.

"Hey." He grabbed her arm. "Stay beside me." He pulled her close again.

Torture. Sofie wished he really wanted her close, not

just because she was his job. She licked her ice cream, but now it was tasteless.

"Rome?" a deep, throaty female voice said.

They both looked up.

Sofie's heart shriveled. A gorgeous African-American woman stood in front of them. She was nearly six feet tall, statuesque, with curves for days. She had a beautiful face, and shining, dark skin, topped with a head full of glorious, black curls.

She smiled at Rome like she'd just won the lottery.

"Tara," Rome said. "It's been a long time."

"Too long." Totally ignoring Sofie, the woman leaned in and kissed his cheek. Then she glanced at Sofie and blinked. "Oh, hi."

"Hello."

"Tara, this is a friend of mine." Rome paused. "Sam."

"Nice to meet you." Tara looked back at Rome. "You look great."

"You too." He glanced down at Sofie. "Tara is a private investigator."

So, beautiful, smart, *and* badass. Sharp pricks poked Sofie in the belly. The woman was gorgeous, vibrant.

Tara talked, mentioning some joint friends they shared. She put a hand on Rome's arm. They looked gorgeous together, and worked in similar businesses.

Sofie glanced away, feeling miserable.

She stared off into the distance. It was stupid to have even considered for a second that Rome would break the rules for her.

He could have this smiling, beautiful woman who could do whatever she wanted, whenever she wanted to.

Sofie was bound by the chains of duty and position, whether she liked it or not.

She usually never resented her royal status. Being part of the Caldovan royal family was a part of who she was. She loved serving her country and her people.

With the added mission of tracking down the people who'd hurt Tori, her life was full.

She realized her avocado ice cream was melting and she had no desire to eat it. Her throat felt like it was filled with sawdust.

"I'm just going to throw this in the trash." She pulled away from Rome.

She saw him frown at her half-eaten cone. She tossed it out. She just wanted to get back to the house and be alone.

She had work to do.

Turning, she saw Rome smiling at the tall, gorgeous Tara, just as the woman slipped her card into his pocket.

"Call me when you're free."

Ugh. Sofie pasted a smile on her face. "I'll wait in the car. It was a pleasure to meet you, Tara."

"Sam—" Rome reached for her, but Sofie dodged.

"Take your time," she told them.

She hurried to the SUV, taking a few deep breaths. It was so silly to weave fantasies about a man she barely knew.

A man who was being paid to be with her.

"Hey." Rome appeared, pressing her against the SUV. "What was that?"

"What was what?"

"Rushing off. You didn't finish the ice cream that you so desperately wanted."

She sighed. This wasn't his fault. She massaged her temple. "I'm just tired. I guess jet lag is hitting me after all."

He eyed her, and she got the impression he didn't believe her. She forced herself to meet his gaze.

"Okay," he said slowly. He bleeped the locks and opened her door.

She climbed in and stared out the window while he slid behind the steering wheel. She unzipped her sweater, toying with the zipper to keep her hands busy.

This was a good reminder that Sofie was here for more important things than parties and men.

She had a job to do.

She'd promised Victoria, standing over her grave, that she'd get justice for her friend.

The doors locked with a click, but Rome didn't start the SUV.

"Okay, now tell me what's going on?" he said.

She tensed. "Nothing. Can we just go?"

"No."

Sofie huffed out a breath. "I liked your girlfriend."

"Tara? She's not my girlfriend. She's the ex of an old military buddy."

Well, Tara was angling for some Rome in her life. "She's gorgeous. You guys suit." Sofie looked out the window.

"I'm not interested in Tara."

Sofie felt him eyeing her. She made an unconvinced sound.

Fingers gripped her chin and turned her to face him. "You jealous, Princess?"

She glared at him. "Are you enjoying this?"

"A little." He paused. "I haven't been interested in anyone else for several months now, because my head's been filled with a beautiful princess who's way out of my league."

Sofie gasped, then sucked in an unsteady breath. The air in the vehicle thickened.

"A princess who kissed me, and left me with the smallest taste of her. One that's been driving me fucking crazy."

Oh. *God.* Her pulse jittered. "You...didn't kiss me back. I was embarrassed. I thought—"

Rome sucked in a breath. "We should go."

She bit her lip and nodded. "That's the sensible thing to do."

"Yeah." But he didn't start the SUV.

"Rome—"

They both moved at the same time. Sofie practically leaped over the center console, but Rome's muscled arms were there, wrapping around her.

She saw the scorching hot glint in his eyes before his mouth crashed down on hers.

Oh.

Oh, boy.

One kiss wouldn't be enough.

Sofie leaned into him and moaned. Rome's tongue slid into her mouth, his hand cupping the back of her head. He was thorough, like he wanted to absorb every bit of her.

"You taste so good," he growled.

She scraped her hands over his short hair, trying to get closer. "Kiss me," she panted.

"I am."

"*More*."

His lips took hers, and the kiss deepened, sensations bombarding her. She felt like she was drowning and she never wanted to come up for air. A groan rumbled through him, thrilling her, and his arms tightened on her. Then he tore his mouth off hers, trailing lower down her neck.

Oh. She arched up. His lips traced along the neckline of her sports top. Her nipples were hard beads under the soft fabric. Desire was an insistent throb between her legs.

A car pulled in to park beside them and Rome lifted his head.

Sofie panted, her hands tightening on him. "Is this where you freak out and tell me this was a mistake?"

He sighed. His hand slid up her jaw, his thumb brushing her kiss-swollen lips. "It was a mistake, but I'm not sorry."

Thank God.

"But you aren't safe here, and I need to get you home. You have interview calls soon."

They stared at each other.

"Later...we'll talk," he said.

A little ball of warmth bloomed in her chest. "Talk. Okay."

He settled her back in her seat, and she zipped up her sweater and pulled her belt on.

She kept glancing his way. Desire made it hard to think. She desperately wanted to touch him again.

Suddenly, Rome reached out and turned up the radio. It was a news report.

"A daring jewelry heist in broad daylight today will leave the upcoming Glittering Court jewelry exhibition short some gems."

Sofie gasped. The words were like a bucket of cold water to the face.

They'd struck. The Black Fox gang had slunk out of the shadows. And while the jewels were being transported. So brazen.

She listened, gripping the edge of her seat.

"Sounds like some of your exhibition jewels are missing," Rome said.

"It's terrible," she said.

But her mind was already whirling.

She needed to get them back. Which meant sneaking out from under her bodyguard's watchful eye.

Guilt pricked at her. One, she hated lying to Rome. Two, she'd been so busy thinking about Rome, she'd forgotten about her work.

But it was time for Robin Hood to make an appearance in San Francisco.

BACK AT THE HOUSE, Rome purposely went outside to check with the guards.

He needed some space from Sofie. Before he dragged

her onto the closest flat surface, tore her clothes off, and fucked her.

"Dammit," he muttered.

He forced himself to study the garden and trees. They were a little too close to the Palace of Fine Arts for his liking. Too much open space, which made security harder.

His gaze narrowed and he looked back at the camera locations on the house. There was a small blind spot. He made a mental note to ask Ace to plug it.

He looked up. Sofie was upstairs somewhere and he wondered what she was doing.

The taste of her was still on his tongue. And he wanted more.

Rome's hands flexed.

Thankfully, the vibration of his cell phone interrupted his thoughts.

He saw who the caller was and smiled. "Hi, Mom."

"There's my boy. Would it kill you to call your mother more often?"

"I've been busy."

"Tell me you've met a good girl, and you're planning to get married and have babies."

Rome rolled his eyes. "Busy at work. Why don't you bug Liana to get married and have babies?"

"You're my firstborn." A gusty sigh. "You'll make a great daddy one day."

He felt pain under his ribs. He wasn't so sure. He hadn't taken good care of Lola.

"Has Vander got you working a job?" his mother asked.

"Yeah." He saw Sofie's shadow walk past a curtained window. "I'm the bodyguard for Princess Sofia of Caldova."

His mother gasped. "I've seen her in the magazines. Liana will lose her mind. That girl is royal crazy."

It was true. Liana had a thing for anything royal.

"We were thinking of coming for a visit soon," his mother continued. "Lia has some time off work coming up."

"I'd love to see you, Mom." His mother had retired, with Rome's help. He'd bought her a cute little house, and she kept busy volunteering at a local shelter.

The throaty roar of an engine caught his ear. A black motorcycle zoomed down the street and parked in front of the house. The rider pulled his helmet off, before swinging his muscular body off the bike.

"Mom, I've got to go. Vander just arrived."

"Okay, baby boy."

Rome mentally shook his head. It didn't matter that he was a grown man, who towered over her, he would always be her baby boy.

"Love you, Mom."

"Love you too, Rome."

He set the phone in his pocket as Vander sauntered up the path. The man had black hair, and a face that showed his Italian-American heritage. He kept his body as fit as he had when he'd been Rome's commander on their Ghost Ops team. Rome had never worked for a better man than Vander Norcross. The guy kept his fingers on the pulse of everything that happened in San

Francisco, and if there was a fight, Rome wanted Vander by his side.

"How are things?" his boss asked.

Rome just nodded. He decided to not tell Vander about the part about having his tongue in Sofie's mouth. "Fine. The princess is upstairs. I'm just about to message Ace about a blind spot in the cameras."

Vander's dark-blue gaze flicked up to study the cameras. "It's not big, but yeah, plug it."

"The princess has several engagements to promote the exhibition this week. I've got prelim security plans done."

"You know what's best. We ran the note from the stalker."

"That was fast."

"No prints, other than yours and hers. Paper's generic."

"Shit." Frustration hit Rome. "So, nothing."

Vander raised a brow. "I didn't say that. Let's go inside."

Vander had found something. Rome let them into the house.

"Nice place." Vander circled the kitchen and living area. No doubt cataloguing every window, door, and exit point. "Hell of a view." He stood with his hands on his hips, looking out at the rotunda.

"So, the note?" Rome prompted.

Vander turned. "Lab found a chemical on the paper. Something unique. It's used for preserving leather."

Rome frowned. "That's...weird."

"Right. Doesn't help us yet, but I'm hoping it might.

If we get any leads on the princess' stalker, this could help narrow it down."

Rome nodded. "Better than nothing. You hear that some jewelry earmarked for the exhibition was stolen?"

"Yeah. Pretty ballsy job."

"I got the sense Sofie wasn't surprised by the theft."

Vander cocked his head. "Sofie?"

Crap. "That's what she likes to be called."

"You think she's involved with the jewelry robbery?" Vander's brow creased.

"No, but I think she knows more than she's telling."

"Senses tingling, Rome?"

"Yeah."

Vander jerked his chin. "We both know it pays to listen to those senses."

It sure did. Too many times in the field, it had saved their lives.

Light footsteps sounded, moving fast. "Rome, tell me you want a smoothie. I'm going to—"

Sofie skidded to a halt and looked at Vander.

Relaxed, smiling Sofie turned into cool, polite Princess Sofia. "Hello. I didn't know we had a guest."

"Sofie, this is Vander Norcross."

"Oh." She relaxed a little. "Mr. Norcross, thank you. Rome's been fabulous."

Vander's gaze flicked between Rome and Sofia. "Call me Vander. It's a pleasure to provide your security. Rome's the best."

"And I prefer Sofie behind closed doors."

"I hope you have a good, safe stay while you're here in San Francisco."

There was a knock at the front door.

Rome frowned. The guards hadn't alerted him. "We weren't expecting anyone." He looked at Sofie. "Stay here."

He opened the front door and raised an eyebrow. "What are you doing here?"

Vander's older brother, Easton Norcross, stood behind a beautiful blonde in a long, fitted skirt in a bright red, and a fancy, white shirt.

"I couldn't stay away *any* longer," Harlow exclaimed. "Can I meet the princess?"

Easton tipped his head to the side. "Sorry, I held her off as long as I could."

"Come in." Rome opened the door wider.

Harlow was Easton's executive assistant. The pair had recently gotten together, after Harlow's father had landed himself in debt to some very bad people. Easton had stepped in to protect Harlow, and he'd taken the very short ride to being totally head over heels for Harlow.

The man would do anything for his woman.

Rome led them to the kitchen. "Sofia, you have some guests."

"Hey, Vander," Easton said.

"Easton, Harlow," Vander greeted them.

Sofia eyed the pair, then looked back at Vander. "So, I'm guessing that you two have to be related."

"Brothers," Vander said.

Easton held out a hand. "I'm Easton Norcross." He shook Sofie's hand.

"I've heard of you, Mr. Norcross. And I know that your company's donated to my charity, so thank you."

"Please, it's Easton. And this is my nosy woman, Harlow."

"Hi, it is *so* great to meet you." Harlow pumped Sofia's hand. "I've seen your picture so many times. You're the best-dressed royal, in my opinion."

"She has lots of opinions," Easton said dryly. "And a lot of clothes."

Sofia laughed. "Thank you." Then she looked down at her leggings and sweater. "Not today, though."

"I love your rings," Harlow said.

Sofie held out her hand, showing off her two silver rings. One had a pearl nestled in the center of it. "My best friend Caro is a jewelry designer. These are her work."

Harlow gasped. "Not Caroline Haller?"

"Yes."

"I love her designs."

Sofie smiled. "I can get you a sneak peek at her collection. They're going to be on display at the Glittering Court Jewelry Exhibition."

"Oh, I can't afford her gorgeous stuff," Harlow said.

From behind Harlow, Easton—an extremely successful billionaire—rolled his eyes. The man had a hard time getting Harlow to accept anything.

"I can get you a discount," Sofie said.

"I have a copy of the Young Royals calendar you were a part of," Harlow said.

Sofie pressed a hand to her cheek. "Really?"

"Calendar?" Rome asked.

Sofie's cheeks pinkened. "It was a few years ago, and for charity."

"I'll have to get you to sign it. That Givenchy dress you wore..." Harlow slapped a hand to her chest. "Magnificent."

"Harlow, we should get going," Easton said.

Harlow sighed. "Duty calls. My man is a tyrant at work."

Easton yanked Harlow close and kissed her.

Rome saw Sofie watching the pair, a wistful look on her face. His gut tightened.

"If you have time, let's do drinks," Harlow said. "And you need to meet Easton and Vander's sister, Gia, and her friend, Haven, who's also with the final Norcross brother, Rhys."

"I'd love that," Sofie said, smiling.

"I'll bring my calendar."

After Easton and Harlow left, Sofie glanced at Vander and Rome. "I'm feeling a little tired. I think I'll head up and read for a bit before my final interview calls for the day."

Rome frowned at her. She didn't look tired. "You okay?"

"Fine. Totally fine." She waved. "Bye, Vander."

"I'll head off, too," Vander said. "If I hear anything else on the note, I'll let you know."

Once Vander had gone, Rome did some work and messaged Ace about the blind spot in the cameras. Then he went to check on Sofia. She should have finished her calls by now.

With each step, he felt a little more tense. It was just the two of them now.

How the hell would he keep his hands off her?

He knocked on her bedroom door, but there was no answer. He quietly pushed the door open and his heart squeezed.

She was asleep on the bed.

She was on top of the covers, still in her leggings, but her shoes were kicked off on the floor. Her breathing was deep and even.

Jet lag must have caught up with her. He found a blanket draped over a chair and placed it over her.

She was so beautiful.

Fighting the urge to touch her, Rome left her to sleep.

CHAPTER SIX

Carefully, Sofie climbed out the ground floor window, trying not to make a sound.

She was dressed all in black—black leggings and long-sleeved shirt. Black cap and a black backpack on one shoulder.

She was focused and determined.

She had a job to do.

Guilt nipped at her. She'd pretended to fall asleep to avoid Rome. She sighed. She knew he was sleeping somewhere downstairs in a guest room.

Sofie had spent the last hour disconnecting this window's security sensor to ensure that it wouldn't show on the security system. She'd reactivate it when she returned.

She crouched near a tree and glanced at her Garmin Tactix Delta watch. The hands were luminous in the darkness. She needed to wait twenty seconds.

Locked in her room, she'd worked on her laptop. She'd run an encryption program that she'd paid a paranoid and brilliant Ukrainian hacker a small fortune for. It allowed her to anonymously surf the web, and send encrypted emails.

She dug up everything she could on the theft of the jewels today. It was definitely the Black Foxes.

Her belly clenched. *Bastards.*

After some clever hacking, even if she did say so herself, she'd tracked the car involved in the theft. They'd removed the license plates, but the sedan had a scratch on it.

That had led her to Dante Luzzago.

She'd suspected Dante was a member of the Black Fox gang for a long time. He was a smarmy, self-important asshole.

He'd rented a house in the waterside suburb of Seacliff.

And tonight, she was going to break in and steal back the jewelry.

A guard walked past and she held her breath, willing him to keep walking. She was getting ready to move, when she heard a deep rumble.

"Everything all right?"

Rome's voice made her freeze. Her pulse rabbited.

"All fine," the guard replied.

The men talked some more, her nerves stretching taut, then Rome finally headed back into the house.

She released a soundless breath. She waited, checked again, then sprinted through the minute blind spot in the cameras.

She hit the sidewalk in front of the house and fell into

a relaxed walk. Her pulse was fast, and she took a few breaths. *Just out for an evening stroll.*

She smiled, exhilaration filling her. Excitement hit her with every heartbeat.

This was an unconventional pastime for a princess, but she felt no guilt stealing from thieves.

For Tori.

She turned down a side street, and ahead, a blue Tesla was parked at the curb.

Perfect.

She'd arranged the car anonymously online. She glanced around, reached under the wheel well on the back passenger side, and found a magnetic key box.

She pulled out the key, bleeped the locks, and slid inside. She didn't use the car's GPS, but instead, used her burner phone to plug in the address she needed.

Sofie loved driving, but she so rarely got the chance. The Tesla was a beauty.

She navigated toward Seacliff, mentally preparing for the job ahead. She had to focus a little bit on the driving, though, since in Caldova they drove on the left-hand side of the road.

Robin Hood was about to strike.

This had all started two years ago. Still grieving for Tori, she'd been at a ball when a tiara had been stolen by the jewelry thieves.

Sofia had been in the right place at the right time. She'd seen the thief—he'd been one of the guests—with the stolen crown.

It'd been left on a desk for a second, and Sofia had stolen it back.

She'd left it for the owner to find.

The next robbery she heard about, she'd researched who could be responsible for the stolen gems. She'd planned out the job and stolen them back.

Robin Hood had been born.

The European press had gone nuts over the jewel thief who stole *back* stolen, priceless jewelry and returned it to museums or its owners.

Her first jobs had been messy and not well planned. She'd smartened up. She'd spent time training with palace security, and scoured various sources for information.

She'd met a retired French thief who'd taught her to pick locks and evaluate security systems, and she wasn't too bad at cracking a safe.

The world loved Robin Hood. The mysterious thief who returned stolen jewels and pointed authorities in the direction of several members of the jewelry gang.

Some had been arrested, some had wriggled off the charges, but not all.

Many were from the aristocracy of Europe—bored, spoiled men and women, a few who were desperate to reinvigorate their dwindling family wealth.

But the men responsible for attacking Tori were proving elusive.

Sofie kept a cool, slightly bored face in public that drew as little attention as possible. She needed to keep what Robin Hood did behind-the-scenes strictly secret.

Once she reached Seacliff, she parked the car several streets away from the house. She swung her backpack on her shoulder and power-walked toward Dante's rented house. She was just a woman out exercising.

After a few minutes, she spotted the house ahead. It was a little gaudy. It was painted a terracotta color with cream accents, and had delusions of being a Mediterranean mansion. She suspected it would have a million-dollar view out the back.

Pausing in the shadows, she lifted a set of binoculars. There was a guard at the front door, but none roving around that she could see. She'd already checked, and learned that the house had no dogs, and no window sensors on the top floor.

She scanned the upper level of the house. *There.*

Sofie smiled. A top floor window was open and she could see a sheer curtain fluttering in the breeze. There was a convenient tree right nearby.

She snuck closer, sticking to the shadows. She quickly scaled the stucco fence and dropped into a crouch on the other side.

She waited, hunkered down on the narrow strip of grass. There was no movement.

Sofie quickly reached the tree, and climbed upward. She was grateful her yoga kept her flexible and in good shape. With a quiet grunt, she edged out along one limb. There were several meters between the tree and the window, but she could make it. She leaped.

Sofie caught the window ledge with her gloved hands and peered over, using all her strength to hold herself.

The muscles in her arms burned. God, okay, maybe she needed to do some more yoga, or get to the gym.

The room was empty, and she climbed in through the window.

It was a bedroom. The king-size bed was a mess of tangled sheets. She heard water running in the adjoining bathroom.

Crap. She dropped to the floor on one side of the bed.

Footsteps. Carefully, she peered around the edge of the bed.

A tall, extremely thin woman in black lingerie emerged, wrapping a silky kimono around her body. Her long fall of black curls hit between her shoulder blades.

She stalked out of the room.

Sofie popped up. She quickly crossed the room and at the door, checked the hallway.

Empty.

She jogged down the corridor, counting the doors.

This one. She checked and found the door unlocked. She shook her head. Dante was careless, considering what he'd stolen.

It was unsurprising; he wasn't the smartest person she'd ever met.

Behind the door was an office. It was dominated by heavy, dark-wood furniture, and lots of shelves crammed with old books.

There was a simple metal lockbox resting in the center of the desk.

Sofia rolled her eyes. It took her three seconds to pick the lock. She flicked the lid open.

"*Hello*," she whispered.

Inside was nestled a necklace, earrings, and a matching bracelet.

She quickly opened her backpack.

She wrapped the jewels in a protective cloth, then pulled out a small makeup bag. It had a false bottom and she set them in place. On top rested a mess of makeup, tampons, and creams.

She slipped the case back in her backpack, then set a small card in the lockbox.

It had a picture of a bow and arrow in it.

Quickly, she headed out of the office. She needed to get back to the bedroom, climb out, and get gone.

She darted into the empty bedroom. She started climbing out the window, just as she heard angry voices heading closer to the room.

Shit. Sofie half fell out the window, gripping the ledge hard, her body slamming against the side of the house.

She peered over the ledge.

The thin woman entered, waving her arms around. Dante followed.

They were arguing, spitting Italian at each other.

Sofie bit her lip. She couldn't jump to the tree, or they might see or hear her.

Suddenly, Dante grabbed the woman roughly and threw her on the bed. He landed on top of her and they went at each other, tearing each other's clothes off.

Ew. Dante had a swarthy, handsome face, but a soft body from too much time spent partying and drinking. She had *no* desire to see it naked.

Sofie looked down. It was a longish drop, but there was a patch of grass below her.

Here goes...

She let go.

She hit the ground and bent her legs. She fell on her ass, hard.

Ouch. Wincing, she rubbed her hip and checked everything. Nothing broken, but she'd have some bruises.

She sprinted toward the fence and climbed over.

A second later, she was free and clear. She lifted her cell phone, pretending to talk to someone about looking for her missing dog.

When she slid into the Tesla, she grinned. As she headed out of Seacliff, she threw her head back and laughed.

She'd done it!

Exhilaration was a little addictive. She had to admit that she liked the thrill.

She had one quick stop to make—to deliver the jewelry back to its rightful owner—then she had to sneak back into her own house.

Sneaking out was harder than breaking into Dante's house, thanks to Rome.

She yawned. She really needed some sleep.

Sofie quickly delivered the jewels, leaving them on the back doorstep.

She left the Tesla parked a few blocks from her rental house, then she snuck past her guards, and climbed back into the house. She crept upstairs and made it into her bedroom.

Phew. Releasing a breath, she dumped her gear and stashed it under her bed.

After a quick shower, she was still feeling pumped. She looked at herself in the mirror and grinned.

She pulled on her sexy, silky, blue night gown. Perfect for a princess. It felt good on her skin.

Then she climbed into the big bed, nerves still shimmering with excitement.

She was all worked up and shifted restlessly on the sheets.

She imagined Rome's hands on her body, him caging her to the bed. She sucked in a breath. *Danger. Danger. Danger.*

But her mind wouldn't stop.

If he'd caught her, he'd have to punish her, right? Sofie closed her eyes and shivered. She let her hand drift down her body.

"Yes. *Rome.*" She arched. She bunched the nightgown up, then set her fingers between her legs.

She was already wet.

She stroked and moaned. When she pushed two fingers inside, she imagined it was Rome's hand.

Sofie came hard, biting her pillow.

Oh. *God.* Sucking in air, she fell on her back and stared at the ceiling.

It was sad that her own touch was as close as she'd get to Rome making love to her.

She punched the pillow. *Stop obsessing, Sofia.*

She closed her eyes and willed herself to go to sleep.

ROME LAY on his back in the guest room, the early morning light spilling through the cracks in the curtains.

He had one hand wrapped around his cock, pumping. His mind was filled with Sofie.

He groaned and imagined his mouth on her, between those slender legs. She wouldn't be cool with him. She'd be hot and sexy, all that passion spilling out.

He groaned, stroking faster.

Fuck.

With a roar, he exploded. He tugged hard, coming on his gut.

Sucking in a breath, he sank back on the pillows.

Damn. He wasn't supposed to be doing this. Picturing Sofie under him, taking his cock.

He scowled. He should consider having Vander replace him.

His gut rebelled. She was in danger, and he wouldn't entrust her safety to anybody else.

He released a breath, scrounged up some control, then rose. He needed to clean up and shower.

When he came downstairs, he heard Sofia clunking around in the kitchen. He stepped in to see her at the coffee machine.

Her back was to him, her slim body wrapped in a blue silk robe.

Shit. His cock throbbed and he ruthlessly locked down the reaction.

She turned. That strawberry-blonde hair was a tangled mess around a makeup-free face, and her eyes were still sleepy.

He'd never seen her look cuter.

"Good morning," he said.

She grunted and sipped her coffee.

His lips twitched and he took in the dark circles under her eyes. Apparently, princesses had bad mornings too. "Jet lag?"

She looked at him blankly, then blinked. "Yes. Jet lag." Her voice was still husky with sleep.

"You going to be awake for your interview this morning?"

She waved a hand and sipped more coffee.

"Well, you have an hour."

She nodded and flopped on the couch.

Slowly, as she drank more coffee, she started to show signs of life. She started going through a stack of mail that had arrived.

Suddenly, she froze, and let out a sharp gasp.

Rome strode over.

There was a letter tucked in between the envelopes. There was no postage, and just *Princess Sofia* written on the outside.

"It's from him?" Rome asked.

She pulled in a breath. "That's his handwriting."

Rome mentally cursed. He had to have a word with the exterior guards. They needed to make sure things like this didn't get through.

A spark of anger showed on her face. "How *dare* that bastard think that he can terrorize me." She set her coffee mug down on the coffee table with a click. She ripped the envelope open.

Rome grabbed her wrist. "Let me—"

"No!" She tossed her head back. "I'm not letting him make me cower."

Such inner strength. Rome nodded.

She read it and her face went white. "*Asshole.*" Her tone was broken.

Rome snatched the letter from her, then scooped her up. He sat on the couch with her on his lap. "Hold on."

She burrowed into him. "I...don't hold on. A princess lifts her chin, smiles, and deals."

"Today, you hold on." He tightened his arm around her. She was so small.

She sighed, and her breath puffed against the side of his neck. "I can't get used to this, because in just under two weeks you'll be gone."

He scowled over her head. The thought left a rock in his gut.

He flicked open the note with one hand and read the ugly words.

The asshole was escalating. Now he was detailing how he was going to rape and murder her. Frowning, Rome read the last line. *I'll leave you broken like Victoria.*

"Who's Victoria?"

Sofie let out a small noise. Her hands twisted in his shirt.

"Victoria Cavadini, one of my bestest, most beautiful friends."

He remembered her talking about the Tori she'd lost. "The Victoria Foundation?"

Sofie nodded. "I named it after her." She gripped his wrist, stroking his skin. He didn't think she even realized she was doing it. Her fingers were so small and delicate compared to his.

"She was so much fun. She used to elbow me when I was being too serious. She made me laugh."

"What happened?"

"Three years ago, she became the target of a gang of jewel thieves. Her family are Caldovan aristocracy, wealthy, with an amazing jewel collection second only to the Royal jewels." Sofie paused. "Tori was on a trip to Paris when they attacked her. They didn't just take the jewelry…two of them raped her. She never recovered. She didn't give herself enough time."

Rome heard the mixed emotions in her voice—fear, love, hate, anger.

He understood. He felt them, too. Every single day since the time a six-year-old Lola was snatched off the street by a predator.

It had been Rome's job to protect his baby sister, and he'd failed. "I know it hurts, beautiful. Hold on."

Sofie turned her face to his neck. He felt the tears on his skin.

"Tori took a bottle of sleeping pills."

He tightened his arms. He wanted to comfort her, to take away the pain. He rocked a little.

"Her poor boyfriend, Lorenz, was heartbroken. I was heartbroken," Sofie said quietly. "I started the charity to help other victims of violence. I couldn't help Tori, but I can help save others." She lifted her head and he saw her eyes were dry now. "That's why the jewelry exhibition is important. It raises money and awareness for the foundation."

"You're pretty incredible, Princess Sofia of Caldova."

Pink spots appeared on her cheeks. "Hardly. I'm doing what anyone with my resources and influence would do."

No. He'd met all kinds of wealthy people. He didn't believe that for a second.

She glanced at her watch and squeaked. "I need to get ready for the TV interview." She tried to scramble off him.

But Rome held her in place. Her robe parted, showing him a flash of slender leg. He noticed an ugly bruise on her knee. "What's this?"

She stilled. "Ah, I'm not sure."

He parted the silk a little more and he saw another bruise on her lower thigh.

"I must have got them doing yoga."

Rome's brows drew together. "I didn't see you fall, or bump into anything."

She waved a hand. "Maybe I bumped the dresser in my room. Yes, that was it."

He got the distinct impression she was lying to him.

"Interview." She leaped off his lap.

"Okay." His phone pinged. He grabbed it and read the message from Ace. His eyebrows rose. "Well, I have some good news for you."

She turned. "Oh?"

"The jewelry that was stolen, it was returned safely to its owner last night."

For a beat, Sofia's face didn't change. "That's great news." Then she smiled, although it didn't quite reach her eyes.

Rome was good at picking up little details, and he was quickly becoming an expert at reading Sofie. He frowned. Something was off.

"Truly, it's wonderful," she said. "I'm glad to hear it."

"It looks like it was the work of Robin Hood."

Sofie gasped. "The mysterious jewel thief?"

Rome grunted. He wasn't a big fan of people taking the law into their own hands.

"I'm just glad the jewelry is back safe and sound." She tightened the belt of her robe. "Now, I have to get ready or we'll be late."

"Takes a while to put the 'princess' mode on, huh?"

"It sure does." She raced up the stairs.

Rome slid his hands into his pockets. The woman was such a fascinating puzzle.

But he liked her relaxed and snuggled in his arms most of all.

He was in so much trouble.

CHAPTER SEVEN

Sofie pinned her smile in place and walked into the television station offices. She wore a lovely white dress with a blue pattern on it, and a thin blue belt at her waist. Luis had done an outstanding job selecting clothes she loved.

Rome was right behind her, with his bodyguard face front and center.

She leaned into him. "You know, if I have a princess face, it's nothing compared to your bodyguard face."

He shot her a look. "Behave."

"Princess Sofia, welcome," a voice said.

She took a deep breath and turned. There was a small group who made up her welcoming committee. A woman with a headset stepped forward with a smile.

"It's a pleasure to be here," Sofie said.

"I'm Gloria Mattson. We're thrilled to have you on *Good Morning, San Francisco.*"

"Thank you. I'm very excited to talk about the Glittering Court and my charity. And this is my bodyguard, Mr. Nash."

Gloria nodded and waved a hand. "This way."

They went up several floors in an elevator, and when the doors opened, she saw the studio. People bustled around, and cameras were lined up in front of the brightly lit set.

Rome stepped closer to Sofie, pressing a hand to her lower back. He scanned around.

"The lovely Princess Sofia," a deep, masculine voice drawled.

One of the hosts of the show, Matt Grable, stepped forward. He wore a sharp suit, and had a wide, perfect smile that had to make his dentist proud. Combined with his square jaw, brown hair, and dimples, he looked perfect for television.

He took Sofia's hand but didn't shake it, just held it. "You're even more beautiful in real life."

"Thank you." She saw the glint in his eye. A man used to women tumbling at his feet. She tugged her hand free, and gave him a cool, regal look.

"Princess, we have a private green room where you can wait, with snacks and refreshments," Gloria said.

Sofie inclined her head.

"Jenny, my co-host, and I are real pleased to have you on the show." Matt smiled again.

Rome steered her away. Gloria showed them to a green room with a large couch and small kitchenette.

"I'll come and get you when it's time. It won't be long. Makeup will be along shortly."

Sofia waited for the door to close behind the woman,

then dropped onto the couch. “Mr. Grable’s teeth were so white they almost blinded me.”

Rome grunted, but it sounded like he was hiding a laugh. He walked around the room, checking everything. “You like these sorts of things?”

“Interviews?” She shrugged. “Some are better than others. It’s a chance to increase awareness of the exhibition and the Victoria Foundation, so I take any inconvenience that comes with it.”

There was a knock at the door. Some makeup artists and a hairdresser arrived to touch-up Sofia’s face and hair.

After they’d left, there was another knock, and the door opened. Gloria’s head appeared. “Ready?”

Sofia rose. “Ready.”

They walked out. More lights were on, washing the set in bright light. There was a couch and two armchairs. The two hosts were being fitted with their mics.

“I’ll stand over there.” Rome pointed to the left of the set. “If you get worried about anything, you head there.”

“Thanks, Rome.”

“Go and kill it.”

His quiet support made her straighten.

As a technician fitted her with a mic, Jenny Jackson, the second host, strode over to meet her. She was an attractive African-American woman with her hair in a dark bob.

“A pleasure, Princess Sofia. Welcome.”

“Thank you.” Sofia settled on the couch.

“Ready?” Matt winked at her.

She kept her calm, serene smile in place, and nodded.

Cameras blinked on. The two hosts smiled.

"Good Morning, San Francisco," Matt boomed.

"I hope your day's off to a great start," Jenny followed.

The pair bantered, talking about some local topics of interest. They made some jokes.

"Well, we have a truly special guest today. Royalty right here in the studio." Matt waved a hand. "The beautiful Princess Sofia of Caldova."

Sofie smiled. She glanced to her right, but couldn't see Rome due to the bright lights. "Good morning. It's a pleasure to be visiting your gorgeous city."

They made small talk. The pair asked her about her favorite places in the city.

"But you're not just here on vacation," Jenny said.

"No. I'm here for a wonderful reason, one very close to my heart. The upcoming Glittering Court royal jewelry exhibition and gala."

"What woman could pass up the chance to see diamonds and famous gems?" Jenny said, with a smile.

"It's going to be entrancing." Sofie gave her practiced spiel on the exhibition. "The event launches with a special gala night in just a few days."

"I hear tickets are already sold out for that," Jenny said.

"Yes, but still plenty of tickets for the exhibition. The jewelry will be on display for several weeks."

"There will be lots of guests at the gala." A sly look covered Matt's face. "Will your former fiancé be there?"

Sofie stilled and fought back her annoyance. They'd been asked to stick to questions on the exhibition, not personal items or gossip. "I'm sorry, Matt, I've never been engaged."

"Prince Crispin."

"Oh, we were never engaged." She leaned forward. "I would've thought you knew this, being in television, but you shouldn't believe what you read in the tabloids."

Jenny stifled a laugh and Matt looked disgruntled.

Asshat. Sofie kept her smile in place.

"You were almost engaged to the prince, though, right?" Matt persisted. "Until he was caught in a compromising position with supermodel Paulina Rocco."

Sofie kept her cool, but she really wanted to punch him in his perfect teeth. "Our relationship had run its course. I wish Crispin very well. I don't believe he'll be at the gala, though." Sofie looked at the camera. "Remember, you don't need to be royalty to come and see the jewelry. The gala is sold out now, but please come to the jewelry exhibition and see the crowns, tiaras, even some cursed diamonds."

"It sounds amazing," Jenny said.

"And the proceeds go to the Victoria Foundation. A charity that helps victims of domestic violence."

Jenny nodded. "A very worthy cause."

The two hosts finished up the segment, and the cameras stopped.

"Thank you." Icily polite, Sofie rose. "I appreciate you talking about the exhibition." She pulled the mic off.

Matt smiled. "Princess, you know—"

Rome appeared. "Your Highness, we need to go."

"Hey, man, we were talking," Matt said.

Rome speared the man with a look. "You're done."

He swiveled and hustled Sofie back to the green room to collect their gear.

"You okay?" he murmured quietly.

She lifted her chin. "Yes, it comes with the territory."

"Sorry he dragged up your ex."

She shrugged. "Crispin was a mistake I clearly needed to learn from."

She'd fooled herself into thinking he really felt something for her, and had set aside his playboy ways to be with her. She'd believed that their shared background of being raised royal, of duty to their people, would be a good foundation for a relationship.

She snorted. It definitely hadn't been.

Grabbing her bag, she looked at Rome. "I wasn't engaged to him. Contrary to what the press says, I've never agreed to marry anyone."

Rome grunted. "None of my business."

Sofie swallowed. "But I'd like it to be."

He shot her a hot look. "Got everything?"

She lifted her bag, and he held the door open for her.

"Wait." She rummaged around in her bag. "My phone must have fallen out."

"I'll get it." He strode back into the room.

As Sofie stood in the hall, she felt a prickle along the back of her neck and turned.

The corridor was empty.

She looked back, but couldn't shake the feeling that someone was watching her. She glanced back into the waiting room, and saw Rome searching the cushions on the couch.

"Princess." A hand gripped her bicep.

She looked up and saw Matt. "Mr. Grable."

"Look, I hope there are no hard feelings. I was just doing my job out there. Giving our audience what they want."

Sofie fought not to roll her eyes. Chasing ratings, more like it. "It's fine."

Matt leaned in. "There's a new nightclub opening tonight. I'd love your company. I know you like that kind of thing."

She did not. Crispin had dragged her to several clubs during their short time together, and made sure they were photographed.

"I don't, and I'm very busy."

Matt reached for a strand of her hair. He rubbed it between his fingers. "You're very beautiful. I'd love to spend more time with you."

"Step back, Mr. Grable." She fought back her annoyance.

"Sofia—"

"That's Princess Sofia," she snapped.

"Back off." Rome appeared, pushing between them. "Don't touch her." With one hand to Grable's chest, he shoved the TV host back.

Matt almost lost his balance, but caught himself at the last second. "*Careful*. I was just being nice."

Rome just glared at the man.

Matt shifted nervously and straightened his jacket. "No one gives a fuck about jewelry. They just want to know who she's fucking."

Rome moved, lightning-fast. He punched the guy in the gut and Matt fell on his ass.

"Rome!" she cried.

"Stay back, Sofia." Rome advanced, towering over the TV host.

Matt scuttled back. "Not the face!"

"Touch her again, and I'll break your fingers. Your teeth will be next."

Rome took Sofia's arm and led her down the hall.

Her body felt electric. The way he protected her... She shivered.

An angry vibe was coming off him in waves.

"Wait." She tugged on his arm. He stopped, and she glanced over and spotted an empty office. She pulled him in and shut the door.

"What is it?" he asked.

"I just wanted to say thank you. For punching him." Her voice was a little breathless.

Then she went up on her toes and kissed him.

Rome made a deep sound in his throat. His arm wrapped around her, and he yanked her closer. His mouth opened.

Oh. *Goodness.*

He took control. The force of the kiss bent her head back. She slid her tongue against his and moaned.

He lifted her off her feet, holding her easily against his body, and making her realize just how much bigger he was than her.

And how that made her feel safe and protected.

Sadly, he broke the kiss, and set her on her feet.

Sofie licked her lips, waiting for her head to clear.

He tucked a strand of her hair behind her ear. "For the record, you're welcome."

She smiled.

"Sofie—" He sucked in a breath. "You should be with some prince. Some guy who can give you everything."

Her smile morphed into a scowl. "That's hogwash."

"You're a princess, you're meant to be in a palace."

She growled. "A prince like my ex, Crispin? Who cheated on me? Who dragged me to nightclub openings and parties I had no interest in attending? Who doesn't work, doesn't achieve anything, who just uses people, and goes on ski trips or rents yachts?"

Rome's lips flattened. "No, not like that."

"Being royal doesn't make someone special, or a good person, Rome."

He touched her jaw. "Okay, beautiful. I'm sorry."

"I don't want to hear any more about princes."

"Okay. Now, let's go. I've got just enough time to feed you some lunch before you have to be at the photo shoot."

ROME STAYED CLOSE to Sofia as they walked up the steps of City Hall.

The massive, grand building was a Beaux-Arts monument, with a long and varied history. They stepped inside. It was even grander than the outside, with marble everywhere. The magnificent, arched windows let in lots of light.

"Oh, it's stunning," she murmured.

Rome counted people on the mezzanine level above, along with lights and other photo shoot equipment. He also noted the Norcross guards stationed at the stairs leading up. One caught his eye and gave him a nod.

The jewelry for the shoot had already been brought here under heavy guard. Rome had planned out every detail of the security himself.

A woman jogged down the stairs toward them. "Princess Sofia."

The woman was tall, with long legs clad in dark jeans. She had an attractive face, with eyes that were different colors—one brown and one green. Her long, black hair was pulled back in a ponytail. A camera hung around her neck.

"Dani!" Sofie cried. "It is so lovely to see you again."

The women embraced.

Sofie stepped back. "This is Rome, my bodyguard. Rome, this is Dani Navarro Ward. A *brilliant* photographer." Sofie squeezed the woman's hand. "Thanks for doing this." Sofie looked back at Rome. "Dani is primarily a landscape photographer. She travels the world taking pictures of exotic, beautiful locations."

A man followed the woman down the stairs at a slower pace. Rome tensed. He recognized former military when he saw it. His gaze met the other man's blue one. This guy had been special forces, for sure. He had a rangy body, dark hair that was overdue for a cut, and scruff on his hard jaw.

Rome frowned. The guy looked familiar.

"Sofia, you've never met my husband. Cal, this is Princess Sofia of Caldova. Sofie, my hubby, Callum Ward."

"Nice to meet you, Callum."

"It's Cal, please."

"And this is Rome Nash, my bodyguard," Sofie said.

Rome straightened. "Ward? Treasure Hunter Security? You must be Declan's brother."

The man lifted his chin. "Yeah. Nash. You from Norcross Security?"

Rome nodded and shook the man's hand. "I know Dec. Good SEAL."

Callum smiled. "He was. Now he's running THS, keeping his wife happy, and spoiling his daughter."

"I've heard good things about Treasure Hunter Security."

"We keep busy. We're mostly all former SEALs. And I hear good things about Norcross."

Rome inclined his head. "We're mostly all former Ghost Ops. And we keep busy, too."

"If you badasses are finished communing," Dani said dryly, "we have photos to take."

Sofie shot Rome a smile, and headed up the stairs arm in arm with Dani.

At the top, Rome stayed to the side, watching carefully. He glanced down at the main floor. People were coming in and out of the main doors of City Hall. He would have preferred to shut off public access completely, but they didn't have that luxury. Still, he had guards stationed at all the entrances to the mezzanine level.

Sofie disappeared behind a large folding screen. Dani checked her cameras and equipment. An assistant brought things around for Sofia. Cal Ward perched on a large box, watching the comings and goings.

A fur rug was laid out on the stone floor—it was beige and fluffy. Dani set a silver umbrella thing by the rug, then fiddled with her camera.

One of the guards brought a heavy-duty case over. He clicked the locks and opened it.

Hell. Rome wasn't into jewelry, but these pieces were impressive.

There were diamonds—a lot of diamonds—and other jewels. There were earrings, necklaces and tiaras.

Behind the screen, he heard Sofie laughing with a hairstylist. A few minutes later, she stepped out.

Every muscle in Rome's body tensed.

She was wearing a black fur coat, although, knowing Sofie, it wasn't made of real fur.

Her hair was piled up with a plait circling her head. It vaguely made him think she was a winter Viking princess. It looked like she had no makeup on her face; her skin and lips were dewy, and her eyes were smoky.

"Here you go, Your Highness." An assistant held up a diamond-and-ruby necklace. The earrings were next, and Sofie carefully fastened them in her earlobes.

"Gorgeous," Dani breathed. "Okay, Sofie let's start over here against the railing."

Sofie moved over and leaned against the stone railing. She let the coat fall open.

She wore a column of silver underneath. The dress hugged her gentle curves and made her look like a glittering statue. The neckline dipped low, showing the creamy swells of her breasts. Rome squeezed his hands together, his knuckles tight.

She posed, looking into the camera.

Dani took some shots, then checked the screen. "Gorgeous." She took some more with Sofie smiling, frowning, looking away from the camera.

"Absolutely gorgeous," Dani said. "Let's change up the jewelry."

Next was a delicate-looking tiara, and some dangly, sparkling earrings that Rome knew must be diamonds.

Sofie ditched the coat and her shoes. They did some walking shots next, with her laughing, the light catching the jewelry.

"We have to hurry, Sofie," Dani said. "Storm clouds are moving in, so we'll lose the light soon."

"Okay."

The next shots of her, she was perched on a bench, the huge, arched windows behind her. This time, she had sapphires in her ears, at her wrists, and at her neckline.

She was so beautiful.

Rome knew her real beauty was within. That smile, her generosity, the way she thought of others, and still grieved for her lost friend.

Sofie was easy to be with. Rome didn't like loads of people close, up in his space. He liked his solitude.

He got on well with all his Norcross buddies, and he also liked the women that some of them had claimed. At least, he liked them in small doses, but they were all good women.

"Okay, let's get the last shot done." Dani clapped her hands.

Sofie was back behind the folding screen. She came out in the fur coat again.

She had diamond studs in her ears. Big ones. And a

necklace of pink-and-white diamonds draped around her neck. It looked stunning with her hair.

"Can you lie on the rug," Dani said.

Sofie dropped gracefully onto the fur rug. Dani arranged her.

"Hey, that's a nasty bruise on your leg," Dani said, her voice full of concern.

"Sorry," Sofie said. "I bumped something."

The photographer waved the makeup artist over. "No problem. It can be hidden."

Rome frowned. How the hell had she gotten the bruises?

When Dani and her assistant stepped back, he couldn't breathe, all his thoughts scattering. He felt like there was a rock on his chest.

Sofie was sprawled on her back. The fur coat covered a lot of her, but not all. Her shoulders were bare, as were the tops of her breasts, and he could see the necklace resting there, supposed to grab the eye, but all he saw was her skin.

Her slim legs were bare, resting on the fur. She looked like she'd been ravished by a warrior king, and left sprawled in the furs. What was she wearing under that coat? Was she naked?

"Beautiful." Dani moved around, the camera clicking. "So sexy, Sofie."

Sofie smiled—a mysterious half smile. Like a woman who knew a secret.

She shifted, tilting her head back and her gaze met Rome's.

"Perfect, Sofie. Imagine you're a queen, and your king will be back soon."

Her legs moved restlessly. Her glossy lips parted.

"Hmm, no, not your king," Dani said. "Your captain of the guard. Ready to do your bidding."

Rome saw need in Sofie's eyes. Desire was like a vicious punch to his gut.

He normally had rock-steady control. He liked women just fine, but he never kept any around long. And he'd never felt a desperate need for any of them.

But this one...

What he felt for her was a fucking inferno.

"Not sure you should be looking at your charge like that."

Rome barely controlled a jolt.

Damn, Callum Ward had snuck up on him. He didn't look at the former SEAL, but kept his gaze on Sofie and grunted. He didn't need the reminder.

Cal gave a low chuckle. "I fell for Dani on a job. We were in the middle of the Cambodian jungle, being chased by black-market antiquities thieves."

Now Rome looked at the man. Cal was watching his wife with a warm expression.

"Couldn't have stopped falling for her if I tried. Hell, I didn't want to try by the end. She's the best thing that ever happened to me." Cal's gaze met Rome's. "Protect your princess, Nash, and don't be an idiot."

Cal moved to help Dani with some equipment.

There was a boom of thunder from outside.

"That's a wrap," Dani called.

Applause broke out.

"Well done, Your Highness." Dani helped Sofie up.

Sofie pulled the coat around her and smiled. "You make it easy." She glanced at Rome, then disappeared behind the screen.

Helpless to stop the urge, Rome followed. He scanned the space, ensuring the guards were all in place and everything was in order.

When he paused at the screen, Sofie turned.

She was still clad in the fur coat.

He just stared at her.

"Rome."

"What's under that?" he said between gritted teeth.

She gave him a faint smile. "Not much."

"Fuck," he muttered.

"Did you like the jewelry?"

"Barely saw it. Your skin is prettier."

She flushed. "I like your skin better."

"Sofie—" Need pounded through his bloodstream. He was conscious of the people moving around on the other side of the screen.

She parted the coat a little and his gut tightened. His cock was as hard as a rock.

She wasn't wearing a bra, and he saw the inner curves of her breasts, her flat belly, the twinkle of her piercing, and tiny, gossamer panties in pale pink.

"Sofie," he breathed.

"I ache for you, Rome. So much."

With a growl, he stepped forward. He slipped an arm around her and pulled her close.

The coat opened more, those pretty breasts topped with pink nipples displayed to him.

The last of his restraint evaporated.

He cupped her breast, his thumb flicking over her nipple. It hardened for him. His hands were large, but her breast filled his palm just fine.

Sofie bit her lip and moaned softly.

"Damn you for being so beautiful," he growled.

"*Please.*" She arched her back.

He kissed her, feeling a deep, primitive need to stamp his ownership on her. He opened his mouth on hers, tongue thrusting deep. He was lost, and fuck, he didn't want to be found. He used his tongue to tease, taste, and stroke every part of her delectable mouth.

He dragged his lips down her neck, peppering her skin with kisses.

She shivered.

"I love when you do that," he said. "When your body shows me how much you want me."

She moaned, her nails biting into his shoulders.

Finally, he closed his mouth over one nipple.

"*Rome*," she panted.

Someone dropped something on the other side of the screen with a clatter.

"Crap, sorry," someone yelled out. "It's okay, I've got it."

Rome lifted his head. Sofie blinked, eyes dazed.

Hell. He had his mouth on a naked princess in the middle of a photo shoot.

"Get dressed." He set her down.

She blew out a breath. "Dressed?"

His lips twitched. "In clothes."

She grabbed the lapels of the fur coat. "I know what

it means, Rome Nash. Your kisses aren't *that* brain scrambling."

"Really? Do I need to kiss you again?"

Her brown gaze dropped to his lips. "Maybe?"

He rubbed his thumb along her jaw. "Later."

"You promise?"

His gut throbbed at the need in her voice. "Yes. Now get dressed, beautiful."

She nodded.

As he left her to change, more thunder sounded outside. Rain spattered against the windows.

Rome shoved his hands into the pockets of his pants.

It was time to admit that, right or wrong, he wanted Princess Sofia of Caldova.

And he wasn't going to let anything—not their roles, her stalker, or crazed fans—stop him from claiming her.

CHAPTER EIGHT

Rome kept his hands clamped on the wheel as he drove through the city, heading back to the Marina District.

Rain poured down, the sky a heavy gray, with clouds the color of bruises. The bad weather had cleared the streets, people taking cover.

"The photos from the shoot should turn out well," he said.

In the passenger seat, Sofie bounced a little and smiled. "They'll really help us raise awareness of the exhibition. The more people who buy tickets, the better."

He grunted. He hated the idea of anyone seeing the beautiful, sexy shots of her.

The song on the radio ended, and a news report started.

"Another jewelry robbery took place in San Francisco today," the announcer said.

"Oh, no." Sofie turned the volume up.

"A house in Nob Hill was firebombed, as thieves

targeted jewels that were scheduled for the Glittering Court exhibition," the newsreader said. "The jewelry exhibition is being spearheaded by Princess Sofia of Caldova. The thieves made off with a tiara, worth millions of dollars."

"*Bastards*," Sofie muttered.

Rome watched her sink back in her seat, her gaze turning inward. There was something working in that head of hers.

"You want to share what you're thinking?" he asked.

She shook herself. "Just thinking some very unkind thoughts about thieves."

"What about Robin Hood?"

"Robin Hood is excluded. He's a thief with honor."

Rome grunted.

She turned in her seat. "You don't admire the mysterious thief? Even a little?"

"He should leave it to the cops."

She arched a brow. "Do you always follow the letter of the law exactly?"

Rome's lips twitched. "No. Sometimes you have to color outside the lines to get a job done."

She nodded. "Exactly. Robin Hood returns stolen jewelry. I don't see anything wrong with that."

"Maybe your thief will get this tiara back, too."

She nibbled her lip. "I hope so."

Something in her voice made him narrow his gaze. "You know something about this theft?"

"What? *No*."

He was about to question her some more when movement in the rearview mirror caught his gaze.

A dirty, gray SUV was following them. The streets were pretty empty, thanks to the storm, but the SUV was staying right behind them.

Rome took the next turn.

The SUV followed.

He glanced over. Sofie's belt was on. Ahead, another SUV turned from a side street in front of them. It was the same gray, and make and model, as the one behind them.

Fuck. Boxed in.

Rome's focus narrowed. He had to keep Sofie safe.

He thumbed a button on the wheel. He felt Sofie glancing at him.

"Yeah." Vander's deep voice answered.

"It's Rome. I'm driving the princess back from City Hall, and we picked up some friends."

Sofie gasped, and looked back.

"Two gray Escalades have boxed us in."

"I've got your location," Vander said. "I'm on my way with Saxon and Rhys."

"I'll try to lose them. Weather's shit, Vander."

"Yeah. Lose them if you can, or stall them. See you soon."

Rain splattered against the windshield.

"Rome?" There was fear in her voice.

He reached over and squeezed her hand. "It's going to be okay."

"Really? It doesn't feel okay."

"Hold on and keep your head down."

He sped up. The Escalade ahead of them braked, while the one behind them accelerated.

Rome dodged around the one in front and yanked the wheel.

The X6 responded like a dream. It shot down the street, and ahead, traffic thickened a little, but he turned another corner.

"They're following," Sofie said, voice tense.

He sped down the street. Thankfully, this one was nearly empty.

The Escalade was right behind them. Rome braked hard, then jerked the wheel.

Sofie screamed. Their sleek SUV skidded on the wet road, and he whipped them through a 180-degree turn.

He stomped a foot on the accelerator, then they careened down the wrong side of the road, past the pursuing SUVs. Then he jerked them back to the right side of the road.

"Oh, my God!" Sofie pressed one hand to her chest, the other braced on the dash. She let out a laugh. "That was *incredible*."

Rome shook his head. He couldn't rattle his princess.

But they hadn't gone far when he saw the SUVs pull in behind them again.

Fuck. Where the hell were Vander and the others?

Rome turned again, then suddenly, a garbage truck pulled out of an alley, blocking the street.

He slammed on the brakes, the SUV skidding to a stop.

"Oh, no," Sofie said. "This isn't good."

"No." Rome gritted his teeth. *Come on, Vander*.

The two SUVs stopped behind them. Through the

driving rain, he watched the doors open, and several men get out.

They were all wearing black masks over their faces.

Shit.

Ahead, two men leaped out of the garbage truck. They wore masks, too.

Rome opened his door. "Stay here."

"Rome. You're outnumbered!"

"I don't think so. It'll be okay."

He'd deal with whoever the hell was trying to hurt her, and do whatever he needed to do.

The rain hit his face and immediately soaked into his jacket. The guys from the garbage truck reached him first. One was big and muscled, but it looked more for show. He'd be slow. The other was smaller and leaner.

Rome looked back and assessed. The other four guys were advancing slowly. No one had pulled any weapons.

He stayed silent, and saw the guys from the truck shift restlessly.

"The woman's coming with us," the big one said.

"No," Rome replied.

Over his mask, the man's brow creased. "There are six of us, and one of you."

Rome shrugged. "I don't care. She's not going anywhere with you."

The man beside the taller guy slammed his fist into his palm. "This should be fun."

The other four were hanging back for now, but the two from the truck advanced.

Rome just breathed slowly, and waited. The lean guy

moved in. Even with a mask on, Rome could tell the guy was grinning.

The man charged, fist swinging.

Rome sidestepped, and rammed his fist into the man's lower back. He yelped, and Rome whipped his elbow up into the guy's face.

With a crunch of a broken nose, he went down, hard. He made a gurgling noise.

The big guy tensed.

Rome just stared at him.

"Fuck you." The big guy lunged.

Two punches and a kick, and the guy hit the road and curled into a ball. Rome had been right. He was slow.

The rain intensified and Rome's clothes were drenched. He turned and saw Sofie's face through the window of the SUV.

The four men behind him advanced. One pulled a handgun.

Fucking hell. Rome wrenched open the X6 driver's-side door. Bullets pinged off metal, and he ducked down.

"Rome!" Sofie yelled.

"Come on." He pulled her out.

Bent over and curled around her body, he pulled her around the front of the SUV.

He scanned, hearing more gunshots. He spied the entrance to a narrow alley.

He gripped her face. "I need you to run."

Her eyes widened. "What?" Rain drops dripped down her cheeks.

He shoved his phone into her wet palm.

"Run. Don't look back. Call Vander."

"I can't leave you!"

"I won't let them hurt you." He kissed her hard.

A bullet shattered the windshield and she cried out.

Rome pulled his own weapon. "Go!"

She hesitated, then turned and ran.

Rome fired on the attackers, buying her some time.

SOFIE RAN, rain pelting down on her. She stumbled down an alley and came out on another street.

A car drove past, spraying her with water.

She looked back, and spotted the shadow of someone chasing her down the alley.

God.

She turned, running down the sidewalk. Her low heels and dress were not good for running.

Was Rome okay? It had been him against multiple attackers. Pain and worry twisted in her gut.

She tripped, and fell on her hands and knees.

Ow. She had to keep moving.

She heard the wet slap of footsteps running behind her. She had to get somewhere safe so she could call Vander, and get help for Rome.

Pushing up, she turned and started down another alley. The bulk of a dumpster appeared, and she ducked down behind it.

She heard someone pause at the entrance of the alley.

Heart pounding, she curled into a ball and didn't dare breathe.

Then, she heard whoever it was move off.

She shivered. Her dress was soaked and stuck to her skin. The white fabric was smeared with grime. She pushed her sodden hair off her face.

Carefully, Sofie peered around the dumpster. The ripe stench of rotting food was almost overwhelming. She couldn't see anyone through the sheets of rain.

She pulled out the phone, her hand shaking, and saw Vander was the first contact. She pressed it.

"Rome, we're almost there." Vander's voice was sharp.

"It's not Rome, it's Sofie."

"You okay, Sofie?"

She heard the sound of a gunning engine through the line.

"Rome—" her voice cracked. "He made me run. There were six of them. He took two down, but they had guns—"

"Calm down, Sofia. Easy."

Panic was slick in her veins. "They were shooting at him, Vander."

"Don't worry about Rome. He can handle himself. Let's worry about you. Leave the phone on. I'm going to send someone to your location."

"All right. But you need to help Rome."

"Hang tight, Princess."

She swallowed. "You promise you'll help Rome?"

"We're almost to him. Keep your head down."

"Okay, Vander." She sank back against the brick wall.

Then she heard a scrape.

She froze.

Oh, God. Her heart lodged in her throat.

A big body loomed over her.

"There you are." The man grabbed at her.

Fear driving her, Sofie threw herself sideways and scrambled to her feet.

The man lunged, and Sofie spun and ran deeper into the alley. She kept her hand clenched on the phone.

Soon she was panting, running as fast as she could.

"There's nowhere to go, Princess." Hard arms wrapped around her from behind and lifted her off her feet.

She kicked and jerked. "Let me go!"

"Nope." He shook her. "We want that sparkly tiara and you're gonna help us get it."

"Not happening," she yelled. "You'll regret this."

"If you think that big bodyguard of yours will help you, he ain't coming."

The words were like a punch to her gut.

Anger welled, growing into a horrible churn. *They'd hurt Rome.*

Her brain shied away from the thought. She lifted her legs, then kicked at her attacker.

He grunted and stumbled.

Sofie grabbed his hair and yanked.

"Bitch!"

She scratched at his face, thinking of Tori. Thinking of Rome. She dislodged his mask, shoving it over his eyes. She raked her nails down his cheek.

He roared and dropped her.

Sofie ran.

She pumped her arms and legs. She'd lost her shoes, and sharp things pricked at her feet.

She didn't stop.

The rain was still falling, and there was another crack of thunder that made her jolt.

She wasn't stopping.

She wasn't giving up.

She had a life to live, and a man she was totally entranced by. She wouldn't let anyone jeopardize that.

Sofie spilled out of the alley and turned left.

Where the hell was everyone? The driving rain was keeping people off the sidewalk.

She heard the man coming after her.

Her chest was burning, a sob welling in her throat.

The man was gaining on her. His heavy, wet footsteps were getting closer.

A hand sank into her hair.

Ow. Ow. Tears pricked her eyes, and the sting in her scalp was horrible. She turned and rammed her fingers into his eyes.

He slapped at her, the blow catching her chest and sending her stumbling backward. The phone flew out of her hand. *No.*

Sofie caught herself, spun, and ran again.

And rammed into a hard chest.

"You okay, Princess?"

Oh no. Not another one.

She looked up. Blinked.

The tall man wore a suit, and even wet, he was smoking hot. She thought his hair was light brown, but it was hard to tell in the rain. It was well cut around a handsome, aristocratic face, and gorgeous green eyes.

"I'm Saxon Buchanan. From Norcross."

Relief punched through her. "I'm okay."

With a nod, Saxon pushed her behind him.

"Fuck off, asshole," her attacker growled. "This is none of your business."

Saxon cocked his head. "It's very much my business. You get off knocking women around?"

The man lifted his hand, fingers curling into a fist. "I said, fuck off."

"I don't think so," Saxon drawled. He sounded like he was having a polite conversation at a party.

The man advanced.

Sofie sucked in a breath.

Then Saxon *moved*.

He slammed several blows into her attacker.

Wow. He looked...almost elegant. He whirled, planted a kick in the man's gut. The guy groaned.

Saxon followed through with two punches, then a vicious chop to the back of the man's neck.

Her attacker dropped to the wet sidewalk, tried to pull himself up, then flopped down.

Saxon pulled something from his pocket, then tied the man's hands behind his back.

Sofie shivered. She was cold. Nervous energy jittered through her body.

"You're safe now." Saxon rose.

She nodded. "Rome? Is he okay?"

"I'm sure he will be. Rome's faced a lot of tough situations."

She grabbed Saxon's shirt. "Please, I need to know. I lost the phone—" She glanced around, but there was no sign of it.

Saxon eyed her, then nodded. He pulled out his cell phone.

"Vander? Yeah, I got her. She was busy beating up a bad guy." A faint smile crossed Saxon's handsome face. "Yeah, okay." He ended the call. "Rome's fine. They're on their way."

Sofie couldn't quite believe it, wouldn't, until she saw him.

A violent shiver wracked her.

"Come here, Your Highness. You're freezing."

Saxon pulled her to his hard chest. He was wet, but warm. She held on.

"Thank you for the rescue."

"You were doing a damn good job of rescuing yourself, Princess."

She felt a spurt of pride. "Please, call me Sofie. That's what my friends call me."

"You did good, Sofie."

Saxon smelled good, and he was so warm, heat pumping off him. She held on until she heard the screech of tires.

Two black X6s jerked to a halt beside them. She saw Vander leap out of one, his face set with a dark look.

Sofie shivered. That man was a little scary.

Then another door slammed, and she swiveled to see Rome.

All she saw was Rome.

He looked fine. His dark gaze zeroed in on her like a laser.

She broke free of Saxon and ran.

Then she was in Rome's arms.

He lifted her off her feet, holding her against his chest. He was hot as well, and she pressed her face against his neck.

"I've got you, Sofie."

She gripped him tightly, and finally, she felt safe.

"I'm taking you home," he said.

CHAPTER NINE

Rome sat in the backseat of the X6, Sofie cradled in his arms. Vander was driving.

She was soaking wet and shivering.

But she was alive.

Rome released a slow breath. For what felt like an eternity, he hadn't known if she was all right.

He'd taken down their attackers, but he'd known one had followed her.

Hunting her down.

He tightened his hold. She made a sound and burrowed deeper.

"I was so worried," she murmured.

"You're safe now."

"I was terrified they'd hurt you."

Rome stilled. She'd been worried about him? *Fuck.* Emotion swelled in him.

He met Vander's gaze in the rearview mirror. His boss shot him a knowing look but didn't say anything.

Fuck it. It wasn't protocol to get personally involved

with the person he was guarding, but it was too fucking late for that.

He wasn't backing away from Sofie.

"I'm fine," he told her. "You're fine."

She nodded.

"The attackers?" he asked Vander.

"We gathered them all up. Rhys is with them, waiting for Hunt to arrive. They'll take them in and get them booked. Hunt will question them. Hopefully, we'll know who they work for soon."

Rome noticed that Sofie's palms were grazed badly. "Oh, beautiful, that must hurt."

"They'll be fine. They just sting a little."

He shifted her. Her knees were grazed, too, and her bare feet were too dirty to tell, but they were probably scratched up as well.

"Vander, she needs someone to clean her scrapes."

"I'm okay," she insisted. "I don't need the media attention of visiting a hospital. I—"

"Ryder," Rome said. "He's a paramedic friend. Can you get him, Vander?"

"On it," Vander replied.

Vander made the call quietly in the front, and finally, they made it to the house.

Two guards appeared, staying close and watchful.

Rome got out and then pulled Sofie into his arms. He carried her inside.

"I'll help her get showered and clean," he told Vander. She was clinging to Rome like she would never let go.

Vander nodded. "Take your time. Ryder will take a while to get here. We'll be down here when she's ready."

Rome took the stairs two at a time. Overwhelming, possessive urges clawed at him.

She'd been threatened.

Someone had tried to take her from him.

He wouldn't let that stand.

Sofie made a noise and he hugged her tighter. The first priority was getting her warm, clean, and calm.

In her room, he strode straight into the bathroom.

He set her on the edge of the deep tub, then turned on the huge shower.

She was shivering, her dress a mess, her wet hair plastered to her head, shades darker than it normally was. His gut twisted. "I'll wait out—"

"No." She stood and swayed.

Rome grabbed her.

"No." Huge brown eyes met his. "Don't leave me."

Shit. Steeling himself, he reached out and started unzipping her dress. He pushed it off and it hit the tiles with a wet splat.

Trying to be businesslike, he quickly flicked open her bra, and pushed her panties off.

He didn't let himself look. She needed to get warm. He had to keep his unruly cock under control and take care of her.

He opened the shower stall.

She grabbed his hand. "Rome—"

"*Shh.* Get under the water, Sofie." He shed his wet jacket, then followed her in, uncaring that the spray hit his already-soaked clothes.

He urged her under the warm water, and she made a happy little sigh.

His gaze dropped. Damn, her body was gorgeous—delicate but strong, slender, but with curves at her hips and ass.

He moved up behind her and grabbed some shampoo.

He worked it through her hair. Her head tipped back, and he smoothed the shampoo through the strands, separating the tangles. He massaged her scalp.

That earned him a low moan.

Desire was a scorching fire in his blood, tempered only by the need to look after her. He helped her rinse her hair out. Then he repeated with the conditioner.

Next, he checked her abraded palms, making sure they were clean. He kissed one, then the other.

He heard her voice hitch. Being so much taller than her, he had a clear view over her shoulders. He saw her nipples peeking out through her hair.

Suddenly, she spun and tugged at his sopping shirt. "Off."

Together, they unbuttoned it. He let it drop into a wet pile on the floor of the shower.

Sofie attacked his belt, but he pushed her hands away. Working quickly, he let his pants and boxers hit the tiles.

"*Oh.*" Her mouth opened, hunger in her gaze as she looked over his chest. "You're so big and muscled."

Shit. That sexy, cultured voice made his desire spike.

Her gaze met his. "Can I touch you, Rome?"

"Anything you want, Sofie." Hell, he'd never deny her what she wanted.

She smoothed her hands over his chest, fingers tracing over the intricate tattoo on one side of his chest. It curled down his side.

As she explored him, flames licked at his gut.

She dragged her fingers down the ridges of his abdomen. "You're so strong, Rome. I wanted you the first time I saw you."

Her hand moved south, but he caught it before she grabbed his cock. If she touched him, he'd go off like a teenager.

Besides, he wanted this to be about her.

He spun her again so her back was pressed to his front, and ignored her sound of protest.

He squeezed some liquid soap that smelled fresh and sweet onto his palm. He smoothed it over her shoulders, and down her arms. She leaned back against him, her eyes closing and her lips parting.

Rome cupped her breasts. *Hell.* He let out a shuddering breath. Her breasts fit perfectly in his hands and she pushed into him. He played with her nipples until they were hard and beaded.

Then he let one hand slide down her belly, and she undulated against him.

"Yes. *Please*, Rome." Her eyes opened.

"You're so beautiful, Sofie." Every part of her was beautiful.

He let his hand go lower and dip between her thighs. He toyed with the strip of curls he found.

"Oh, God." She clamped a hand on his wrist.

"You feel so soft. I bet you're sweet."

Sofie made a hungry, inarticulate sound. She rubbed against his hand.

"What does my sexy princess need?"

"*You.*" She moaned. "Please. Touch me."

He parted her folds and slid a finger inside her.

She cried out.

Damn, she was tight. He stroked her, loving her wild, abandoned moves. Soon she was riding his hand. His thumb found her clit and her husky cries filled his ears.

Need was a wild sensation riding him hard.

He needed to taste her. Was desperate for it.

He withdrew his hand and shut off the shower.

"No," she cried.

He scooped her up and swallowed her gasp with his mouth. Still wet, he strode into the bedroom and lay her on the bed, so just the lower parts of her legs hung over the edge.

"Rome?"

When she tried to sit up, he pushed her back down and knelt by the edge of the bed. He pushed her thighs apart and she quivered.

"There's that sexy, little shiver. Drives me crazy." He stroked her thighs, dropping gentle kisses on her bruises. "I knew you'd be pretty."

Then he slid his hands under her curvy ass and lifted her to his mouth.

Her cry filled the room.

Rome used his lips, tongue, and teeth, reading every little move and moan she made to find what she liked best.

She tasted like spicy honey, and he licked harder, pulling the taste of her in.

"*Rome.*" A moan. "You're *so* good at this." Her body tensed, twisting in his hold.

He plunged his tongue into her, tightening his grip to hold her in place. Then he moved his tongue back to her clit.

"It's... *Oh*... Rome!" Her back arched, thrusting her into his hold.

As she shuddered through her orgasm, he watched her, absorbing every detail.

When she dropped back on the bed, panting, little aftershocks made her twitch. She smiled. "I'm feeling very warm now." Her gaze skimmed down his body. "Are you—?"

He slid his hands up her thighs. "I'm not going to fuck you."

Her face fell.

"Not now." He kissed her. "You've had a rough afternoon. You're hurt—"

"I'm fine. *Really*."

He smoothed her damp hair back. "When you finally take my cock, Sofie, it won't be rushed, with my boss waiting downstairs."

"Oh."

Rome gripped her chin. "I can't wait to watch your pretty face when I sink inside you."

She squirmed. "I look forward to it."

He smiled. "Get dressed. Ryder will be here to treat your grazes soon."

AS SOFIE DRESSED, her body was still tingling. She grinned.

Somehow the worst afternoon of her life had turned into the best.

Rome wasn't holding back anymore. She shivered and pulled on some loose trousers and a tank top. What he'd done to her... She closed her eyes and smiled.

She pulled her hair up in a simple ponytail. Her scrapes stung and she winced. Her feet were a little cut up, too, but she'd had worse.

She headed downstairs, the murmur of deep male voices growing in volume as she approached.

When she entered the kitchen, she stopped in the doorway to appreciate the view.

Rome's broad back was to her, but still made her pulse leap. He'd changed into dry clothes, and was wearing a white shirt and another set of black pants. She'd seen all the hard, defined muscles hidden under his clothes. And that fascinating tribal-like tattoo on his chest. Her gaze ran up over his close-cropped hair.

Vander looked dark and dangerous as always. His pitch-black hair was damp, and he leaned against the kitchen island, his rugged face set in hard lines.

The third man was rough and sexy, a bad boy designed to lure good girls into dark corners.

He lifted his head.

Yikes. The Universe help whoever caught this man's eye. His light-brown hair was shaggy, his jaw covered in dangerous scruff, and his green eyes promised pure sin.

He had a long, powerful body clad in jeans and a tight, burgundy Henley that was snug enough to showcase his muscled biceps.

Rome spun. "Sofie." He held out a hand.

She took it and moved closer.

"This is Ryder Morgan. He's a former Air Force combat medic who now works as a paramedic."

"Hello, Mr. Morgan," she said.

"It's nice to meet you, Princess Sofia. And it's Ryder."

"Thank you for coming at short notice."

He lifted his chin, his gaze dropping to her hands. "Why don't you take a seat? We can take care of those nasty scratches."

Rome gripped her waist and lifted her onto a stool.

She smiled at him. Beside her, Ryder opened a huge, black bag resting on the island. Then he lifted one of her hands and started cleaning.

"Sofie," Vander said. "I spoke with the police. Ryder's brother, Hunter, is a detective with the San Francisco PD. Hunt said the guys who tried to grab you aren't talking. He'll keep trying, but these guys are professionals. Hunt got the impression that they were afraid of whoever hired them."

She nodded. Another swipe of the antiseptic made her wince.

"Feet next." Ryder crouched and started on her feet. The man grinned at her. "Never said this to a woman before, but you have pretty feet."

She laughed at the man's teasing. When she looked up, she saw Rome scowling.

"Your Tetanus shot up to date, Princess?" Ryder asked.

"Yes. I had one last year. And call me Sofie."

"We need to increase security," Rome said. "Take guards with us when we travel. Beef things up around the house."

Her pulse jerked. That would make things trickier when she needed to sneak out. She cleared her throat. "Whatever's necessary."

Ryder finished putting bandages on the worst of her scratches.

"Her knees are scratched up too, Ry," Rome said.

Ryder pushed up her trousers. "Ouch."

Her knees were scraped up badly.

"You've got some bruises, too."

She waved a hand. "That's just from my own clumsiness."

The paramedic tipped some more antiseptic solution onto a cloth. "Sorry if this hurts."

"I'm sorry to hear more jewelry was stolen from your exhibition," Vander said.

"It's a real shame," she murmured.

"I heard today that the fire killed someone in the house. They found a body in the ruins."

She gasped, her heart kicking against her ribs. "Oh, no."

"A young man. He was asleep in an upstairs bedroom."

God, a life cut short. Sofie's hands balled into fists. The Black Foxes had no regard for life.

When she looked up, she found Rome watching her. She blew out a breath and made herself relax.

But inside, anger burned.

She had to get the jewelry back.

And those responsible had to pay.

A poor man had lost his life. Like Tori. The bloody Black Foxes.

"They need to be caught," she said.

Rome cocked his head. "They?"

Crap, had she given away the fact that she knew more than she should? "The thieves."

"Ace is poking around," Vander said. "Discreetly."

Ryder finished and patted her leg. "Maybe Robin Hood will get the jewelry back again."

"We don't need some adrenaline junkie vigilante involved," Rome said.

Sofie kept her face blank. Then she feigned a yawn. "I think I need some rest. Thank you, Ryder."

"My pleasure." He shot her a killer grin.

Rome tipped her chin up. "Okay?"

She nodded.

"You did good today, Sofia," Vander said. "Kept a cool head."

"Not really, but I was aware that if I didn't fight back, they'd take me."

"You've had some self-defense training," Rome said. "Heard you hit all the right spots on your attackers."

She nodded. "I've worked with the palace security a little."

"Get some sleep. If you need anything, I'm down here."

She saw no glimpse of anything personal in his face. She really wanted to see that heated desire again.

But maybe not with two other men in the room.

With a smile and a nod, she headed upstairs. She locked her bedroom door and pulled out her black laptop.

Her belly hardened. She had a job to do. She needed to find the tiara and get it back.

Needed to find out who was responsible for the death of an innocent man.

Tonight.

It was time to get to work.

She did a little creative hacking and read the police reports.

There. There were security pictures of the masked thieves. They weren't great quality, but they were clear enough to see that one had a tattoo on his forearm. She tapped her nails on the edge of her laptop. It was a coat of arms.

A specific coat of arms. For the old Russian Empire.

She knew someone with the same tattoo, but on his bicep. Andrei Petrovich. A Russian prince.

Sofie pulled up information on his family and associates.

He was a loud man, who'd copped a feel of her butt at a ball once. He didn't like hearing the word no.

There.

There was a photo of Andrei with his cousins. He had an arm around a man with a coat of arms tattoo on his forearm.

Boris Petrovich.

She did a quick search. The man didn't work, just

seemed to attend parties around Europe. It was also mentioned that he was going to be attending the Glittering Court gala.

She smiled. "Gotcha."

He was staying at the Ritz-Carlton in the city.

Looked like Robin Hood was going to pay a visit.

But she knew she needed to be very careful with Rome increasing security around her. She wouldn't let anything stop her.

It was time to get to work.

CHAPTER TEN

Rome checked in with the exterior guards.

"All quiet, Rome."

"That new camera get installed in the blind spot?" Rome asked.

"Yeah, Ace sent a guy. It's not tied into the main system yet, so you need to check the feed separately."

"Thanks, Mike."

Back inside, Rome fired up his laptop and activated the security system. He glanced up at the ceiling, thinking of Sofie upstairs, sleeping.

He paused. Memories of her sweet ass in his hands, and the taste of her on his lips, cascaded through his head. Damn, the way she called out his name... Desire was hot and heavy in his gut.

Tonight, she needed to rest.

But tomorrow...

Well, they'd see. He couldn't keep his hands off her for much longer.

His phone rang. It was Vander.

"Hey," Rome said.

"Sofia okay?"

"Yeah, she's sleeping."

"Saw the way you looked at her, Rome. And the way she is with you."

Rome dragged in a deep breath. "She's mine."

Vander made an amused sound. "Damn, you going to take the fall, too?"

"Don't know where it's going, but I can't stay away. She's mine." He paused. "I know it oversteps the bounds of my work, but I'm not leaving her safety to anyone else. You try to take me off her security, I'll quit, and guard her anyway."

Vander was silent a moment. "Are you sure you can keep your cool? That you can be her lover and her bodyguard?"

"I'll protect her with my life."

"Okay. We've been through too much together for me to doubt you. You know I trust your judgment, Rome, and at Norcross, we've never followed the rules exactly. We both know life is never neat and tidy. But if you need help, or things get sticky, you tell me. I've got your back, and Sofie's."

Relief rushed through Rome. "Thanks, Vander."

He checked the security system again. He put on some music—some low, bluesy jazz—and got to work going over the security plan for the gala. There was a ping on his computer and Ace's face popped up in a chat window.

Born to Brazilian parents but raised in the US, Ace had dark good looks that made him popular with the ladies, and his long, dark hair was pulled back in a short ponytail. The man was sitting in his lair at the Norcross Security office—the walls were covered in flat screens.

"Working late?" Rome asked.

"No rest for the wicked, *amigo*. How's the princess after the attack?"

"Fine. A little scraped up, but sleeping now."

"Vander said she looks like a perfect princess, but she has a spine of steel."

"Yeah." A good description. "Heard you got the extra camera set up."

"The blind spot is plugged. I'll get the camera integrated into the main controls tomorrow. I ran a system diagnostic while I was at it."

"And?"

"There's a problem with a downstairs window. Someone very cleverly hacked it so it won't set the alarm off when it's opened."

Hair rose on the back of Rome's neck. "Someone got in?"

"Nope." Ace sat back in his chair. "Someone got *out*."

Rome's chest locked.

"I'm guessing you didn't climb out the window in the middle of the night, *amigo*?"

"No, I did not." It was only himself and Sofie inside.

"So, your princess snuck out."

A muscle in Rome's jaw twitched. "I'll find out."

Why the fuck would she sneak out? Why would she risk herself like that? His gut felt like sludge. Was she meeting a lover?

No. She'd come alive for him. She'd been hungry for

his touch. He couldn't believe that was a lie, or that she was seeing someone else.

"Thanks, Ace."

His friend saluted him. "Good luck. Go easy on her."

Rome closed the laptop and headed upstairs.

It was silent.

He didn't bother to knock, just pushed open the door to her bedroom. It was shadowed, moonlight streaming through the window.

Illuminating the empty bed.

He flicked on the light.

No Sofie.

There was a black laptop sitting on her bed though. He frowned. It wasn't the shiny, silver one she'd showed him the other day.

He opened it. It had a heavy-duty casing...and a heavy-duty encryption on it.

His cell phone pinged and he pulled it out. It was a notification from the security system.

The downstairs window had just been opened.

Anger flared, but he banked it down. He jogged down the stairs. Quickly, he slipped out the front door and pulled out the second app showing the new camera feed.

He watched a slim figure in black dart through the former blind spot to the trees.

Fuck.

Rome signaled one of the guards, pressing a finger to his lips. "Keep watch," Rome whispered. "There's something I need to follow up."

The guard nodded and Rome stuck to the shadows.

As he reached the street, he saw Sofie out on the sidewalk, a ball cap pulled low on her head. She was walking away from the house, totally relaxed. Like she was just out for an evening stroll. She had a black backpack slung over one shoulder.

Rome scowled. *Where the hell was she going?*

He jogged to his X6, bleeped the locks, and slid behind the wheel. As he pulled out onto the street, he hoped Sofie didn't spot the vehicle. He drove slowly and saw her walk down a side street.

He pulled over, then nosed forward enough to spot her.

He saw her get into a blue Tesla.

What the hell?

Moments later, she pulled out onto the street ahead of him. A second later, Rome followed.

He was experienced at tailing people, and she didn't notice him. When she pulled up at the imposing façade of the Ritz-Carlton hotel, he frowned.

He watched her hand her keys to the valet. Once she'd entered the lobby, Rome pulled in.

"Checking in, sir?" the uniformed valet asked.

"Yeah." He handed over his keys and quickly strode into the hotel.

The lobby was opulent and modern. There was lots of shiny, veined marble and everything was decorated in shades of gray.

Rome scanned around. Crap, if he lost her...

There.

She was standing with some people at the elevators.

Rome circled around the lobby, moving closer, but staying out of her view. The elevator doors opened.

An old lady with a walking frame fumbled with her key card near the door to the elevator.

"Can I help you?" Sofia asked.

"Oh, that would be lovely, dear. I'm going to the top floor."

"Me too." Sofie helped the woman into the elevator.

Rome whirled and found the stairs. He broke into a run, taking them two at a time. Thankfully the Ritz-Carlton buildings only had a few stories. He reached the top floor, and cracked open the door.

Out in the corridor, he saw Sofie helping the old lady to her suite.

"You're so kind," the woman said. "Thank you."

"Have a great night." Once the lady closed her door, Sofie's smile disappeared.

She scanned the empty hall, then Rome watched her stride to the housekeeping closet and pick the lock.

It appeared his princess was hiding some pretty interesting skills.

Moments later, she came out dressed in a housekeeping uniform, with a brown wig on, and pushing a cart. Cogs turned in his brain and a suspicion formed.

Rome ground his teeth together. He had no idea what she was up to, but he planned to find out.

Sofie had a lot of explaining to do.

He watched her knock on a suite door. "Housekeeping."

Rome shot off the text to Ace.

Need to know who's staying in the Presidential Suite at the Ritz-Carlton.

Sofie opened the door and disappeared inside.

Rome strode down the hall. His phone vibrated.

Boris Petrovich. Russian. Here for the gala.

Rome's gut hardened. *What the hell?* This couldn't be a lover's meet-up, or otherwise there'd be no need for her housekeeping disguise. He pulled a card out of his wallet. It took a second to override the electronic lock and he slipped inside the suite.

It was silent.

Place was stylish, with gleaming, wooden floors, more shades of gray with a few touches of blue. There was a nice view of the Coit Tower out of the windows.

Rome turned left and followed the faint sounds down the hallway. He moved silently, and saw a door ajar. He pushed it open.

It was the master bedroom.

Sofie was crouched in front of an open safe, a sparkling tiara in one hand, and a small card in the other.

"Resting well, beautiful?"

Sofie's head whipped around, blank shock on her face.

NO. Oh, no.

Sofie squeezed her eyes shut, praying that Rome was just a figment of her imagination.

She opened her eyes.

No. He was still standing there, looking very pissed off.

He couldn't be here. If he was caught...

"Rome, I—"

He strode across the room, and snatched the card out of her hand. As he looked at it, something rippled across his face.

"Get the tiara packed up," he said.

He set the card in the safe and closed it.

"You can't be here," she said. "Go."

His green gaze met hers—hot, angry. "Pack up the sparkler."

"If you get caught—"

"I won't."

"I have diplomatic immunity," she whispered furiously. "You don't."

"So, the quicker we get out of here, the better."

Dammit. He was so stubborn. She pulled out her makeup kit from her backpack and lifted up the false bottom. Rome watched with interest as she set the tiara inside.

"Resourceful," he said.

She noticed he was careful not to use her name. Probably worried about any recording devices.

She zipped up her backpack and Rome took it.

"Let's go."

She nodded. Then she heard the distinct click of the front door and voices.

Oh, crap.

A muscle in Rome's jaw ticked. "Go. Do your maid

routine."

"What about you?" Her pulse was racing.

"Don't worry about me. I'll keep this." He jiggled the backpack. "If they suspect you, they won't find the tiara on you."

"What if they see you—?"

"They won't." He touched her cheek, then pushed her out the bedroom door.

Sofie resisted the urge to fiddle with her wig. She walked into the luxurious bathroom and grabbed some towels.

She walked out and headed down the hall.

"Hey," a man barked from the living room. "We need more towels in the other bathroom, too."

Sofie nodded her head. *Boris Petrovich.* He had clean-cut features but an ugly scowl.

She hurried to the front door and reached the cart. She grabbed more towels, wishing she could just walk away.

Where the hell was Rome? There was no possible way for him to get out unseen.

She took the fresh towels in, her heart pounding. She so desperately wanted to get out of there. What if one of Petrovich's entourage recognized her?

In the living area, the group was gathered around the built-in bar, pouring drinks and laughing. Petrovich was in a chair, a scantily-dressed woman in his lap.

Sofie set the towels down and hurried out. No one paid her any attention.

In the outside hall, she blew out a breath and quickly pushed the cart down the corridor. She reached the housekeeping closet and suddenly, the door opened and she was yanked inside.

Sofie gasped.

"You all right?" Rome asked.

"*Rome.*" How had he gotten out?

"You okay?" he repeated.

"Yes." She yanked her wig off, then she was pulled up on her toes.

"*Never* risk yourself like that again," he growled.

Warmth bloomed in her chest. "I'm fine—"

He shook her. "*Never* again, Sofia. Someone tried to snatch you today. You have a stalker. You don't fucking sneak out."

"It was important, Rome. I know what I'm doing."

He leaned close, their faces inches apart. Her heart knocked hard in her chest.

"Playing Robin Hood?" he asked silky.

She lifted her chin. "Righting wrongs. A man was killed. Others have been hurt."

There was a flash in his eyes. "We'll discuss this more once you're safe, back at the house."

"There is nothing to discuss. This is my life, Rome."

He growled, then backed her against the shelves full of cleaning products, towels, and linen.

Then his mouth was on hers.

Sofie moaned and threw her arms around his neck. His hands slid under her ass. Their tongues dueled.

God, he tasted better than anything. Heat flooded her.

Then he tore his mouth free. She was very pleased to see his chest rising and falling faster than usual. Knowing that she affected the strong, contained man so much left her lightheaded.

"I'll follow you back to the house."

She pouted. "You trailed me here in the X6? I never saw you."

"I wouldn't be any good at my job if you had."

"Rome, I need to return the tiara to its rightful owner."

"I'll see you home, then I'll return it."

She wanted to argue, but the look on his face warned her not to. She nodded.

"Get changed," he said.

He slipped out and Sofie quickly changed back into her own clothes. She stuffed her disguise in her backpack. It didn't take long for her to collect her car.

This time, she noticed the black SUV staying behind her on the drive back to the house.

She parked the Tesla on the side street where she'd picked it up from. The X6 stopped beside her and the passenger door opened.

She climbed in. Rome was quiet as he pulled up in front of her rental house.

He opened the window and waved at one of the guards.

"Get inside, Sofie."

"Rome—"

"We'll talk when I get back."

She sucked in a breath, then slid out of the SUV.

One of the guards opened the front door for her. She was filled with nervous energy and leftover adrenaline from her little jaunt. She stomped up the stairs.

How dare Rome take over? She'd been retrieving stolen jewelry for years now. She knew what she was doing.

She stormed into her bedroom and kicked off her shoes, then she started pacing.

Had he returned the tiara yet? What if someone spotted him?

Ugh. She hated the stress. It was different when you were only risking yourself.

Rome hadn't thought highly of Robin Hood. Would it change how he thought of her?

How he felt about her?

She paced across the room, swiveled, then paced back.

It felt like an eternity, but finally, she heard the door downstairs. She didn't hear his footsteps; Rome was too quiet for that. Her bedroom door slammed open.

Rome stood there like some avenging god.

"It's done?" she asked.

He nodded. Then he closed the door and strode toward her.

Sofie suddenly felt like prey. She backed up. His burning gaze ran over her.

"Rome—"

"Quiet." His arms circled around her waist and he lifted her off her feet. She loved it when he did that. Used his strength to move her around.

Then his mouth was on hers.

Sofie clung to him, clamping her legs around his waist.

He bit her lip, then took her mouth, rough and hard.

She *loved* it. She gripped his head, kissing him back.

Yes, yes, yes, her body chanted.

Then his hands were on her shirt. He yanked, and the buttons popped off.

She gasped, their gazes met. Desire was reflected back at her. What she saw was hot enough to melt steel.

"Rome, I need—"

"I know what you need." His voice was low and guttural.

They tore at each other's clothes. She got his shirt open. *Yes*. Instantly she put her mouth on his tattoo.

He growled, then shoved her leggings and panties down. Her bra followed.

"So damn beautiful, Sofie. And sexy."

He pinched one nipple and she squirmed. She went for his belt.

"You want my cock, Sofie?"

Her belly contracted. He was talking dirty. No one talked dirty to her. She wanted more. "*Yes*."

His hands ran down her sides. "You going to take all of me? Scream my name when I'm moving inside you?"

She rubbed her thighs together. She was so wet, so turned on.

His fingers skimmed along her thigh, then between her legs. He toyed with the strip of hair at the juncture of her thighs. She widened her stance a little and he stroked her. A shiver wracked her.

"Love those sexy shivers. Just for me." He thumbed her clit. "Fuck, so damn wet."

She let out a husky cry.

"I know, baby. I'll make it better soon."

He picked her up like she weighed nothing, and set her on the bed.

He quickly dealt with his belt, then kicked his pants and boxer shorts off.

Oh. *God*. Sofie froze.

He was so beautiful. So strong, so big. She ran her gaze hungrily over his hard stomach, solid thighs, and the heavy erection between them.

She was almost panting. She'd never wanted someone so much.

He climbed on the bed, sitting with his back to the headboard. He grabbed a packet from his wallet and she watched him slide the condom on his large cock.

His gaze met hers. It made it impossible to breathe.

"Come here, Sofie."

Her belly pulsed, need making her mindless.

She crawled across the bed.

"Yes, come right here." He gripped her hips, pulling her to straddle him. Sofie gripped his broad shoulders, her fingers biting into his dark skin. She spread her thighs wide.

The fat head of his cock nudged her folds and she moaned, her eyes closing.

"No, look at me," he ordered. "I want those eyes on mine."

She opened her eyes. She saw her need echoed in his own.

He fisted his cock and nudged her hip.

Finally. Sofie sank down.

Oh, God. "Oh...*Rome*."

"I'm big, I know. You can take me, beautiful."

She kept her gaze on him, panting. "It feels so good." He stretched her, but she loved the pleasurable burn.

Finally, she sank the last inches, taking him deep.

"Fuck, beautiful," he breathed.

Then his big hands cupped her ass. He lifted her up, then slammed her down.

"Rome!" Sofie moved her hips, riding him. She ground down, but it was a joint effort. Rome used his strength to move her.

She had enjoyed sex before, but this was something much more raw, powerful. This was primal, wild fucking, and she loved it.

Rome groaned. "You're so tight, Sofie. You feel so good around my cock."

She made a sound—part cry, part moan.

"Rub your clit, beautiful. I want to watch you come."

She dug her nails into his shoulders, then moved one hand down her belly.

Her clit was swollen. With each rub, she felt the flex of his stomach muscles as he thrust up inside her.

"*Oh*." Electricity skated through her. "Rome, I'm..."

"Can feel your sweet pussy squeezing me. *Fuck*. Come, Sofie."

Her orgasm hit. She screamed. She might have begged. Pleasure was a hot rush, her body shaking wildly.

Rome's hold on her ass turned bruising. He pumped up into her, once, twice.

"Sofie...*fuck*."

His big body arched beneath her, his cock pulsing inside her. His face twisted as he came.

CHAPTER ELEVEN

Breathing heavily, Rome tried to get his brain functioning.

He'd wanted Sofie—wanted to claim her, tie her to him. Mixed with the volatile emotions of the night, it had been hotter and rougher than he'd intended.

Hell, she was a *princess*. First, he'd mauled her in a hotel closet, then he'd come in here and fucked her hard.

Rome hadn't expected to lose any semblance of control. To be swept up in his own clawing needs.

She was sprawled over him, face hidden by her cloud of strawberry-blonde hair. His cock was still inside her, and he felt tremors running through her.

He slid his hand up her back, feeling the delicate knobs of her spine. Jeez, she was so finely made, and he'd taken her hard.

Had he hurt her?

"Sofie?"

"*Mmm.*" She stirred a little.

"You okay?"

She lifted her head, her eyes dazed, a little smile on her face.

Something inside him eased.

"Okay doesn't come *close* to describing how I feel right now," she said.

She'd matched him in bed, meeting every kiss, caress and stroke with her own. And as his worry cleared, he remembered her begging him, her husky cries.

Right now, her face was flushed with pleasure, her hair tangled, and she'd never looked more beautiful.

He fingered the strands of her hair. "I was rough."

"I know." She shivered. "I hope you will be again."

Rome shook his head. "You never do what I expect."

He certainly never expected her to be an infamous international jewel thief.

She sat up, straddling him, her pretty breasts snagging his gaze. She ran her hands over his chest. She was staring at his tattoo, fascination on her face.

"Roll off, beautiful. I need to deal with this condom."

She shifted to the side.

He strode straight into the bathroom and was back as fast as he could. Sofie was lying on the bed, smiling.

Hell, she was glowing.

There was no way he would regret breaking his own rules to be with her.

Her chin lifted. "I'm guessing you've changed your mind about me needing a boring, proper prince—"

Rome flicked the sheet off her body, gripped her ankles and yanked her to the edge of the bed.

She let out a squeal.

He pressed his hands on either side of her body, their faces inches apart.

"Those princes lost out. They were too slow to realize what a sexy beauty they had right under their noses. Too bad for them. Their loss," he nibbled her lips, "is my gain."

"No one's ever wanted me the way you do," she whispered.

"Then all men are idiots." He pressed his lips to her jaw and she arched into him.

"You *really* want me. It wasn't polite, or nice, or elegant." Her smile widened. "It was hard and rough."

Shit, she brought him to his knees. Rome lay back on the bed, pulling her close.

Sofie propped herself up on one arm, eyeing his chest again.

"You need something, Sofie?"

She licked her lips. "Your body is so... I want to explore."

He shoved a pillow under his head. "Have at it, beautiful. But be warned, I only had one condom in my wallet. I've got more, but they're in my bag downstairs."

"Okay." She pressed into his side. She stroked a hand over his pecs, over his tattoo, tracing the lines. She toyed with his nipple.

She was totally absorbed and he loved the way she looked at him. She spread her hands over his abs, and stroked down his thighs.

His cock twitched, already hardening.

She made a sexy little sound. Those elegant fingers circled his cock.

Shit. His hips jerked.

She smiled and stroked. Tightening her grip, she took her time, exploring and experimenting. She leaned over him, the curtain of her pink-gold hair blocking his view of her face.

He groaned. "Put your mouth on me, beautiful."

She eagerly closed her mouth over his cock.

Rome locked his muscles. She licked, that pink tongue so damn sweet.

"That's my greedy princess."

She looked up at him, her eyes blazing.

It was a hell of a picture. He almost came.

She shifted, and he realized she had one hand between her legs.

"You working your clit, beautiful?"

She nodded, her mouth still on his cock.

"You want more?"

She moaned.

"Open wider, Sofie."

She opened and Rome pushed his cock deeper.

She sucked harder, her cheeks hollowing. He tangled his fingers in her hair. "Baby, *God*."

He surged up, and her mouth slipped off him. He pushed her onto her back and replaced her hand with his between her legs.

"*Rome*." She writhed on the sheets.

He worked her clit, sinking one finger inside her. With his other hand, he pumped his cock.

She detonated.

She cried out, the words inarticulate. Damn, watching her come was the best damn thing ever.

"I'm going to come," he growled. He stroked his cock faster and started to shift away.

"No." She gripped his head. "Come on me."

Rome groaned. "Sofie." His orgasm hit, so hard the pleasure hurt.

His body jerked as he spurted. His come hit her belly.

Then he couldn't think, could only feel. He collapsed beside her, pulled her close, and pressed his face to her hair.

SOFIE WOKE SLOWLY. *Mmm.* She was so warm. She snuggled into the hard body holding her tight.

Her eyes popped open.

Rome's big body was curled around her. She was part under him, like he wanted to make sure she would stay exactly where he'd put her.

Pure, undiluted happiness filled her.

She absorbed the feel of him—the hardness, the heat, the heavy arm at her waist. Keeping her pressed into him.

It was a little strange to be sleeping naked, but she had no complaints when he was naked as well.

She was pretty sure they hadn't moved after the last time they'd gone at each other.

She shivered.

After the first time, and their sexy exploration on the bed, Rome had rallied to clean off her skin with a washcloth, then get more condoms. When he'd returned, he'd gone down on her with that clever mouth, giving her another earth-shattering orgasm before he covered her, hitched her legs around his waist and taken her again.

Mmm-mmm. She shifted, her bottom rubbing against the cock nestled against the cleft of her buttocks.

As she felt it hardening, she guessed Rome was awake.

"Good morning," she murmured.

"Morning, beautiful."

She loved the husky edge to his deep voice.

"Sleep well?" he asked.

"I did."

"I guess all that jewelry robbery took it out of you."

That startled a laugh out of her. "I don't think it was that." She paused, glancing back over her shoulder. "You aren't upset? About me being Robin Hood?"

His arm tightened, and he pressed his lips to her neck. "I understand, Sofie."

Relief hit her.

"But I won't let you put yourself at risk."

She frowned. "Rome—"

His hands slid down her belly, then lower, arrowing between her legs. She gasped.

"We'll talk more over breakfast," he said.

She gasped. "Okay."

"You want to get up and shower?"

She shimmied on his hand. "Later."

"Later," he echoed.

She felt him reach to the side of the bed, then heard the crinkle of a wrapper. Then she felt his hard cock prodding her.

"Damn, Sofie, I love your ass."

She was thrilled. She'd had compliments on her beauty, her elegance, and her poise before, but never her ass.

He lifted her thigh and pushed closer. Then his cock surged into her from behind with one hard thrust.

She cried out, gripping Rome's arm.

"That feel good, Sofie?" he murmured in her ear.

"Yes, *so* good." With a whimper, she pushed back against him.

"So damn hot."

She tipped her head back, her body shuddering with each thrust.

"Can't get enough of you, Sofie." His hand found her clit.

"*God.*" She gasped for air, pleasure coursing through her.

"Find it, Sofie."

She couldn't take anymore.

Then suddenly, he slowed. Each thrust was still firm, deep, but blissfully slow. She rode the edge, trembling so close to her orgasm. He filled her up completely. Just Sofie and Rome.

On that thought, she broke.

Pleasure crashed over her and her vision grayed, her chest locked.

Rome's hand tightened, almost painfully on her thigh. He bucked against her, thrusting deep and groaning loudly. Then he bit her neck. She jolted, the final spasms of her own climax pulsing through her.

He pulled back, but kept his tight hold on her. She felt his deep breaths against the back of her neck.

Her pulse was racing like crazy.

"I want to wake up like this every day," she said.

He chuckled deeply. "Is that an order, Princess?"

She rolled to face him. He looked relaxed and sated.

"Yes, it is." She used her best princess voice. "I demand that you, Rome Nash, give me delicious orgasms every day."

A beautiful smile crossed his face. "Yes, Your Highness." He kissed her.

She cupped his strong jaw, emotions tightening in her throat. She realized she hadn't been this happy for a long time. Since before she'd lost Tori.

"How about some breakfast?" he asked.

She nodded.

They showered together and Sofie pulled on some fitted pants and a top with ruffled sleeves in a pretty blush pink.

Rome changed into fresh suit pants and a blue shirt. It made his eyes stand out.

In the kitchen, he made coffee while she whipped up some omelets. She hummed as she cooked.

"So, you have a lunch today." He set a mug down beside her.

"A luncheon," she said. "Lots of San Francisco socialites. Wealthy ones." She set the plates with the omelets on the island. "I'm *starving*."

"I wonder why," he said dryly.

She grinned at him. "So, at the luncheon today, I smile, hobnob, and hope to get some new supporters for the gala and charity."

Rome nodded. "It's at the Palace Hotel. I've done a

preliminary security plan, and I have the schematics for you to memorize. I want to go over an evacuation plan, in case something goes wrong. And we get separated."

She took a bite of eggs and swallowed. "You'll stay close."

He touched her hair. "Yes. That's no hardship." His phone pinged and he pulled it out. "Robin Hood's exploits hit the news."

She pressed her tongue to her cheek.

"The tiara is back safely."

"You can count on Robin Hood," she said.

"Yeah. But promise me you won't sneak out again. If Robin Hood needs to get something done, I'll help you, and keep you safe."

She couldn't find any words. She'd always done this alone. It was kind of nice to have a partner.

But worry nipped at her.

"I have diplomatic immunity, Rome, as Caldovan royalty. I won't let you get into trouble."

He grabbed her hand. "Let me worry about that. Your safety is what I'm most concerned about."

"Thank you."

"I also need to talk to Vander about this. I need to tell him about Robin Hood."

"Rome—"

"I promise you that he won't mention it to anybody. There's no one who can keep a secret like Vander."

She nibbled on her bottom lip, but nodded.

"We'll also find a way to anonymously tip off the police that Petrovitch was involved in the firebombing and the man's death."

"Good." She paused. "I was worried this would... change how you think about me."

"I told you that I understand why you do it."

"I do it for Tori. Losing her left a hole. Being Robin Hood, righting these wrongs, helps fill that hole. Along with my charity work." Sofie shook her head. "She was so wonderful, and then she was just gone. It broke her boyfriend, Lorenz. He's a rare book dealer and she used to travel with him sometimes. They were like chalk and cheese. She was bubbly, and he was quiet and reserved. They reminded me of my parents." She pressed her hands to her chest, to the hurt in her heart. "Being Robin Hood stopped the grief from dragging me under."

"I get it."

There was something dark in his voice. Frowning, she grabbed his arm. "Rome?"

He took a deep breath. "When I was eight, I was looking after my younger sisters— Lola and Liana. They're twins. They were six. We were walking home from school. My mother worked two jobs to feed us after my dad ran off."

Sofie hated the terrible look in his eyes.

"I stopped to talk with some buddies from school. Lia was picking flowers, and Lola walked on. She was skipping." Rome shook his head. "She was always skipping, dancing, singing, never sitting still."

Sofie's belly hardened. "What happened?"

He was silent for a moment. "I was only a minute behind her. But by the time Lia and I followed, there was no sign of her."

Sofie grabbed his hand and squeezed.

"She was just gone. I searched everywhere, but nothing. It was like she'd disappeared into thin air. I gave Lia to a neighbor to look after and then ran blocks to where my mom worked." He met Sofie's gaze. There was so much heartbreak in his green eyes.

Sofie threw her arms around him. He hugged her close, so tight it hurt, but she didn't pull away.

"Lola was missing for three days. Three hellish days. They found her body in an abandoned lot. She'd been raped and murdered."

"*No*." Sofie hugged him tighter. "I'm so sorry, Rome. I know how much it hurts."

"Yeah."

"Did they catch the bastard?"

"They did."

But her big, protective man wouldn't forgive himself. Even though he'd been just a child himself.

"It wasn't your fault."

"I was supposed to take care of her."

Sofie cupped his cheeks. "It was *not* your fault. You were a child yourself. You were all doing the best you could." Realization hit her. "This is why you joined the military? Became a bodyguard?"

He just stared at her.

This big, rugged, protective man was paying his penance and honoring his sister.

Like she did for Tori.

"Tell me about Lola," Sofie said softly.

His eyes changed. "She loved to sing. Drove us crazy."

As they finished their breakfast, he talked about his sister, telling stories that made them both smile.

Then the doorbell rang.

Rome rose and went to answer it. He came back with a large bouquet of flowers. They were huge, exotic blooms in shades of white and purple.

"Sorry, these aren't from me," he said.

"I get stuff like this all the time." She grinned. "Besides, you've been a little too busy to order flowers." She searched the blooms. "No card."

"Yeah, the guards checked it. The florist said it was a cash sale."

"Wait." She crouched a little. There was a small envelope on the bottom of the vase. Sofie recognized the handwriting. Her gut cramped, and all her happiness drained away.

Rome cursed and set the flowers down. He took the envelope and flicked open the note. His face hardened.

She held out a hand.

He shook his head. "You don't need to—"

"Rome, I won't bury my head in the sand."

A muscle twitched in his jaw.

She took the note.

You're mine, Princess. No one else can have you. Only I will touch you. Only I will choke you and see your fear.

"Lovely." She wrapped her arms around herself.

Rome hugged her. "I'm not letting this sicko close to you. *Ever*. I'll protect you, Sofie, whatever it takes."

CHAPTER TWELVE

As Rome walked with Sofie into the Palace Hotel, every one of his nerves was tight. The extra guards who'd followed them from the house were two steps behind them.

He was still pissed about the flowers.

He'd spent an hour trying to find who'd sent them. All he'd found were dead ends.

The stalker was here in San Francisco. Rome could sense it.

Just like he could sense the bad vibe in the air.

Cameras clicked. Sofie, dressed in pants a color between gray and purple, and a pretty, billowy blouse made of shiny purple fabric, waved to the cameras. She looked elegant and beautiful. Her hair was out today in a gorgeous fall of strawberry blonde.

He wanted to scoop her up and carry her away.

What he hated most of all was the fact that the glow from their night together had dimmed. He saw a hint of fear in the back of her eyes, the stress in her body.

But she didn't want to let her fans down. Or her charity. She waved and smiled graciously.

He hustled her into the hotel. Built in the late 1800s, the place was grand. He felt like he'd stepped into an emperor's palace, with all the cream marble, arched ceilings, and enormous chandeliers.

There was a small line of people working its way into the luncheon. The charity luncheon was being held at the Garden Court restaurant. It was the main restaurant of the hotel, and on the first floor, but it was closed to the general public for the luncheon today.

The extra guards broke off to take up their assigned places. When a couple spied Sofia and started forward to talk to her, Rome scowled until they stepped back.

"Rome! That was rude," she whispered.

"Don't care. Your security is my main concern."

"I don't think that couple was my stalker."

He grunted.

"You look so good in a suit." She pressed a hand to his chest, a private smile on her lips. "I miss seeing the tattoo though."

"Cameras and keen eyeballs," he warned.

She winked and stepped back a little.

He liked seeing her more relaxed. "I didn't tell you that you look beautiful."

"But you prefer me naked?" Her voice was a low, private whisper.

He leaned in. "Yes."

She shivered—that sexy, little wiggle that he loved. Finally, they reached the doorway to the Garden Court, and he watched her put on her princess face and straighten.

"Let's do this so we can go home," she said.

Home. He liked the sound of that.

It was even more opulent than the lobby, with a huge, curved-glass ceiling arching above. The chandeliers dangling overhead were even larger. There were some jewelry pieces displayed under glass on pedestals around the restaurant.

Rome walked a step behind Sofie, staying quiet and unobtrusive. This crowd was wealthy, and comfortable with bodyguards. He earned a few gazes. Some just gave passing glances, others barely seemed to notice him, and a couple of well-dressed women shot him speculative looks.

He ignored them all. He kept his focus on Sofie, and continued to scan the large room.

Sofie started talking with some people, but soon a blonde woman stepped up to the microphone at the front of the room.

"Welcome to the Stevens Charity luncheon." The woman had a fancy British accent. "I'm Chantal Lockwood, your host for today's event. We're extremely happy to support the Victoria Foundation and the Glittering Court jewelry exhibition. I am *very* honored to welcome our special guest and a friend of mine, Princess Sofia of Caldova." There was a round of applause.

Chantal Lockwood smiled at Sofie and Sofie waved.

"Please, take your seats and enjoy the luncheon," Chantal said.

Sofie leaned into Rome. "Here we go."

He followed her to the head table. He held the chair out as she greeted the other guests.

"Sofia, you look wonderful." Chantal Lockwood swept forward in a cloud of perfume and kissed both of Sofie's cheeks. "You always do."

"As do you, Chantal. Well done on today, the place looks fabulous."

"All the better for raising lots of money for our charities." Chantal squeezed Sofie's arm. "Enjoy."

After Sofie sat and Rome leaned over her shoulder. "I'll be to your left." He nodded his head.

She glanced at the grand columns off to the side and nodded.

"Have fun," he said.

She turned her head, shooting him a warm look. "I'll be counting down until it's over and we can get out of here."

The look in her eye told him exactly what she was thinking about.

Hell. He fought the urge to touch her. He headed to the spot near the columns where he could watch.

The luncheon started, uniformed servers bringing out fancy plates with fancy-looking food on them. There were some speeches on the various endeavors of the charities. Everyone wanted to talk with Sofie. She shook hands, smiled, chatted.

As the food was served, there was a talk on the history of royal jewelry from some expert. They referenced the famous tiara that Sofie would wear to the gala.

Rome scowled. Wearing a tiara like that was like painting a goddamned target on her.

He still had that bad vibe. He scanned around. Those fucking flowers had unsettled him. He scrutinized everyone—the guests, the waitstaff, the charity organizers.

"My God, we need help!"

He glanced sideways down the row of columns and through some glass doors into a side room. A man had collapsed on the tiles, and a frantic middle-aged woman was crouched over him.

She looked at Rome. "Help him!"

Rome didn't move. He spied the closest server. "Hey, there's a medical emergency."

The young man jerked, almost spilling the drinks on his tray, then spotted the fallen man. "Oh, God. I'll get help." The man raced away.

Rome looked back at Sofia. She was still chatting, but he saw that some of the tables closest had heard the ruckus.

He met Sofie's gaze and gave her a slow nod. She relaxed, and turned back to her table.

Then he sensed a presence behind him. Something sharp jabbed into the back of his jacket. A knife. *Fuck.*

"Should have helped the guy," a man drawled. "Then we would've taken you down the easy way, without an audience."

"I don't go down easy." Adrenaline spiked in Rome. He breathed through it. He'd been trained how to use it.

Sofie. He wouldn't let them have her.

Rome whirled. He swung at the man, but the guy dodged. They rammed into each other, shoving for advantage.

Rome felt a flash of the knife at his side, cutting through his jacket and shirt.

Fuck.

Suddenly, the woman who'd been crouched over the fallen man leaped onto Rome's back, wrapping an arm around his throat.

Screams broke out in the restaurant. People had noticed the fight.

Rome prayed that Sofie stuck to the plan he'd drilled into her.

He rammed the woman into a column. He saw the man who'd collapsed was rising. He looked perfectly fine.

Rome grabbed the woman over his shoulder and tried to pry her loose.

"Who are you assholes?" he growled.

"Nobody," the woman said. "We were just paid to keep you busy."

His gut knotted. Suddenly, the screaming increased. Rome turned and saw smoke rising in the center of the tables.

Dammit, smoke grenades.

In the chaos, he found Sofie. She looked worried, her face pale. She took a step toward him, but he shook his head.

The woman on his back shifted, and then Rome felt a prick in the side of his neck.

Fucking hell. He managed to rip the woman off and threw her. She hit the first attacker and they collapsed to the floor in a tangle.

Dizziness hit him. His legs weakened and he went

down on one knee. The smoke was thickening through the Garden Court.

People were panicking.

"Go!" he roared. He hoped Sofie heard him. His consciousness wavered.

He saw her. She hesitated.

"Now!" She was the target, and now he wouldn't be able to protect her.

Something rippled over her face, then she spun and ran.

Rome tracked her as she dodged around tables, then she disappeared into the smoke.

The edges of his vision went black, like slime crawling in.

He slumped sideways and hit the tile floor.

Sofie.

She was his last thought as darkness poured in on him.

SOFIE KICKED off her shoes and sprinted across the smoke-filled restaurant.

Every step away from Rome was painful.

A sob lay trapped in her throat. He'd gone down. He must be hurt.

Her eyes were blurry with tears.

He'd drilled her on the hotel layout. She needed to get back to the lobby and find their other guards—Mike and Dan.

People were screaming and panicking. She got jostled

by the crowd and she wasn't sure where she was. Dammit, she'd left her handbag—and phone—behind on her chair.

She saw a door and slipped through it.

The marble-lined corridor was empty. This wasn't the way to the lobby. Biting her lip, she hurried along it, looking for another way out. She found a stairwell and opened the door. She heard loud voices echo behind her.

Keep moving. Rome had warned her not to let herself get trapped. She started up the stairs. He said if he was incapacitated or they were separated, she had to run and find the other guards.

She hadn't realized how hard it would be to leave him behind.

Please be okay, Rome. Please. He meant more to her every day.

She rounded the landing, puffing.

Almost there.

She heard a noise, footsteps.

She froze. She had no idea if the person in the stairwell was friend or foe.

Screw it. She wouldn't be trapped in a damn stairwell. She shoved open the door and exited on the next floor.

She spotted a sign. This level contained a ballroom and meeting rooms. She thought about the hotel maps Rome had made her memorize. That meant she was one floor above the lobby. The place was empty and silent, and a little creepy.

Right. Find the elevator and get down to the lobby

level. Then find her guards, alert security, and call Norcross.

She reached the elevators and pressed the button. Nothing happened.

Dammit. She stabbed the button multiple times. It wasn't working.

She whirled and tried the first door she found.

It opened, and she stepped into a lovely ballroom. It wasn't as grand as the Garden Court, but it had an ornate ceiling, and equally pretty—if smaller—chandeliers. The place was filled with empty, round tables.

"*Princess.*"

The husky whisper echoed in the air around her.

She whirled, heart pounding. She couldn't see anyone.

"Who's there?"

"*I told you that we were meant to be together,*" a man whispered.

Her stalker.

Her stomach dropped to her feet.

Stay calm. She couldn't see him anywhere. His voice was just a whisper, and didn't sound familiar.

She heard a muffled thump, then smoke started rising.

She backed up. She gripped the door and tried the handle. It was locked. She yanked on it but it didn't budge.

The trickle of panic was like acid in her veins.

She was trapped.

Smoke filled the room and she coughed. She edged along the wall. There had to be another door out of here.

"Sweet, sweet Sofia. With hair like a sunset."

The eerie whisper chilled her blood. She wanted to snap back at him, but she didn't want to help him pinpoint her location.

She bumped into a chair. Her chest was starting to burn and the smoke was stinging her eyes.

She kept moving.

Her fingers touched another door and her pulse leaped. But when she tried the handle, it was locked as well. She stifled a cry of frustration.

A window, then. She glanced through the smoke and saw faint light. She'd jump if she had to.

"You can't escape me. I can see you."

"You're a coward," she said. "Come out and face me."

"We'll have so much fun. Your neck will feel so good under my fingers."

"You're sick."

"You shouldn't have let your bodyguard touch you, Sofia. You're mine."

She froze, staring at the smoke. "What?"

"I've been watching you. I've always watched you."

A nasty taste filled her mouth. He'd been watching her and Rome.

"He can't have you." The whisper was furious now.

Sofie dropped to her knees and crawled. There was less smoke down here, and she could breathe a little bit easier. She could see a bit better too.

She crossed the room, dodging chairs and tables.

"I'm going to find you," her stalker whispered. *"You'll die here, by my hands. It's time."* Now his voice was

excited. *"I can't wait to watch you fight, and smell your fear, show you a sweet death."*

Bastard. Fear was ugly and slick inside her, but she let her anger drown it out.

She was getting out of here. She was getting back to Rome.

She reached the far side of the room and saw a window. She rose.

She knew they were one floor up, so she wasn't sure she'd survive the fall in one piece. She looked back. But if she stayed in this smoke-filled room she was guaranteed to die.

Glancing around, she noted that the smoke was thinning, and for a second, she saw a menacing shadow of a man. She also smelled a sharp chemical smell that was vaguely familiar.

Her pulse went crazy. It was now or never.

She grabbed a chair, and swung it at the window.

Glass shattered.

"Princess! You can't escape me."

The shadow came at her. She swung the chair again.

It connected with something and she heard a groan.

She didn't stop to look.

Heedless of the broken glass, Sofie scrambled out the window.

There was a wide ledge outside and she rose, walking along it. She kept her back pressed to the building.

Oh. God.

Down below, she saw cars on the street, and a cable car rattling past.

A fire truck was also coming down the road, sirens blaring.

Sofie kept moving, and then saw the curved metal-and-glass awning over the entrance to the hotel.

She could drop onto that, then lower herself down to the street.

She kept moving. Finally, she was in position. Gut churning, she took a deep breath. She prayed the glass panels would hold under her weight.

Releasing a breath, she jumped.

Sofie landed on the glass awning like a starfish, her arms and legs spread.

She heard shouts, and her knee throbbed where she'd banged it. She crawled to the edge of the awning, then rolled over the side.

She dangled there, holding on by her fingers for a second before she dropped.

She hit the sidewalk hard, her bones rattling. *Ow.*

"Miss, are you okay?"

She looked up and saw a firefighter in full gear.

"Please." Sofie scrambled up. "There was a man chasing me. And smoke in the Garden Court." She thought of Rome. "My bodyguard is hurt."

"Calm down." The firefighter paused. "You're bleeding."

"A man was chasing me." She felt a little dizzy now. "He wanted to kill me."

The firefighter looked at her face. "You're...Princess Sofia."

She nodded.

"Come on." The man took her arm gently. "We need the police and a paramedic."

"I have some other guards here too." She looked around, but didn't see Mike or Dan.

As they neared a throng of police cars and ambulances, a man broke away from the police cruisers. He wore a dark suit, with a badge clipped to his belt.

He looked an awful lot like Ryder Morgan. A slightly more clean-cut, but still outrageously attractive version of the paramedic.

When the man saw her, his eyes widened. "Princess Sofia?"

She nodded. "Please, I need help—"

"Where's Rome? And your other guards?"

"Rome—" Her voice cracked. "They attacked him. He went down and told me to run." Tears welled in her eyes. "I don't know if he's okay."

"We'll find him." The detective took her arm.

She grabbed at his jacket. "You're related to Ryder, aren't you?"

The man nodded. "I'm his brother, Detective Hunter Morgan. Wish we were meeting under better circumstances."

"Detective, my stalker found me. I...jumped out a window."

The detective looked up, scanned, and saw a broken window. "Rome's going to be pissed. Come on, we'll get someone to look at your cuts. I'll also call Vander." Detective Morgan waved at some uniforms. "Dixon, Carr, I need you guys to guard the princess."

The uniformed officers—one man and one woman—jolted, staring at her. Sofie started to shake.

"You're safe now." Detective Morgan took her to the back of one of the ambulances, barking orders at some of the paramedics.

"Princess Sofia." Mike shouldered through the crowd, Dan on his heels.

"Watch her," the detective said to the guards and the uniforms. "No one gets close."

Sofie grabbed the man's arm. "Detective Morgan, please, Rome—"

"Call me Hunt." He met her gaze. His eyes were a deep green flecked with gold. "I'll find him."

She nodded.

Hunt strode toward the hotel.

As the paramedic started work on pulling tiny shards of glass from her hands, all Sofie could think about was Rome.

CHAPTER THIRTEEN

Rome opened his eyes and groaned.

His head was throbbing, and his mouth was as dry as the desert. *Where the hell was he?* He smelled smoke and heard agitated voices, screaming.

Was he in Afghanistan? Libya? Had the mission gone bad? Was his team okay?

"Rome?" A man knelt beside him. "Take it easy."

Rome sat up and Hunt's face swam into view. The detective's brow was creased.

"Hunt?" He looked past his friend and his gaze focused on a huge chandelier.

Everything rushed back in like a flood.

"*Sofie.*" He gripped Hunt's arm.

"She's safe. She's downstairs, with your guards and a couple of uniforms. She's worrying about you."

All the air rushed out of Rome.

"The paramedics are patching her up," Hunt added.

Rome whipped his head around. "She's hurt?"

"Like I said, she's fine. Just a few cuts."

"Cuts?" Rome heaved himself to his feet. He had to see for himself that she was okay.

"Rome, take it easy."

Fuck that. He fought off the dizziness and fog of whatever drug they'd hit him with. He walked across the mostly abandoned dining room. There were a few cops helping crying people out.

"You hurt?" Hunt stuck close by.

"Assholes drugged me."

"Hell, you need to get checked out."

Rome grunted. What he needed was to get to Sofie.

Hunt muttered under his breath as they moved toward the doorway. A trio of firefighters rushed past them.

"She's in danger," Rome said.

"I know. Like I said, I've got two officers on her, and the Norcross guards. I called Vander." Hunt paused. "She was chased by someone."

"What?" Rome's muscles went rigid and jerked to a halt.

"He attacked her in the ballroom upstairs. I assume he orchestrated this whole mess and took you down to get to her."

Shit. She must've been terrified. This had to be her stalker. Rome's head filled with mental curses. The fucker was going down.

"She hit him with a chair, broke a window, and jumped out."

Rome's heart did a hard squeeze. He ran through the hotel schematics in his head and met Hunt's green gaze.

"You're telling me that she jumped out of a second-floor window to escape the asshole terrorizing her?"

Rome's deadly tone made Hunt wince. "She's fine. Settle down."

Rome rushed into the lobby, shoving through the crowd of people. Outside was chaos. There were crying guests, most of them red-eyed from the smoke.

Police cars and ambulances filled the street. Rome scanned, then spotted a small form in purple at the back of an ambulance. Two officers, Mike and Dan, and Vander, were standing nearby.

Rome didn't say anything. He jogged through the throng, heading straight for her.

He bumped into someone.

"Hey, watch—" The man saw Rome's face and wisely sidestepped out of the way.

As Rome approached, Sofie sensed him coming. A paramedic was wiping blood off her hands.

When she saw Rome, she leaped to her feet and pushed the man away. Her gaze locked with Rome's.

Then she was running.

She dodged a couple and broke into a sprint.

Rome caught her, wrapping his arms around her.

"Rome. Oh, God. *Oh, God.*"

"Shh." Rome dropped to his knees, and pressed his face to her hair. It smelled of smoke.

"He was hunting me..." Her voice broke.

"I'm sorry, beautiful. I should've been there."

She lifted her head. "You were hurt." She cupped his cheek.

"I'm fine. You okay?"

She nodded. But he touched the new bandages on her hands.

Her fingers stroked his cheek. "Just cuts. I'll heal."

If her stalker had succeeded, she could be dead.

Rome's gut rebelled. No fucking way. He was not going to let her be hurt.

"Rome, we've got reporters around," Vander murmured.

And Rome had the princess clutched to his chest like she was his.

She *was* his, but they didn't need the world to know.

He rose with her in his arms.

"Rome, the stalker... He mentioned that he's been watching the house. I...I can't go back there right now."

Dammit. Rome met Vander's gaze. "I'm taking her to my place. No one will expect her to be there. I've got a good security system, and we'll get more guards assigned outside. At least until Sofie has had a chance to calm down from this."

Vander nodded. "Do it."

"Can you organize some of her stuff to be brought over?"

"Sure thing." Vander handed Rome a set of keys. "Go. Get her out of here." He pointed to Mike and Dan. "They'll tail you."

Rome got Sofie into an X6.

"How many of these does Vander own?" she asked.

"A few."

As they pulled out, he watched the guards fall in behind them, driving another X6. He scanned for anyone else following. He took a circuitous route to his place.

"My condo isn't very big."

She glanced over at him. "I don't take up much room."

That wasn't what he meant. "My condo only has one loft bedroom. It's not far from the Norcross Security office."

"Okay," she said.

Hell, she'd been born and raised in a palace. "It's right for me, but—"

"Rome." She rested her hand on his thigh. "It's fine. I'm excited to see where you live. Do you think I'm an elitist snob?"

"No. But you're royalty, and I'm not."

She withdrew her hand, her mouth moving into a flat line. "I thought I was just Sofie to you."

He cursed and grabbed her hand back. "You are, but I can't pretend the differences in our backgrounds don't exist."

"They don't matter to me."

He felt those words deep.

Then he shoved all this aside. He needed to focus on keeping her safe, not worrying about the differences in their bank accounts and houses.

He reached his building, and saw her looking out the window at the old factory building and its prominent clocktower.

"It's called the Clocktower Lofts. It was once the headquarters of a printing company."

"It's *fabulous*."

He parked in the garage and led her upstairs. As they

waited for the elevator, it opened and a man in a business suit stepped out, swiping at his phone.

"Hey, Rome," the man said.

"Ed. This is Sofie."

The man lifted his chin for a second, and his gaze narrowed. "You look familiar."

She just smiled.

Ed shrugged. "Got to run, Rome and Rome's girl. Big trading deal." Ed strode off, still swiping his phone.

They rode up in the elevator, and Rome led her to his condo. He unlocked the door.

Suddenly, he felt nervous. He watched as she walked in, looking around. Then she grinned.

"Rome, I *love* it."

The loft was all white, with wooden floors and beams, along with black pipework. It had high ceilings that he loved, and stairs leading up to his loft bedroom. He scrutinized her face and all he saw was happiness. She meant it.

She walked over, studying the exposed brick wall in the living area and his bookshelves.

"The perk of working at Norcross is that Easton helps us invest our money. I would never have afforded this place back when I was in the military."

"It's got such good light and character. It's really great."

Huge, narrow windows faced an internal courtyard, so the place never lacked for light.

"Let me check in with the guards."

She nodded and kept wandering. Rome made a short call to ensure Mike and Dan were in place, and monitoring everyone entering and leaving the building. He slipped the phone back in his pocket.

"Kitchen and bathroom are at that end." Rome pointed past his black dining table. "Why don't you shower and—"

"You could join me." She shot him a sexy smile.

"I could." He felt his chest lighten for the first time in hours. "Let's—"

There was a knock at the door.

Rome frowned. "Vander can't have gotten to your place and back that quickly." Rome checked the peephole, then rolled his eyes.

"Rome?" Sofie asked.

He swung the door open.

The doorway was filled with three women.

Gia Norcross lifted a hand and smiled. "Hi."

SOFIE SHIFTED and looked at the three attractive women in the doorway. She recognized Harlow instantly.

Rome scowled.

"We heard what happened at the Palace Hotel." Harlow barged past Rome. "We wanted to check that you're okay, Sofie."

Sofie lifted her bandaged hands. "A little banged up, but I'm alive and breathing."

"God." Sympathy crossed Harlow's face. The woman opened her arms, then hesitated. "Is it okay to hug you? Is that against royal protocol?"

Sofie felt a rush of warmth. "It's fine. I could do with

a hug, although I still smell like smoke."

Harlow gently wrapped her arms around her. "I've just been through some scary times with a bad guy after me. I know how much it sucks."

Sofie hugged the woman back. She had Caro, and for many years, she'd had Tori, but she didn't have lots of close girlfriends. It was hard when she traveled so much, plus being a princess didn't make it easy. People had to be vetted, and even then, lots of people just wanted her for her money and influence.

Harlow patted her shoulder.

"You have Norcross Security looking after you," the tiny, curvy brunette in a killer blue suit said. "So, you'll be fine." The woman smiled. "I'm Gia Norcross."

"Oh, it's a pleasure." Sofie gingerly shook hands. "Your brothers are—"

"Hot. Gorgeous. Badass. I know, believe me, growing up with them has been a trial."

Sofie liked Gia already.

The final woman stepped forward. "I'm Haven, Rhys' girlfriend, and Gia's best friend."

Sofie shook the other woman's hand. She was another brunette with a slender figure and a pretty face.

"Don't you three work?" Rome grumbled.

Gia waved her arm. "Take a chill pill, big guy. We were all worried about you and your princess."

"Please, call me Sofie."

Gia smiled. "Sofie. Besides, I own my own business, so I can make my own hours."

Haven tucked her hair back behind her ear. "And mine and Harlow's boss drove us here."

Harlow smiled. "Easton's parking the car."

"It's nice of you to check on us," Sofie said.

"I'll make tea," Harlow said.

"Tea?" Gia exclaimed. "The woman needs a cocktail."

"It's too early for cocktails," Rome said.

Gia headed for his kitchen and looked back over her shoulder. "It's never too early for cocktails."

"I only have beer," Rome said.

Gia spun, undeterred. "Well, luckily, I have a bottle of wine in my bag."

Sofie watched Gia open her huge—and super cute—handbag and pull out a bottle of white wine.

Rome made a choked sound. "What else do you have in there?"

When Gia opened her mouth, Rome held up a hand. "Don't tell me. I don't want to know." He sighed. "I have some wine glasses from my mom and sister's last visit."

He stalked off to the kitchen with Gia. Soon, Sofie found herself on Rome's comfy gray couch, sipping a glass of Chardonnay.

There was another knock at the door, and Rome let Easton in.

The billionaire nodded at Sofie. "I'm glad you're okay, Sofie."

"Thank you."

The oldest Norcross brother sat in a black armchair, then pulled Harlow down to sit on the arm. He kept a tight hold on her. With a smile, the blonde dropped a kiss to his lips. They looked beautiful together, and clearly happy.

Gia leaned forward. "So, tell us everything."

Rome moved behind the couch and rested a hand on Sofie's shoulder. "She doesn't need to relive it. She needs to shower, change, and rest—"

Sofie reached up and touched his fingers. "It's okay. You need to know the details. It was my stalker. He's here." She shuddered. "And it might be good to talk it out. Get it off my chest."

There was another knock at the door. Rome huffed out a breath and went to open it. Vander walked in with two of her suitcases.

Sofie froze. "Who packed my stuff?"

"I did," Vander said.

Sofia blinked, having trouble picturing badass Vander Norcross packing her clothes. And her underwear.

Oh, God.

She prayed he hadn't thought to check under the bed. All her Robin Hood stuff was stashed there.

Vander also handed over her handbag. "Recovered this from the Palace Hotel."

She took it. "Thanks, Vander."

"Up here." Rome led his boss up the stairs to the bedroom with the suitcases.

Once the men were back, Sofie sipped her wine. "So, the luncheon started off fine..." She launched into the story.

Rome sat beside her and when she reached the part about being trapped with her stalker, he tensed. Harlow, Haven, and Gia made shocked exclamations. Easton and Vander scowled.

"God, Sofie," Harlow murmured.

A muscle worked in Rome's jaw. "It could've turned out very differently." He could have lost her.

She grabbed his hand. He tangled his fingers with hers.

She turned her head, conscious of the others watching them. Vander looked impassive, Easton looked amused. All the women were smiling, not even bothering to hide their glee.

Gia looked pointedly at Rome and Sofie's joined hands and winked.

"We need to step up work on finding the stalker," Vander said.

Sofie jolted. "But that's beyond the scope of just guarding me."

"Don't care," Rome said. "I'm going to find the asshole."

"Rome also shared... About the jewelry thefts being linked." Vander gave her a pointed look, but was careful to keep the identity of Robin Hood to himself. "I think the Black Fox gang deserve a closer look."

Sofie pondered. "You think my stalker is part of the gang?"

"It's a possibility," Rome said. "I want to check it out."

She straightened. "I want to help."

He looked like he wanted to argue.

"I know more about them than anyone."

Reluctantly, he nodded. Then he glanced at their guests. "I think it's time for Sofie to rest now."

"That sounds like our marching orders." Harlow stood and hugged Sofie. "Feel better." The blonde ran her tongue across her teeth and rolled her eyes at Rome.

Sofie grinned, enjoying the playful teasing.

Rome showed everybody out.

"I like your friends, Rome."

He grunted. "They grow on you. Like mold."

She giggled, and then her stomach growled.

"Hungry?" he asked.

"I didn't get to eat much before the luncheon got interrupted."

"I'll see what I've got." He headed for the kitchen.

"Actually—" she fiddled with her hair "—I'd love a burger and fries."

He smiled and pulled out his cell phone. "I can order you a burger, Princess."

"And fries."

"How do you stay so slim?"

"Princess secrets."

He ordered. While they waited for the food, she showered and changed. The bandages made it a bit tricky, but she was just really glad that apart from a couple of deep cuts, her hands weren't as bad as they could have been.

They ate the burgers on his couch and watched Netflix.

Apart from Rome regularly checking in with the security guards outside, Sofie felt like they were just a normal couple, doing normal things on an easy night at home. Just the two of them.

She leaned into him.

It was perfect.

CHAPTER FOURTEEN

The next morning, Rome woke in his own bed, with Sofie plastered to his side, and her hair spread all over his chest.

Sofie was in his bed.

It felt damn good.

He glanced at the clock on the bedside table. *Crap*. She had a press conference at the Norcross Security office in an hour, to talk about the attack at the Palace Hotel.

He slid his hand down to cup her hip. He wanted to stay in bed all day, but duty called.

He slipped out of the bed. She murmured, but didn't wake. He smiled. He'd kept her up a little late, testing out his bed.

When he returned from the bathroom, she'd moved into his spot in the bed, hugging his pillow.

A bolt of emotion punched through him. He liked Princess Sofia of Caldova right there.

He crouched beside the bed. "Sofie?" He pushed her hair off her face.

Her pretty brown eyes opened the tiniest crack and she grunted.

Shit, she was cute. "You've got a press conference in one hour."

She blinked, then exploded off the bed.

"I have to shower. And do my hair." She gasped. "I hope Vander packed my hair dryer."

Rome grabbed her, and kissed her long and slow. "You look beautiful all the time."

Her face softened. "Who knew you could be charming?"

"I have my moments." He spied a bruise on her neck and touched it. "Crap, looks like I left a mark."

She smiled. "I can hide it, but we'll both know it's there."

He gave her butt a light slap. "Go and get ready."

When she came downstairs, she wore a long, black skirt and a cream top. A jaunty scarf was tied around her neck, hiding the hickey. Her hair was piled up on her head, and her makeup emphasized her eyes.

They kept breakfast simple—toast and cereal—before he hustled her into the X6 under the watchful gaze of the guards.

It was a short drive to the Norcross Security office. The street outside the converted warehouse was lined with news vans, but Rome drove straight into the underground parking.

Sofie dragged in a breath. "Time for Princess Sofia mode."

"I'll be right with you."

They walked upstairs, but before they reached the top, he stopped and pressed a quick kiss to her lips.

Her tense body went lax.

"*Mmm.*" She had a dazed, smiling look on her face.

"Go and do your thing," he said. "Once it's done, we can get to work on researching the Black Fox gang."

She nodded.

When they stepped into the main level of the warehouse, reporters were sitting in chairs that had been set out. The central space was all open, with a polished concrete floor and industrial metal touches. Glass walls enclosed the offices along the sides.

Rome led her over to the microphone. Vander stood nearby, nodded. There were various Norcross Security guards dotted around.

"Good morning," Sofie said. "I wanted to talk a little about the terrible attack at the charity luncheon yesterday."

Rome folded his hands in front of him and listened as she spoke. She spoke well—clearly, keeping things simple. She smiled at the right moments, appeared grave at others.

"Princess Sofia?" A female reporter raised her hand. "Is this the work of the thieves targeting the jewelry of the exhibition?"

"I don't know," Sofia answered. "I'm leaving it to the experts. The San Francisco police have been wonderful. I appreciate all their hard work."

"Princess?" A male reporter stood. "You're lucky you weren't hurt, or worse."

Rome glared at the weasel. He could already see the hungry look on the man's face. He wanted to relive the salacious details of the attack.

"Yes, I am very fortunate to have amazing protection provided by Norcross Security." She nodded at Vander.

"Princess Sofia?" another woman said. "There have been some photos circulating of you in your bodyguard's arms. Can you tell me about your relationship? You appear very close."

Rome stiffened and felt some gazes glance his way.

Sofia's smile cooled. "When you spend twenty-four hours a day with someone, and trust them with your life, yes, you get close. Especially after a frightening attack. As I said, I'm extremely grateful for the work of Norcross Security." She looked around. "That's all, thank you. I look forward to your support of the gala, and the Glittering Court Exhibition. We're raising money for a very worthy cause. Thank you." She stepped away from the microphone.

Rome stepped in and took her arm. More reporters shouted out questions, but he ignored them and led her away.

He took her down to Ace's computer room. It was one of the few spaces with no windows or glass walls, and offered more privacy.

Once they were inside, she blew out a breath.

Ace was kicked back in a chair, a coffee mug in hand. "Vultures gone?"

"Not soon enough," Rome said. "Sofie, this is our tech guru, Ace Olivera."

"Hello, Ace."

"Nice to meet you, Princess Sofia. Although I hear you go by Sofie." The man shot her a wide smile.

"I do."

On-screen, Rome watched the guards herding the reporters out of the office.

"So," Ace said, "ready to get to work on the Black Fox gang? If that's exciting enough for Robin Hood." Ace winked.

Sofie flushed prettily.

"What have you got?" Rome knew Ace would have already been digging.

Ace tapped the keyboard and data filled the screens. There was a global map covered in red dots.

"I've got a lot. The gang's been operating for years, and growing bolder over recent months."

Sofie studied the screens, her face serious. "I have a few more of their jobs to add." She pulled her laptop out of her bag.

She and Ace swapped data. They sat at Ace's desk, heads pressed together, and Rome leaned against the wall and watched.

Ace pulled up some of the files he'd collected. Sofie studied the screen.

Rome suddenly saw her stiffen. He glanced over and saw a picture of an attractive brunette on the screen.

"Sofie?" He moved up behind her.

"That's Tori." A sad smile crossed her face. "I miss her so much."

Rome didn't care that Ace was there, he pulled her out of her chair and to his chest.

She held on for a second, then patted his chest. "Thanks, I needed that."

"Vander picked up some chatter from some informants," Ace said.

"I did." Vander strode in. "My informant said the thieves are after the Sapphire Wave Tiara."

"I already suspected as much," Sofie said.

Vander crossed his arms. "And they're going to target the gala night."

Rome cursed. "You're not wearing it."

Sofie straightened. "It's the centerpiece of the exhibit. I'm not going to let these cowards dictate my actions."

Rome cursed again.

She grabbed his hand. "I have faith you'll keep me safe. Besides, doesn't it make sense to lure them out?"

He growled. "I'm not fucking using you as bait."

She turned to Vander. "Is there any progress on identifying my stalker?"

"Guy's a ghost," Ace said.

"No one's a ghost," Vander said.

"I've been analyzing all the CCTV from the Palace Hotel security," Ace said. "Seeing if anyone popped coming in and out. Tedious, and it's totally possible he slipped in without being spotted by a camera."

"So, you've got nothing?" Rome said.

"I didn't say that." Ace grinned. "I am brilliant, after all."

An image appeared on the screen. It showed a room filled with smoke, with the dark shape of a man.

"This was taken from the ballroom where Sofie beaned the guy with a chair," Ace said.

Vander stared at the screen. "Not much to go on."

"He's about six feet tall, give or take. Slim build."

"It's a start." Rome glared at the shadowy shape. *You can't have her, asshole. I will stop you.*

"I got something else via Hunt," Ace continued.

A picture of a trim woman with ash-blonde hair flicked up on screen.

Sofie straightened like she'd been prodded. "That's Chantal Lockwood. She organized the luncheon at the Palace Hotel. She's a British socialite. She's pleasant, friendly. We move in similar circles."

Ace crossed his arms. "She purchased the makings of a firebomb a few days ago. Likely used in the firebombing at the first robbery."

Sofie gasped. "*No*. It can't be. I like her. I *trust* her."

Rome gripped Sofie's shoulder. "What do you know about her?"

Sofie swallowed. "She's in her mid-forties, and married to a wealthy British viscount, and travels around the world doing her charity work. Her husband is in his eighties and it's rumored she likes men." Sofie wrinkled her nose.

"What?" Rome prompted.

"It's just gossip..."

"Tell us."

"She likes her men young...and a little kinky. Look, she can't be involved with this."

"Is there anything linking Lockwood to the Black Fox gang?" Vander asked.

"Nothing overt," Ace conceded. "But my search did find this."

It was a still from a CCTV security feed. It showed Chantal and Boris Petrovich meeting at a coffee shop at Fisherman's Wharf.

"Could be a coincidence," Vander said, sounding unconvinced.

Rome studied the way the pair kept a low profile. "They didn't want to be seen together."

"She's part of the Black Fox gang." Sofie's voice vibrated with anger and disbelief.

"We can't prove that, but I think we need to do some surveillance on her," Vander said. "This is incriminating, but not solid enough evidence."

"I'm in," Sofie said.

Rome stiffened. "Sofie—"

"*No*. I won't stay hidden, and locked up, and doing nothing." Her chin lifted.

Vander raised a brow. "I think if you stay with Rome, and go undercover, some surveillance work will be fine."

Rome grunted. "You just don't want the surveillance job."

Vander shrugged.

"What?" Sofie asked.

"Surveillance is boring," Rome said.

"Surely not. This could prove that Chantal is involved or not. It could help us bring down the thieves."

Rome shook his head. "Let's go, Sherlock."

EXCITEMENT WHIPPED along Sofie's veins.

She and Rome walked down the street. She was

wearing khaki cargo pants and a sweater. She looked a little dowdy, because the sweater was way too big. She also wore a black wig in a bob style. Her hair was tucked underneath and hidden away.

No one would recognize her. In fact, her parents could walk past and not recognize her.

Rome had changed into jeans. When she'd first seen him, her mouth had watered. He looked *so* fine. The denim cupped his muscular ass. He also wore a black polo shirt, with a battered leather jacket on top.

Yum.

"Here." He stopped beside a nondescript, white sedan and unlocked it.

Their surveillance vehicle.

"You bring a book?" he asked as he settled into the driver's seat.

"No. I'm planning to use those big binoculars you brought."

He grinned at her.

She rolled her eyes. "That did sound a bit naughty, but I really do want to use those binoculars."

He handed them to her.

He started the engine and pulled out. "Lockwood's staying at the St. Regis Hotel."

They reached the hotel and circled the block a few times. Finally, he got a parking spot a few doors down from the front entrance.

Sofie rubbed her hands together. This was so cool. She lifted the binoculars and zoomed in on the front doors. It was busy, with crowds of people coming and going.

"If Chantal is involved..." Sofie shook her head. "I just don't understand being part of something illegal, something that destroys lives."

"Not everyone is good, Sofie. And sometimes good people do bad things." His gaze turned inward.

"Rome?" His dark mood throbbed off him.

"Sorry. When I was in the military, the last two years I was part of a covert special operations team."

"It was hard?"

"We had some rough missions. I saw some desperate people forced to do bad things, bad people who were rotten to the core, and some good people, too. Those good people gave me hope."

Sofie nodded. "You're right. I can't just focus on the bad."

Rome ran a finger down her nose. "Chantal just exited the hotel."

"What?" Sofie looked out the window and lifted the binoculars. Sure enough, Chantal—stylishly dressed in black slacks and a blue blouse—was talking to a uniformed concierge.

"How did you see her? You were looking at me."

"I'm good at my job," he said.

He sure was.

A big, silver SUV pulled up and Chantal slid into the backseat.

Rome waited for the SUV to pass them, then pulled out.

They trailed behind it. For a while, Sofie was sure they'd lose them, as Rome didn't get too close. But he doggedly stayed on their tail. He made it look easy.

They headed north.

She glanced out at the greenery of the Presidio. The waters of the Bay lay to their right.

The Golden Gate Bridge stretched ahead. Soon they were driving onto the bridge and Sofie took a second to absorb the stunning view.

"Looks like she's going to Sausalito," Rome said.

The SUV drove into the pocket of houses set on the hill looking over to the Bay toward San Francisco. It stopped in front of a modern, white house with a curved roof. The place would have wonderful views back toward the city.

Rome parked several houses away.

Sofie watched Chantal climb out and the SUV drove off. The woman jogged to the front of the house and knocked. Like she didn't have a care in the world.

A part of Sofie really hoped Chantal was innocent.

The door opened, and Chantal smiled and walked inside. Sofie couldn't see who'd opened the door.

"Now what?" she asked.

"We wait."

She stared at the house. Rome started texting and she raised a brow.

"I'm getting Ace to check whose house this is," Rome said.

"Good idea."

They waited.

And waited.

After two hours, Sofie was dying of boredom. "Surveillance is boring."

"I warned you."

She sighed.

His phone pinged and she watched him read the message.

God, he was so purely masculine. She could happily sit here and watch him for hours. She'd prefer to do other things with him, if she had the choice. Her belly coiled. Being with Rome was just easy. There was no pretense; she didn't have to be anything special to him.

"Anything?" she asked.

His brow creased. "Ace said the house is being rented by a company called Antiquarian. It's European. Heard of it?"

The name tickled something in the back of her head, but nothing came to mind. "No."

"Ace is going to keep digging."

She flopped back in the seat.

"He said the Black Fox gang is planning another theft. He found info on the Dark Web."

She gritted her teeth. "They're so greedy."

Suddenly, the front door of the house opened.

"*Rome.*"

They watched Chantal skip down the steps. Her hair was no longer up in a ponytail but mussed and loose. Her face was flushed and she was smiling.

"Three guesses what she's been up to," Sofie muttered. "She's married, with two kids, and her husband and family are back in England."

The woman started down the sidewalk in their direction.

"Shit." Rome turned his head.

Sofie followed suit and saw the silver SUV driving

down the street toward them. Chantal was walking to meet it. She was going to see them.

Rome grabbed Sofie, yanked her across the center console, and kissed her.

Oh. This was *much* better. She kissed him back.

He cupped the back of her head and she leaned farther over the console, ready to crawl into his lap.

Then he bit her lip and smiled at her. "She's gone past."

She blinked. "Who?"

"Chantal. The person we're surveilling."

"Oh, right." Sofie sat back in her seat. "I really suck at this private investigator stuff."

Ahead, Chantal got into the silver SUV.

"Luckily you're better at jewel thiefing." Rome pulled the car out to follow.

"Thiefing isn't a word." Sofie paused. "I'd stop if the Black Fox gang was brought down."

"You know it won't bring Victoria back."

"I know that." Sofie sighed. "I guess I hoped that it would lessen the pain."

"Time does that, Sofie." There was so much understanding in his voice and she knew he was thinking of Lola.

She touched his thigh.

"I read once that grief is like a box with a ball inside it," he said. "Inside the box is a button, and when the ball hits the button, you feel the pain of your loved one's loss."

She nodded.

"At first, the ball is huge and hits the button all the

time." His hands flexed on the wheel. "But over time, the ball shrinks. It doesn't hit the button as often."

He stopped at some lights and looked at her. "But every now and then, it still manages to hit that button, and it still hurts."

"I like that analogy," she said.

"We'll always miss them, Sofie, but we still need to live."

"And accept that there was nothing more we could have done to save them," she added.

He watched her for a beat, then set the car in motion. He held her hand as they drove back to San Francisco.

They watched Chantal head back into her hotel.

"Surveillance is over," Rome said.

"Thank God. It's so boring."

He smiled. "Come on, Princess, we'll find you something more exciting to do."

CHAPTER FIFTEEN

The next day, Sofie had no engagements.

They spent the day at his place, and she dove into her charity work. Rome leaned against his kitchen island, watching her. She'd spread papers all over his coffee table, and sat cross-legged on the couch, with her silver laptop close by, and her phone pressed to her ear.

"That's great. If we can add additional funds today, that would be amazing." She was quiet a moment. "Priya, you are a *miracle* worker. Okay, let's discuss the event in London next month."

She was so organized. He knew that she was discussing millions of dollars' worth of charity funding, and scheduling events to help so many people.

Incredible. She was beautiful, funny, generous, kind, and he wasn't anywhere near good enough for her.

His hands clamped on the edge of the island. She was a princess, she traveled the world doing these charity events, not to mention stealing back stolen gems.

He didn't like that last part so much. It was dangerous.

What the hell did he have to offer her?

She looked up, caught his gaze, and smiled at him. He felt it move through him.

He pushed the questions away. Whatever happened, for now at least, she was his.

His to protect and his to pleasure.

She ended the call. "Done."

"You have a lot of work going on."

She nodded, sticking a pen behind her ear. "The more I do, the more money I raise for the Victoria Foundation, and the more people we can help. I'm lucky to have amazing staff, like Priya in London. That woman could organize a space invasion."

Rome walked toward her. "You're pretty amazing, you know that?"

Sofie blushed. "I think I'm pretty normal. A bit boring, even."

He leaned down to kiss her. "Not even a little bit."

She gripped the front of his shirt and hauled him closer. As he deepened the kiss, she moaned. "*Now*. I need you."

"Yes," he growled.

He dragged her off the couch and onto the rug on the floor. Papers rustled. He tore at her clothes and heard something rip.

"Shit, sorry."

"Don't care," she panted.

He needed her, was desperate for her.

"Rome, Rome, Rome," she chanted.

He kissed her again, thrusting his tongue into her mouth. She made a sexy sound and he savored the taste of her. Desire seared through him.

Finally, he got her naked, that sexy little piercing on her belly winking at him. She tore his shirt open, and then her hands stroked his chest.

Rome fumbled for his wallet. He stopped for a second to admire her, naked, and spread out on his rug.

"Fuck, you are beautiful."

"*Hurry.*"

He flicked open his pants. When he pulled his aching cock free, her gaze latched onto it. He opened the wrapper with his teeth and rolled the condom on.

"*Rome.*"

When he looked up, she'd turned onto her hands and knees.

"Sofia." His voice was guttural with need. Her beautiful ass was on display.

She looked back at him, face flushed, need stamped on her features.

"Sofie, baby." He moved in behind her. He ran his hand over her ass, loving how she quivered beneath his touch. He gripped his cock, and rubbed the head through her wet folds. He wanted her so badly and he was having trouble holding it together.

"Rome, *please.*" She shoved back against him.

And he had no rational thought left.

He shoved forward, thrusting into her.

She cried out.

Damn, she was hot and tight around him. She was perfect. She was everything.

He stayed there for a second, lodged inside her. His fingers dug into her golden skin and he looked over her sweet ass, then lower, right where his cock was embedded inside her.

Sofie moaned. "Move. *Please.*"

Rome drew back, then rammed in.

Her back arched, her head flew back. "*Yes.*"

He gripped her hips and found his rhythm. She took every hard thrust, rocking into him. The sound of their flesh slapping together filled the room as he powered into her.

Christ. He couldn't think, could barely breathe.

There was only Sofie and the sweet, hot pleasure.

Rome slid a hand beneath her and found her clit. He thumbed it and felt her pussy clench on his cock.

"*Yes.* Please. Yes, Rome." Her movements turned wild, desperate.

He kept thrusting into her, driving deep.

"Fuck, Sofie." He felt his orgasm building—huge and big.

"*Rome.*"

She started coming. Her breathless cries pushed him over the edge.

He rammed deep, hips bucking as he imploded. His low roar filled the room.

Fuck, he loved coming in his Sofie.

She collapsed forward on the rug, panting.

He stroked his hand down her back. He could just sit here and touch her all day. He'd never wanted to just pet and caress a woman before.

She made a contented sound, and he leaned down and kissed her shoulder blade.

"Okay?"

She turned her head. "Rome, I'm awesome. That was exactly what I needed."

He arched a brow. "You needed to get fucked hard, doggy style, on the floor?"

Her smile widened. "Yes. All these things that I've been missing out on."

The thought of her doing this with anyone else made him want to growl. "I'll be back."

He made a quick trip to the bathroom to deal with the condom. When he returned, she was standing in the living room, shrugging into his white shirt.

It swamped her and made her look like a little girl playing dress-up. But those sexy, bare legs reminded him that she wasn't a girl at all.

Sofie smiled at him, and he stalked over and kissed her.

"I like this look." She smoothed her hands over his bare chest. "There's something about a man in suit pants and no shirt." She kissed his tattoo. "I'm going to freshen up."

He watched her skip up the stairs to his bedroom.

Yeah, she was totally out of his league, but he didn't care. He wasn't giving her up.

He was tidying up some of her papers when there was a knock at the door. He frowned. A quick glance through the peephole made him groan. *No way.*

He opened the door. "What are you two doing here?"

His mom and sister pushed inside.

"Surprise," Liana said.

His mother eyed his shirtless chest. "Why aren't you wearing a shirt?"

Shit. Rome glanced toward the bedroom.

"We stopped at the Norcross office," his mom said. "Vander said you were working from home."

Thanks for the warning, Vander.

"And guarding Princess Sofia of Caldova!" Lia clapped her hands, her voice excited. "It's *so* cool. I'd love it if she'd sign my Young Royals calendar."

He heard footsteps on the stairs.

"Rome, do you want—?" Sofie froze halfway down the steps. Her eyes were wide, like a deer in headlights.

Hell, she was still only wearing his shirt, her hair loose and her face flushed.

She looked like she'd been well fucked.

His mother's and sister's mouths dropped open.

SOFIE DIDN'T KNOW what to do. Here she was, naked except for Rome's shirt, and there were two women she'd never met staring at her.

"Sofie," Rome rumbled. "This is my mother, Violet Nash, and my sister, Liana."

His sister. And his *mother*.

Both women looked like they'd been hit with a pole.

Sofie didn't need him to introduce them to see that they were related. His mother had the same green eyes as Rome, and his sister had the feminine version of his features.

Mrs. Nash was tall, with a curvy body, and her short hair was a mass of tight, dark curls. Liana was an inch shorter than her mother, a lot curvier, and her black hair was straightened and in a ponytail.

Sofie shook off her shock and embarrassment. "Hello, I'm Princess Sofia."

Rome came to her and wrapped an arm around her waist. It helped her fight the urge to flee.

"Mom, Lia, this is Sofie."

His sister curtsied. "Your Highness."

"Please, it's just Sofie." She held out a hand.

Rome's mom shook it gingerly. Sofie saw something working behind the woman's green eyes.

Liana shook it enthusiastically. "It is *so* great to meet you. I'm a huge fan."

Sofie smiled. "Rome's been wonderful. He's been taking such good care of me."

"Uh-huh," Mrs. Nash drawled.

Heat poured into Sofie's cheeks. "I'll just...go and change."

Rome's fingers squeezed hers, and she managed a smile before she fled.

She stopped in the middle of his bedroom. *Oh, God.* She quickly changed. *Oh, God.* She repaired her makeup, and pulled her hair back into a braid. She tried to tamp down the embarrassment. *Oh, God.*

When she headed toward the stairs, she heard voices.

"What the hell are you doing, Rome Alexander Nash?" his mother bit out.

His middle name was Alexander. Sofie liked it.

"Mom—"

"You're sleeping with a princess!"

"Mom."

"Are you crazy? You're her bodyguard. You're her employee. You're a simple boy from Georgia, and she's a very rich, very well-known princess."

"Mom, keep your voice down."

"She's toying with you. You're just a fun diversion, then she'll dump your ass and move onto the next hot body. You want to be left with a broken heart?"

Sofie's stomach worked into knots and she pressed a hand to it.

"Can I talk now?" Rome asked dryly.

"Let her run out of steam, brother," Liana said.

"I did *not* raise a stupid boy," Mrs. Nash continued.

"Mom, I'm not sleeping with the princess. To me, she's just Sofie."

Sofie leaned against the doorjamb, her heart melting.

"You can't separate the two," his mother said. "And don't tell me that your emotions aren't involved. I can see it a mile away."

Sofie's heart leaped in her throat. *Really?*

"Mom, I like her a lot. She is smart, sweet, kind—"

"Beautiful," Liana added. "Rich."

Sofie heard Rome growl. "I know she's way out of my league. I'll enjoy the time we have together."

Her heart shriveled. That sounded temporary. Was she just a good time to him? It was painful to breathe. Especially when she realized that she was falling in love with him.

Oh, goodness, she was falling in love with Rome. She moved her hand to her chest, felt her heart beating hard.

"You're making a mistake," his mom said.

"Keep your voice down," Rome said. "She'll hear you."

Too late.

"You think she doesn't know all of this already?"

"Mom, she isn't Dad."

Sofie backed into the bedroom and took a few deep breaths. She'd have to think this through. Later. If she could handle the pain.

She headed out, stomping loudly this time so they'd hear her coming.

In the living room the conversation stopped. Sofie pinned on her princess smile. As she descended the stairs, Rome looked at her mouth and scowled. When she got to the bottom of the stairs, he pulled her under his arm.

"Sofie and I are going back to her rental house later. Vander's increased the security there. You guys can stay here."

"Sweet," Liana said. "Sofie, I have a copy of the Young Royals calendar. I was hoping you'd sign it."

"I'd love to."

"I could use some tea," Mrs. Nash muttered.

Rome deposited Sofie in an armchair. "I'll get it."

"I'll help." His sister followed him out.

Sofie fought the urge to fidget. She leaned forward. "This must come as a bit of a surprise."

"Mmm," Mrs. Nash replied.

"Look, Rome is...amazing." Sofie smiled. "So strong, steady, protective. I have a stalker." She wrinkled her nose.

Mrs. Nash's face softened the minutest bit. "I'm sorry."

"It's pretty scary, but when I'm with Rome, he makes me feel safe."

His mother studied her face.

"He sees me. I'm used to feeling like I'm in a fish-bowl. People watching your every move, speculating on everything you do, making things up."

"That sounds horrible."

Sofie shrugged. "I'm used to it. I realized people only see and believe what they want anyway, regardless of the truth. But Rome, he saw the real me right from the beginning."

"Sounds like my boy. He's very observant."

"He's amazing."

Mrs. Nash paused. "He's strong, but he has his own scars."

Sofie nodded. "I know. He's told me about Lola. I'm very sorry for your loss. He's also told me a little bit about his time in the military."

"He told you?" Mrs. Nash whispered, her expression full of pain. "About Lolly?"

Sofie nodded. "No one should ever lose a child, especially like that. I know he feels responsible."

"He was just a baby, shouldering too much responsibility. It was my fault."

Sofie couldn't help but rest her hand on the woman's knee. "It's not your fault, either. It's the fault of the predator who took her. You were doing the best you could in what I suspect was a difficult situation."

Mrs. Nash dragged in a shaky breath. "He really talked about her?"

Sofie smiled. "He told me that she loved to sing."

A sad smile crossed Mrs. Nash his face. "She did. Sofie...Rome hasn't talked about Lola since we lost her."

Sofie's chest locked. "Oh."

Mrs. Nash's gaze turned speculative. "So, you're here for the jewelry exhibition. Lia told me all about it. She's hoping to find a ticket."

"I can get tickets. It's raising money for my charity, the Victoria Foundation."

Mrs. Nash's eyes widened. "I've heard of it. I work at a local shelter back home in Atlanta. The Foundation helped several of our residents, including a friend of mine. She was escaping a bad marriage."

"That's exactly what I'd hoped for when I started it." Sofie sank back in the chair. "I lost my best friend because of an act of unspeakable violence. I wanted to help other women like her, Mrs. Nash."

Rome's mother held Sofie's gaze, and they shared a beat of understanding.

"Please, call me Violet."

"Only if you call me Sofie."

CHAPTER SIXTEEN

Back at the Marina house, Rome did a lap of the outside, staring across at the Palace of Fine Arts. He couldn't argue that it was a top-notch location.

His mom and sister were happily staying at his place. Yesterday, they'd spent the afternoon chatting with Sofie. He'd watched his princess win them over.

She'd also signed the damn calendar for his sister, and gotten them both tickets, not only for the jewelry exhibition, but the sold-out gala, as well.

He'd overheard Sofie telling his sister that she could borrow jewelry, too.

The gala was tonight.

Rome blew out a breath. Sofie was inside doing yoga. This time, in the formal living area, and not on the roof terrace.

A heavy sense of dread settled on him. Being in the military, he'd learned that trusting your gut could make the difference between life and death.

The Black Fox gang would strike tonight.

The stalker would attack tonight.

Everyone was targeting Rome's woman.

Well, they'd have to go through him to get to her.

An X6 pulled up and Vander and Saxon climbed out.

"Hey," Vander said.

Rome lifted his chin.

Saxon eyed the house. "Nice place."

"How's Sofie?" Vander asked.

"Good. She shook off the Palace Hotel attack like it was just a bad shopping trip."

"She's tough," Saxon said. "Didn't know they made princesses from titanium."

Vander was watching Rome steadily. "You're worried."

"I've been over everything for tonight too many times to count." He'd stayed up late, with Sofie asleep in the bed beside him. That was after he'd made love to her. He knew he'd been rough, worry and desperation making him edgy. Not that she'd minded. Hell, she'd liked it.

He'd triple and quadruple checked the security plans for the gala.

"Well," Saxon said. "Easton pulled some strings."

Rome frowned.

"We're all coming tonight," Vander said. "Saxon and Gia, Haven and Rhys, Easton and Harlow, Ace."

Rome's eyebrows rose and his chest tightened.

"The girls are adamant that they wanted to support Sofie," Saxon said.

"Easton got a ticket for Maggie, too," Vander added. "She's out buying a dress."

Maggie was their hotshot helicopter pilot. Rome

wasn't sure he'd ever seen the former Navy pilot in a dress before.

"My parents are coming, as well," Vander added.

Saxon snorted. "Mine will be there too, unfortunately."

Rome's throat went tight. "You're all coming to keep her safe."

"To help you keep your woman safe." Vander grasped Rome's shoulder. "We're a team."

Rome nodded. "Thanks, guys."

Vander's phone rang. "It's Ace." He pressed it to his ear. "Yeah. Hang on, Ace, I have Saxon and Rome here, I'll put you on speaker."

"Hi." Ace's voice. "Just got word, and it hasn't hit the news yet."

"What?" Rome demanded.

"Attempted jewelry robbery. Some big, fancy necklace owned by a woman out of Washington D.C."

"Fuck," Rome said.

"They tried to blow the safe, but couldn't get in."

Rome relaxed. "That's good news."

Ace made a sound. "Gets ugly, *amigo*."

Gut churning, Rome glared at the phone. "Go on."

"They attacked a woman. Attempted rape. A neighbor heard the screams and interrupted. The thieves took off."

"Fucking hell," Vander muttered.

"She's pretty beaten up, but alive," Ace continued. "She's in the hospital, and her family's with her."

Rome scraped a hand over his head. "I want this damn gala over." He wanted Sofie safe.

But a bad taste filled his mouth. Once the gala was over, her time in San Francisco was almost done.

Then what?

Rome wanted her in his bed every night. Wanted to watch her cook, smile, laugh every day, not just on random trips here and there where they could hook up.

He pressed a hand to the back of his neck. He couldn't focus on the personal stuff right now.

He needed to keep her safe. The Black Foxes were getting bolder. Her stalker was growing more unhinged.

And now, Rome had to break the news that a woman was attacked just like the friend she'd lost.

"Anything else on Chantal Lockwood?" Rome asked. "Or who rented the house in Sausalito?"

"Lockwood appears clean," Ace said. "Nothing more on the company that's renting the house. Been watching CCTV footage and haven't seen anyone of interest come in or out."

Damn. "Thanks, Ace. I need to talk to Sofie. She has a stylist and hairdresser arriving soon to help her get ready."

"It's going to be fine, Rome," Vander said. "We'll be with you."

He nodded and Vander's phone pinged again.

"Armored vehicle with the tiara's arriving," Vander said.

"You mean the *three* armored vehicles." Saxon smiled. "Vander put together the most complicated plan to get the damn Sapphire Wave tiara here."

With a rumble, an armored truck pulled up, like the ones used to transport money. Right behind it was a

Range Rover as an escort vehicle. Rome could tell right away that the Range Rover was armored, as well.

A moment later, a second armored truck turned onto the street.

Vander turned and opened his jacket. "They were all decoys." He pulled out a black velvet bag.

Rome took it, but didn't open it. Only Vander Norcross would transport a priceless tiara in his suit jacket.

"I'll see you all there tonight," Rome said.

Vander and Saxon nodded.

"Hope your tux is ready to go," Saxon said.

"It is." Rome waved and walked into the house.

Sofie ran out of the kitchen. She'd obviously finished her yoga and showered, and was now in her silky blue robe.

"Oh my gosh, Luis and the hairstylist will be here soon."

Rome gripped her shoulders. "Take a deep breath."

She did. "A kiss would be better."

He kissed her and she shivered.

"There's my sexy shiver," he murmured.

She smiled up at him. "I'm not usually this wound up. I'm just nervous."

"You should be. You can't get complacent."

She nodded and stared at his face. Her smile dissolved. "What's wrong?"

"There was another attempted jewelry theft."

She pressed a hand to her throat. "Okay. But they didn't actually get the jewelry? So why do you look so angry?"

"They didn't get the jewels, but they attacked a woman. Sexual assault."

"*No.*" Sofie shook her head.

"She's here from Washington D.C. Someone interrupted the attack, she's alive."

"But still violated and traumatized." She closed her eyes. "I should go and see her."

"Sofie, you don't know her. She's with her family."

Sofie lifted her chin. "I'm going to send flowers. I'll get someone from the Foundation to check in with her. We have fantastic therapists."

Such a good heart. He pulled her to his chest. "There's something else."

She stiffened, raised her head. "What now? I'm not sure I can deal with more."

He lifted the velvet bag.

"The Sapphire Wave tiara." She opened it.

The diadem was stunning. It was formed in wave-like loops of diamonds, and set in each loop was a large sapphire—nine in total.

"It'll look beautiful on you." He lowered his mouth and kissed her. His phone pinged. "Sounds like your stylists are here."

SOFIE SAT in front of the mirror. Her hair was up, and it looked like she'd just pinned it up easily, not like it'd taken a good hour of work by an expert hairstylist. Her makeup was dewy and natural, a little smoke at her eyes, and her lips were a glossy pink.

It was almost time for the gala.

She was nervous. She could barely sit still.

Tonight was the culmination of so much planning. But all she could think about was the Black Fox gang.

And her stalker.

Rome would be with her. She knew he'd risk his life for hers. That worried her, as well. She resisted the urge to gnaw on her bottom lip and ruin her lipstick.

After the gala, what then? Would Rome let her fly off? Would he head off on another job and leave her?

"Here we go." Luis settled the Sapphire Wave tiara on her head. "Oh," the man breathed. "You are *breathtaking*. You are going to drive the hunk of deliciousness you call a bodyguard wild."

The tiara was gorgeous. The light caught the sapphires, filling them with blue fire.

"I'm sleeping with him."

"Oh." Luis clapped his hands together. "Good for you, Sofie."

She looked back at the mirror. "I'm falling in love with him too."

Saying it aloud made her jittery.

Luis rested a hand on her shoulder. "Why so sad?"

"I'm a princess. I come with responsibility, duty, the paparazzi, a stalker—"

"Oh, *pfft*." Luis waved a hand. "The man watches you like he's starving, and you're a juicy, prime rib steak."

She laughed. "I don't know if he loves me, or wants me enough to take on the baggage."

"The man has very broad shoulders. And I mean *really* broad. I think he can handle it, especially when he gets you at the end of it." Luis met her gaze. "Follow your heart, Sofie. It's time you do something for you, not always for everyone else. Now—" Luis looked at his watch "—it's time for you to go and wow the crowd."

She took a deep breath and rose.

She was already in her dress, with her sexy Oscar de la Renta shoes on.

"Luis, the dress is stunning."

"You make it that way."

The dress was sapphire blue, to complement the tiara. The bodice was covered in intricate metalwork dotted with crystals. It looked almost like a corset. It sat low, showing off her collarbones, but not too low. A princess never showed too much cleavage. The skirt was a shimmer of blue silk that fell in an A-line to the floor.

She didn't wear a necklace, because she wanted the tiara to be the star of the show. Dangly sapphire and diamond earrings were in her ears, and the tiara nestled in her hair.

"Gorgeous," Luis breathed.

"Thank you, Luis. For all your hard work putting me together."

"It was an honor, not work at all. Go." He shooed her out.

With a smile, she headed carefully down the stairs.

Rome was at the bottom, texting on his phone. When he heard her, he looked up and froze.

She stepped off the last step, and her heart took off, beating a mile a minute.

They both stared at each other.

He stole her breath. He wore a perfectly tailored

tuxedo. It made his shoulders seem wider, his legs longer. The crisp, white shirt was a contrast to his dark skin.

"You look hot," she said.

He shook his head, his lips curving. "You look stunning. Simply stunning, Sofie."

"Thank you."

"I want to put you in the car and drive away. Keep you all to myself."

She heard his unsaid words. *Keep her safe.*

"Maybe after..." she swallowed "...we could go away. Just the two of us."

She saw something in his eyes, but he stayed silent.

Her stomach twisted in knots. "Or not. Forget I—"

"I'd like that," he said. "A cabin in the mountains."

Her stomach relaxed and she smiled. "Or a deserted beach."

Desire flared in his eyes. "You got a little bikini, Princess?"

"Maybe."

"Shit." He adjusted his jacket. "Come on. Quit making me hard, we have a gala to attend." He grabbed her hands. "I'll be right with you. The entire time."

"I know."

"I've got something for you."

He lifted a small box and pulled something out of it. "It's not a million-dollar tiara, or anything like those funky rings you like."

He held up a small ring. It was a simple band with alternating diamonds and sapphires.

"A little something from me," he said.

Her pulse leaped. "I love it."

He slid it on her right hand.

She smiled at it. "It's perfect, Rome."

"Let's go," he said.

That's when Sofie spotted the envelope resting on the table. "What's that?"

Rome's face went blank. "Nothing."

"Rome—" She stepped closer.

He tried to block her.

"Rome, don't hide things from me."

He muttered a curse and let her pass.

She opened the envelope and pulled out a photo. It was of Sofie and Rome kissing.

"It was taken through the windows here, with a telephoto lens."

She looked so small against his big frame. They were kissing passionately. She would have liked a copy of it, except scrawled on the bottom of it in red ink were the words *He will die, too.*

"Oh, God." Nausea crawled through her stomach.

Rome took the picture and threw it onto the table. "Forget it."

"You're a target now," she said woodenly.

"Bodyguards are always targets. I don't care. I *want* the asshole to come for me."

"Don't say that." Maybe she should run. Go back to Caldova and hide. Whatever it took to keep Rome safe.

He cupped her face. "I've got this, Sofie. *We've* got it. Take a breath."

She managed a shaky one.

"We aren't going to let this asshole win. And the Black Fox gang can't have the tiara. Tonight, you'll shine, people will enjoy themselves, and your charity will raise a lot of money. If the Black Foxes or your stalker strike, we'll be ready for them."

She nodded.

"Ready?" he asked.

"I think so."

He held out an arm to her. "Will you give me the honor of escorting you, Princess?"

She slid her arm through his. She'd stand beside him every day for the rest of her life, if he let her.

CHAPTER SEVENTEEN

After the limousine pulled up at the Bently Reserve, Rome exited first. He scanned around.

The historic building was lit up, its impressive façade dominated by a row of huge columns. A red carpet led up the center of the wide stone steps at the front.

The crowds were being held back by temporary fences. Four Norcross guards moved into position, the lead one nodding at him. Cameras clicked and fans shouted.

Vander stepped into view wearing a tuxedo like he'd been born to it. His boss gave Rome a slow nod.

Rome pulled in a breath. He knew the others from Norcross would be around, and he also knew that Ace had a drone in the air, scanning for anyone who shouldn't be on the nearby rooftops. They were all wearing sleek earpieces they could activate if they needed them.

Rome hoped they didn't need them.

Leaning into the back of the limo, he held out a hand.

Sofie took it.

"Ready?" he asked.

She nodded and stepped out. There were cheers, and shouts, and screams. She smiled and waved to the crowd.

Rome motioned for her to walk ahead of him up the steps.

"No." She clamped her fingers on his arm. "You're walking with me, not behind me."

He scowled. "Sofie—"

"I'm not budging. I don't care what people think or say. You're mine. I'm walking with you."

Damn. She cut through every single one of his defenses. He gave a short nod.

She beamed at him.

He tucked her arm against his side and they started up the steps. There were more cheers and shouts.

Sofie looked exquisite. A true fairytale princess.

One who'd captured his heart.

His mom was right. Rome was all in with Sofie. Falling head over heels. The guys would rib him. He'd given Rhys, Saxon, and Easton plenty of shit about being whipped.

Now here Rome was, willing to do anything for a small princess with pink-gold hair.

They reached the top of the stairs, passed through the columns, and followed the crowd inside.

A woman stepped forward, dressed in a forest-green dress. "Welcome, Princess Sofia."

"Helen, the place looks amazing. You've done an incredible job."

"Wait until you see the main hall." Helen's gaze

moved to Sofie's head. "The Sapphire Wave tiara. It's even more stunning than the pictures."

"I feel like a princess." Sofie winked.

The event planner laughed. "Congratulations on the gala. On the entire exhibition. It's exceeded all our expectations."

"Everyone's worked so hard and I appreciate it."

"Go, find yourself a drink."

Rome and Sofie walked into the main hall.

"Oh, Rome."

It looked like a fairytale and perfect for a princess. The huge main hall looked magical and glowed with a golden light. Round tables filled the floor and two huge, circular chandeliers dangled from the high ceiling. By the columns at the sides of the room were cherry blossom trees in huge pots. A dance floor was set up at the far end of the space

As Sofie looked over the decor, Rome studied the people and the layout.

"The jewelry looks amazing," she said.

Like at the luncheon, several pieces were set under glass and resting on pedestals dotted around the space.

"Yeah." Rome saw Vander, along with Saxon and Gia, Harlow and Easton, and Haven and Rhys. With them were his mom and Liana.

Harlow waved and smiled at them. She looked stunning in a column of red.

"Everyone's here." Sofie looked a little stunned.

"They wanted to support you."

She sniffed, a suspicious shimmer in her eyes.

He frowned. "Sofie?"

She smiled and waved a hand. "I really like your friends, Rome."

"I think they're fixing to be yours as well." He led her over to them. "Come on, you haven't met Rhys yet."

"Well, I can guess he's the one who looks like Easton and Vander."

"Sofie, you look gorgeous," Gia exclaimed. The woman was wearing a black dress shot through with silver that left her shoulders bare.

As the women talked, Gia introduced Sofie to her parents and Rhys. Rome hugged his mom and sister.

"This place looks wonderful," his mom said. "I see Sofie's hand in it."

"She looks like a princess," Lia breathed.

"She is a princess," Rome said.

"Who's falling in love with her bodyguard." His sister shot him a smug look.

His gut knotted. Fuck, he hoped so.

Lia leaned in. "Lola would love her, and this."

His heart squeezed. "You look good."

His sister's green dress had a mermaid style bottom and showed off way too many curves.

"I look *sensational*. Especially in emeralds." She touched her ears, and then the emerald studded necklace around her throat. Both were from Sofie's private collection.

"Don't lose them," he warned.

She poked her tongue out.

They moved back to the others and Vander stepped up beside him.

"So far, so good," Vander murmured.

"Won't stay that way."

"Yeah." Vander's dark gaze sliced across the room. "I feel the itch too."

"We'll help you keep an eye on Sofie." Saxon looked like he wore a tuxedo every day. He was from a wealthy family, although he didn't get along well with his parents.

Music started up from the dance floor.

Sofia was showing the women some of the jewelry. Her face was alive, her tiara glittering. She waved her hands as she talked.

Right now, she'd forgotten the stress of the danger looming over her.

Three men in tuxedos moved through the crowd toward them. Titters and whispers followed the trio.

"Oh my God," someone whispered. "It's the Billionaire Bachelors of New York."

The man in the lead was tall and handsome, with thick hair and a strong jaw.

A woman stepped forward to intercept him, but the man sidestepped her with a smile. As one of the famous Billionaire Bachelors of New York, Zane Roth probably had plenty of practice avoiding unwanted attention.

Roth had made his fortune young and was the finance King of Wall Street. Norcross Security did a lot of work for Roth Enterprises. The billionaire had helped them out when Haven had been in danger, and a hundred-million-dollar Monet had been stolen from Easton's museum.

Behind him, the other two billionaires were night and day. One was blond, with an aristocratic, clean-shaven face that probably drove the ladies crazy. He moved like he'd had money all his life. The other man had olive skin, black hair, and a scowl on his rugged, scruff-lined features. He looked like he'd prefer to be somewhere else.

"Zane." Vander stepped forward, holding out his hand.

"Vander."

The men shook hands. Zane turned, smiling at their group.

Rome lifted his chin. He had a lot of respect for Zane Roth.

"I'm not sure all of you have met my friends, Liam Kensington." He gestured to the blond man, then the other. "And Maverick Rivera."

Kensington inclined his head. "A pleasure." He had a British accent.

Rome had heard of the real estate billionaire. He had a British father and an American mother, and was in property, construction, and hotels.

The other man just nodded and lifted his glass of what looked like Scotch.

Maverick Rivera was a tech billionaire and inventor. Rivera Tech developed all kinds of technology, including the best safes and security equipment in the world.

"Liam, Mav, these are the men of Norcross Security." Zane spotted Haven and smiled. "I see the lovely Haven is doing well and looking ravishing."

Rhys shifted. "She was doing really well when I fucked her on our dining room table before we came tonight."

Zane smiled and held up his hands. "I was just making an observation, Rhys. Glad to see you kept hold of her. Beauty, brains, and goodness all rolled up in a gorgeous package isn't easy to find."

Liam sipped his drink. "That's the truth. Although every socialite mama with marriage on the brain in New York is throwing her daughters at Zane since he was voted Sexiest Man of the Year last year."

Zane grimaced.

"Glad you could come tonight," Vander said.

Zane nodded. "I'm in town to do business with Easton."

Easton lifted his drink.

"And I didn't want to miss the gala. I dragged Liam and Mav with me."

Maverick grunted.

Liam elbowed the man. "We have to drag you out of your lab sometimes, Rivera."

"Plus this supports a great charity," Zane continued. "I admire Princess Sofia a lot."

Liam glanced over at Sofie. "There's a lot to admire."

Rome stiffened. Kensington was exactly what people would picture for Sofie. The man didn't have a royal title, but he was rich, successful, and good-looking.

"She's taken," Vander said.

Zane spun, eyebrows raised. "You fell for a princess, Norcross?"

"Not me."

Sofie turned, smiling their way. Her gaze found Rome's and her smile brightened.

"Rome?" Zane shook his head. "You are the *last* man I expected to take the fall."

"She's mine," Rome said.

"And in danger," Vander added.

The faces of all three billionaires turned serious.

"She has a stalker, and jewel thieves are targeting the exhibition," Rome said.

"Hell," Zane said. "If we can do anything, let us know." His friends both nodded.

"Thanks," Rome said.

The music changed and people started heading onto the dance floor.

Rome kept his gaze on Sofie. They'd keep her safe, whatever it took.

"GOD, LOOK AT THEM," Harlow murmured.

Sofie turned to look at the Norcross men. She glanced over the handsome, rugged group but her gaze went straight to Rome. So yummy. She couldn't wait to get him out of that tuxedo. She shivered.

"Oh, Zane's here," Haven said.

Sofie instantly recognized the handsome, dark-haired billionaire. They'd attended some events together in New York.

"Who is that hot, blond god with him?" Gia murmured.

"That's Liam Kensington," Sofia said. "And Tall, Dark, and Grumpy is Maverick Rivera."

"The Billionaire Bachelors of New York," Harlow said.

Gia sipped her champagne. "*Nice.*"

"Don't let your fiancé hear you," Haven warned.

Sofie looked around. The gala was going well. They had a full crowd. She saw that Rome's mother and sister looked like they were having a good time.

"Good evening, ladies."

The throaty, feminine drawl made Sofia look up to see a striking woman striding toward them.

She wasn't classically beautiful, but she sure caught the eye. She had bronze skin and ink-black hair cut in a short style that emphasized her long, graceful neck. Her makeup made her dark eyes stand out and her full lips were blood-red.

"Maggie," Harlow said. "You look like you should be on a catwalk."

The woman ran her hands down her bronze dress that looked like liquid. "I've never owned anything like this before. Very different to my usual jeans."

"Maggie works at Norcross Security," Harlow said. "She's a helicopter pilot." Harlow introduced her around. "And this is Princess Sofia."

"Well, it's my first time meeting royalty." Maggie smiled. "Do I bow or curtesy?"

"Shaking hands is fine. Please call me Sofie."

Maggie shook her hand. "I heard that you've been keeping Rome on his toes." The pilot winked. "Those boys need it. Keep it up."

But as the women continued to talk and laugh, Sofie couldn't quite relax and enjoy herself. She felt like there was a ticking time bomb somewhere. She looked at the well-dressed crowd. Was one of them her stalker? How many were members of the Black Fox gang?

"You all right?"

She smelled Rome's woody cologne, then felt his hand press against her lower back. He dipped his head.

She realized the men had joined them. She watched Easton drop a kiss on Harlow's mouth. Saxon tugged Gia to his side. Rhys pressed a kiss to Haven's temple.

They could be so easy with their affection. Sofie desperately wanted to lean into Rome and do the same.

Right now, they were close, but not close enough to set tongues wagging. She hated even that small distance.

"Sofie?" he asked.

She forced a smile. "Fine. I'm fine."

"You're not alone, beautiful." His face was serious.

She smiled. "I know." She wasn't. She often felt alone at events like these, even surrounded by people. Usually most people wanted the princess, not the woman behind the tiara.

Now she had Rome, and a smiling, good group of people who were here to support her.

She looked up at Rome.

And protect her.

"Your Highness?"

She turned to see an older gentleman in a white tuxedo, with a head full of salt and pepper hair smiling at her.

"Mr. Bradley!" He was a wealthy donor of the Victoria Foundation.

"May I have this dance?" he asked.

She felt Rome stiffen.

"Gia, feel like dancing, darling?" Saxon said.

Gia cocked her head. "Yes, I do feel like dancing with my hot fiancé."

As the pair moved to the dance floor, Saxon nodded at Rome.

"Rome, this is Mr. Bradley," Sofie said. "A very good supporter of my foundation."

Rome gave the man a flat stare. "Enjoy your dance."

Sofie practically heard the "I'll be watching." She took Mr. Bradley's arm.

They chatted and joined the whirl of dancers. She saw Saxon and Gia staying close, and Saxon winked at her.

Finally, the dance finished.

"Thank you, my dear," the older man said. "Always a pleasure."

"Absolutely a pleasure, Mr. Bradley. Tonight would not have been possible without your generous support."

"Truly a wonderful charity. You do such good work."

As he stepped away, she turned...and saw Prince Crispin of Sanovia. He smiled at her, a smarmy look on his face she was sure he thought looked charming.

"Sofie, darling, you look good enough to eat."

Her smile dissolved, but she dredged up her polite, princess smile. "Crispin, this is a surprise. I didn't see you on the guest list."

"It was last minute. I was in the States and knew I couldn't miss it." His perfect white smile widened. "And I am royalty, so I figured I'd give everyone a treat. And now you aren't alone."

She swallowed a snort. "Well, I hope you enjoy your evening." She stepped away.

Crispin grabbed her arm. "Let's give everyone a thrill. A prince and his princess dancing."

"I'm not your anything," she said.

"Paulina is out of the picture." He stroked a hand down her arm. "We were good, Sofie. Let's make up for lost time and have some fun."

"I don't think so." She tried to pull away from him.

His brow creased. "Sofie—"

Saxon appeared and slid an arm around her. "Let's go, Sofie."

She leaned into him, accepting the lifeline.

Crispin's face twisted and he didn't look so handsome anymore. "You replaced me?"

"We were a very short-lived mistake, Crispin. Let's leave it at that."

Vander materialized on her other side, his gaze locked on Crispin. "Sofie, you okay?"

Crispin glanced between Saxon and Vander. "Did you need two men to replace me, Sofia?"

Ugh. What had she ever seen in him? "Just go, Crispin."

Vander leaned in, his tone sharp as a blade. "You don't talk to her like that. Ever."

Vander's voice chilled Sofie's blood. Gosh, she really was glad that it wasn't directed at her.

Crispin froze, then dredged up some bravado. He straightened his tuxedo jacket. "Or what? I'll answer to you?"

One of Vander's dark brows rose. "No. You'll answer to *him.*"

Sofie turned her head.

Rome was striding toward them, his jacket flaring out

behind him, his jaw set, and his green gaze locked on Crispin.

He looked like a warrior ready for battle.

He also looked gorgeous. Sofie's pulse went crazy.

Across from her, Crispin swallowed.

Rome stopped and Saxon shifted her to him. He wrapped an arm around her middle, pulling her against him.

"You all right?" His voice was a deep rumble.

She nodded and pressed a hand to his chest, then slid it under his jacket.

Crispin watched them, his lips twisting. His mouth opened.

"Be careful what you say," Rome said.

"Crispin, this is Rome, Vander, and Saxon. All former military. All former special forces."

Crispin straightened. "Sofia, enjoy your evening." He stalked off.

Sofia had the sudden urge to laugh. She pressed her face to Rome's chest and giggled.

"Not sure this is funny, beautiful."

She looked up. "Oh, it's hilarious."

His lips twitched.

"Thank you," she said.

His fingers brushed her jaw. "I'd do anything for you."

Sofia felt like her insides melted.

Suddenly, Gia appeared.

"Well, after that, I think you need a drink, Sofie."

Sofie nodded. "Absolutely. Where's the champagne?"

CHAPTER EIGHTEEN

Rome watched Sofie chatting with a group of guests. One woman gestured to the Sapphire Wave tiara and Sofie nodded.

Turning away, he scanned the crowd. Nothing was amiss.

Ace arrived at his side, looking sharp in a dark gray tuxedo and a checked, silver bowtie. "Hanging in there?"

Rome grunted.

"I almost want something to happen." Ace crossed his arms, his gaze roving, then it jerked and tracked back to the dancers.

Rome followed the direction he was looking...and spotted Maggie dancing with a tall, tuxedo-clad man.

The man spun her, dipping her back, and Maggie laughed.

"What the fuck is she wearing?" Ace muttered.

Rome thought Maggie cleaned up nicely. Her dark hair gleamed and her eyes were dark and smoky. She wore a sleek bronze dress that showcased her long, lean body, and had a long slit up one side that showed off a toned leg. The dress dipped low in front, but as her entranced dance partner spun her, it showed that the back was virtually nonexistent.

"A dress," Rome said.

"And who the fuck is he?" Ace scowled. "He could be an asshole, a rapist, a murderer. And she's letting him paw her."

The guy was holding the helicopter pilot close, but not overstepping any lines. Maggie would have no problem punching anyone who did something she didn't like.

"I think they're just dancing." Rome let his gaze move across the room to Sofie.

She was with Harlow, Gia, and Haven, as well as Liana. They were all oohing over a jewelry display.

Ace shook his head. "I'm going to tell that pretty boy to keep his hands to himself." Ace stomped off toward the dance floor.

Shit. Ace was going to get a fist to the gut from Maggie if he kept this up.

Rome moved over to Sofie and the women.

"Oh my God," Harlow said. "Look at that ruby and diamond ring. It's to *die* for."

"It's beautiful," Sofie agreed.

"And expensive." Lia sipped her wine. She saw Rome and winked.

"It's a beauty," Gia agreed.

Harlow sighed. "It sure is. At least Easton can't buy it." She fingered the sparkly necklace at her neckline. "He's always trying to give me jewelry."

"Oh girl, you have it *tough*," Lia drawled.

Harlow smiled, and looked over at Easton. "I'm not complaining."

Lia tipped back her wine. "I think I'm going to dance with a billionaire." Her gaze locked on Zane, Liam, and Maverick. "Who gets to say that every day."

Harlow sipped her drink. "Me."

Lia shot the blonde a look. "I hate you." There was no heat in her words.

As his sister strode off, Rome froze. He didn't want his baby sister dancing with anyone.

Sofie appeared at his side. "Zane and the others are decent guys. They'll dance with Lia, but they won't take advantage."

He gave a short nod, and watched Zane smile and lead Lia to the dance floor.

"I want to touch you," Sofie murmured.

Rome's fingers curled into his palms. "Soon."

She looked around and nibbled her lip. "I keep waiting for...something."

He knew the feeling. "Maybe we'll get lucky." Maybe the Black Foxes and her stalker would steer clear.

"A girl can hope."

Rome saw Vander signal to him. "I'll be back." He watched her join the women again.

"Got a ping." Vander held up his phone and on it were two mug shots of two dark-haired men with scowling faces and empty looks in their eyes. "Dragan Tadic and Luka Kezman. Both former Serbian military. They were suspected of being part of the international jewelry thief gang, the Pink Panthers. It was broken up a few years ago and most of the leaders were sent to jail."

Rome had heard of the Pink Panthers. The gang had been made up of ex-soldiers with extensive military and paramilitary backgrounds. They'd carried out some audacious thefts before getting greedy and sloppy.

"Tadic and Kezman were recruited by the Black Foxes," Vander continued. "Both were also hired by tonight's catering company a week ago."

"Fuck." Rome glanced at the nearby waitstaff. He didn't see the pair anywhere. "They're here."

"Yes, but I haven't seen either of them."

"We have to find them." Rome circled the room, staying close to Sofie. He stared at every one of the uniformed servers holding trays of food and drinks. The sit-down dinner would start soon.

A woman bumped into him.

"Ooh, you're a big one, aren't you," she purred.

She was tall and thin, and wore a tiny scrap of a sparkly dress. She had a thick mass of black hair and a heavy accent. Probably Italian.

Rome sidestepped her. Sofie was laughing with Gia. She was fine.

"Easton, what are you doing?" Harlow's sharp voice.

Easton dropped to one knee beside Harlow. The woman went wide-eyed.

"*Oh.*" Gia clapped her hands together.

"Harlow, from the moment you came into my life, you drove me crazy," Easton said.

There was a smattering of laughter from their friends.

"You meet me toe to toe. Make me laugh. Let me take

care of you, and you take care of me in return. You light up my life, and you've made every damn thing I've ever done worthwhile."

Tears welled in Harlow's eyes. She cupped his jaw. "Easton." There was a wealth of love and feeling in her voice.

"You see me," Easton continued. "And you let me see you. I love you. When I think of the future, all I see is you."

"I love you too, Easton Alessandro Norcross."

Nearby, Easton's mom was crying, leaning into her husband.

Easton held up a small box and opened it. "Will you marry me?"

"Oh, Easton, yes—" Harlow's gaze narrowed. "*Wait*. Is that the ruby and diamond ring I saw on display before?"

Easton scowled. "Maybe."

"The very old, historic, and extremely expensive ring?" Harlow pressed a hand to her silk-clad hip.

"So?"

"It wasn't for sale!"

"Everything is for sale," Easton countered.

"Says the billionaire."

"I bought it for you." He blew out a breath. "The woman who is impossible to give anything to. It's damn lucky that I love you."

"Easton—"

He rose. "You liked it. It'll look beautiful on your hand. A symbol that you're mine, that we're a team." He lifted her hand and held the ring up. "It'll look even better when you're wearing just this in our bed."

Harlow gasped. "Easton, your parents are standing right there."

Rome could see that she was weakening.

Easton's voice lowered. "Say yes, Ms. Carlson. Be my wife."

A smile broke out on Harlow's face. "Yes, Mr. Norcross."

Easton smiled and slid the ring on Harlow's finger. Then he swept her into a wild kiss.

Applause broke out.

Sofie, with tears in her eyes, pressed a hand to her throat, watching with a warm look on her face.

Her brown gaze met Rome's.

Then the crowd shifted, blocking Rome's view of her. When he looked again, she was talking with some guests.

He scanned around again, and his gaze snagged on a couple partly hidden by one of the large pillars.

Hell. Ace had Maggie pinned against the marble. The pilot had one long leg wrapped around Ace's waist and the pair were going at each other like there was no one else in the room.

This had trouble written all over it.

Ace went through women fast and easily. He had a hell of a reputation.

Rome glanced back at Sofie, and saw she was talking with a woman. He frowned. It was the dark-haired woman who'd bumped into him before. He saw Sofie's face harden into angry lines.

Forgetting all about Ace and Maggie, he started forward.

The brunette waved an arm, bumping Sofie's champagne and spilling it. *Shit.* Who was this woman?

Laughing people cut in front of him. He saw a server in a uniform stop by Sofie and offer her a fresh flute of champagne.

She took it and when the man turned, Rome saw his face.

It was one of the Serbians. Tadic.

Fuck.

Rome glanced over and spotted another server behind Sofie, watching her intently.

Kezman.

Rome touched his ear and activated his earpiece. "Vander. Tadic and Kezman are on Sofie."

"I'm coming." Off to the left, he saw Vander pull away from his parents.

The Italian brunette said something to Sofie and the color drained from Sofie's face.

Shit. Rome picked up speed. He was almost to her.

Then the lights went out.

SOFIA TAMPED down her annoyance at the tipsy woman who'd spilled a drink on her. Dante Luzzago's girlfriend.

"I think you should sit down," Sofie said. "And not drink any more wine."

Dante had left the country after Robin Hood had

stolen back the jewelry Dante had snatched. Apparently, his girlfriend hadn't gone with him.

A server appeared, holding up a tray of fresh champagne. With a smile, Sofie took a glass and sipped it.

"The tiara is stunning." The woman mumbled in Italian. "It would look better on me."

Sofie stiffened. She spoke fluent Italian. "Good evening. Enjoy your night."

As she turned, her legs suddenly felt weak. A wave of dizziness washed over her.

Sofie frowned.

She looked up and saw a server with heavy features watching her. Her pulse spiked. She wanted Rome.

"Princess, I believe I'll just take the tiara," the annoying brunette drawled.

Sofie turned, panic slicing through her. The woman's gaze was now sharp and focused. *Oh, crap*. She was part of the Black Foxes, not just Dante's ditzy girlfriend.

A strong wave of dizziness hit Sofie, the edges of her vision swimming.

There was something in the champagne.

The lights went out.

She heard someone scream, and people calling out. Sofie knew the woman and the other Black Foxes were after her.

Rome had gone over several contingency plans.

Fighting down fear, she dropped to the floor, and crawled on her hands and knees under the nearest table.

"Where is she?" a deep voice growled.

"Find her!" the woman cried.

Sofie kept moving. She couldn't see well, but she had

to keep moving. She skirted some people's legs and crawled under another table, then another. She sent up a silent apology to Luis for crawling on the floor in her dress.

She had no idea which direction she was headed. She huddled under another table, and pulled the tiara off her head. It caught on her hair and she felt a sting.

The bastards were *not* getting this.

Someone bumped the table, and several women screamed.

Sofie darted out and dived under another table.

"Everyone please stay calm," a voice said over the loudspeaker. "It's just a small electrical issue and we'll have it dealt with shortly."

Sofie pulled out a thin tie from her bra. She tied the tiara to the underside of the table, right in the center.

"Stay safe," she whispered.

She crawled out, her hair half tumbling down. Now she needed to find Rome, or one of the others from Norcross.

Her throat was tight, but she rose. It was so dark, with just faint light near the edges of the room. She thought of Rome's strong arms holding her. His firm lips on hers.

She wasn't alone. She knew he'd be looking for her.

"I'm coming," she whispered.

She moved through the darkness. Anxious, confused voices echoed around her.

"They'll get it sorted soon," a man said.

"I can't see a *thing*," a woman cried.

Sofie bumped into a table, hitting one of her bruises. She swallowed a curse.

"Sofie!"

Rome's deep voice. She turned, her heart leaping. It sounded like he was on the other side of the room. She wanted to call out, but what if the Black Foxes were listening?

"Sofie."

Vander's voice. He sounded closer and she moved in that direction.

Suddenly, there was the sound of crashing plates and breaking glass. Screams broke out.

She bit her lip and heard people jostling. She bumped into someone.

"I'm sorry," she said.

"Sofia?"

Sofie stilled. It was Chantal Lockwood.

Could Sofie trust her? "Chantal, are you all right?"

"I'm fine. I'm *so* sorry this is happening at your gala."

"They'll get it fixed soon, I'm sure."

"Yes."

Another crash sounded nearby.

"Come on." Chantal took Sofie's arm. "Let's get out of the line of fire."

"I need to find my bodyguard. He isn't far away."

"Come," Chantal said. "We'll find him together."

They moved through several groups of people. When a large pillar appeared out of the gloom, Sofie realized they were near the edge of the room.

Not where she'd last seen Rome.

Her pulse spiked. "Chantal, this isn't the right way."

"It's safer out of the crush." The woman's grip tightened on Sofie's arm.

Sofie tried to pull away. "No, I think—"

The woman's nails dug into Sofie's skin. "No, you need to come with me."

Sofie sucked in a breath. "You're with the Black Fox gang."

"What? Black Fox gang? I've never heard of it." Chantal's crisp voice sounded bewildered.

Sofie frowned. The woman appeared genuinely confused, or she was a damn good actress. "The jewel thieves."

"Jewel thieves? You think I have something to do with that? Absolutely *not*."

Chantal sounded so sincere. Sofie's muscles relaxed a fraction, but she still remained worried. "I'm sorry, Chantal. There's so much going on, and maybe I was mistaken."

"It's fine." Chantal paused. "Come this way."

They edged along the room and Sofie strained to hear Rome's voice again. She wanted him so badly.

"Stop here," Chantal said.

"We should—"

"*Well done, pet*," a cultured voice whispered.

Sofie went as stiff as a board. She recognized that whisper.

"I'd do anything for you." Chantal's voice was filled with adoration.

Sofie blinked, fear chilling cold in her veins. "Chantal?"

The woman didn't even look at Sofie. She was looking at the shadowed figure looming over them.

Then the man stepped forward. "*Sofie, finally*."

Her stalker.

A faint chemical smell hit Sofie's senses. Where had she smelled that before?

He moved closer, and there was enough faint light that she could see his face.

"No," she breathed.

Lorenz Stalder. Tori's boyfriend.

The man moved and yanked a black cloth bag over Sofie's head.

CHAPTER NINETEEN

Rome fought back the fear filling his chest like concrete. He couldn't fucking see a thing. "Sofie!"

Where was she?

The lights came back on and he blinked. Worried, he stared at the panicked people. Couples clung to each other. Others looked uncertain and upset.

He frantically scanned the room.

There was no sign of Sofie.

His gut clenched and he felt the same horrible sensation he'd had when he'd lost Lola that long-ago day.

Vander materialized. "You see her?"

"No." *Fuck.*

Saxon, Rhys, and Easton joined them.

"Don't see her anywhere," Saxon said.

"Get everyone looking," Rome ordered.

"I'll ask Zane, Liam, and Mav to help," Easton said.

"We don't have penises, but our eyes work just fine." Gia waved at herself, Harlow and Haven.

"Go," Vander said to his sister.

The group spread out.

"You give her the ring?" Vander asked.

Rome nodded. He'd picked the ring because he knew it would look pretty on Sofie's delicate fingers, and because there was a tracker embedded in it.

"Where the fuck is Ace?" Vander barked.

"Here." Ace appeared. His long hair was no longer tied up, but instead brushed his shoulders. It looked like someone had been running their fingers through it. He had lipstick on the collar of his shirt.

Maggie joined them as well. "What's happening?"

Maggie's cheeks were flushed and her lipstick was gone.

Rome glanced between the two, but he had no time to contemplate them. "Sofie's missing. Track her."

Ace cursed and pulled out his phone. He swiped the screen, tapped. "Shit."

"Ace?" Rome growled.

"There's some sort of interference. Can't get a clear lock."

"Someone's jamming it," Vander said darkly.

Rome scanned and spotted the Italian brunette. "*Her*. She was with Sofie when the lights went out."

They shoved through the crowd.

The woman raised her head and when she saw them coming, her eyes widened.

She spun and ran into the crowd.

Rome broke into a sprint. He ignored the startled cries and shouts. He sensed Vander right behind him.

The woman sprinted out into a marble-lined hall. She wasn't so fast in her sky-high heels.

Suddenly, somebody rushed Rome from the side. A man crashed into him.

Grunting, Rome caught the man's weight and spun. He saw the uniform and recognized the face.

One of the Serbians.

"Where's the princess?" Rome demanded.

"Not with you." The man swung a fist.

Fear and anger coalesced into a horrible ball of rage. Rome blocked the man's punch, then launched his own fist right into the man's jaw.

With a grunt, the man staggered back. Rome kept hitting, his knuckles striking flesh. Soon, the man's teeth were bloodied and he dropped heavily to his knees.

"Where is she?" Rome said.

The man gave a gurgling laugh.

Rome's jaw clenched. He gripped the front of the man's shirt and punched him again, then again. Blood dribbled from the man's mouth.

"Rome, enough," Vander said.

Rome looked up. Vander was holding the brunette in front of him. She struggled, spitting Italian at him.

Vander shook her, and then said something in Italian in a low voice. The woman blanched and went still.

"Where is Princess Sofia?" Rome enunciated each word clearly.

The brunette sucked in a breath and looked away. The man on the ground made a choked sound.

Rome dragged the man up, ready to hit him again.

"She got away," the man bit out.

"When the lights went off, she ran," the woman added.

Dammit. Rome met Vander's gaze.

Suddenly, Ace sprinted toward them. "I got a faint trace. She's upstairs."

Rome released the man and he fell to the tiles. Vander waved some security guards over. "Hold them."

Rome hit the wide stairs at the end of the hall, taking them two at a time. Vander and Ace ran behind him.

At the top was a mezzanine level. Most of it was concealed from the main hall below by textured, lattice screens. Along the walls were loads of doors. As he shoved open one, he saw a stylish meeting room. He guessed the place was a rabbit warren of rooms and offices.

"Rome." Vander gripped his shoulder. "You can't help her if you go in hot, without a clear head."

Rome sucked in a breath. He knew that. He'd seen people die by running in without being prepared.

Right now, the soldier in him was fighting against the frantic man who knew his woman was in danger.

He couldn't fail her.

He locked down the molten emotions as best he could and nodded.

"Good." Vander turned to Ace. "Where?"

"This way." Ace pointed.

Vander pulled a Glock from under his jacket. Rome followed suit and pulled his own.

"Let's move." Vander said.

For a second, it was like being back on a Ghost Ops mission, with Vander giving orders. But this time the stakes were even higher. Sofie, the woman Rome loved, was in danger. Her life was on the line. Some sick fuck had her and Rome was going to make him pay.

Ace nodded at a door.

Rome lifted his foot, kicked the door open, and moved in.

The room was empty. "Clear."

Vander moved fast and silently, weapon up. "Let's find her."

Ace pointed and Rome advanced on the next door.

Hold on, Sofie. I'm coming.

SHE COULDN'T SEE A THING.

The bag over Sofie's head blocked all her vision, and she was being dragged by Lorenz. She stumbled.

"*Come, my sweet Sofie.*"

He was still using the creepy whisper. She still couldn't comprehend that her stalker was *Lorenz.*

She'd always liked the rare book dealer. He'd seemed decent, if a little quiet and staid. Tori had liked him.

But that bland face had been hiding a monster.

He dragged her up some stairs. The noise of the gala dimmed and she heard a door close.

All sound cut off, closing them in a private bubble. As far as she could tell, they were still in the building, but upstairs somewhere.

The bag was yanked off.

She blinked, and Lorenz's unremarkable face came into view.

Sofie took a step back. "You wrote those notes."

"Yes." He cocked his head, reminding her of a predator. "Did you like them?"

"You're sick, Lorenz."

"No, I'm just embracing the real me." His gaze moved to the top of her head. "I was hoping for the tiara as well. I have a buyer lined up, and they're willing to pay a lot of money for it."

Sofie's belly churned. "You're in the Black Fox gang too?"

His smiled sharpened. "Oh, I'm not just *in* the gang, my sweet princess, I run it. It was my brainchild."

She shook her head. "No." He'd been so unassuming.

"In my job, I have access to wealthy families, and the research on valuable, historic jewelry." He shrugged a slim shoulder. "It was so easy to recruit others eager to join me. Eager to bolster their dwindling family fortunes."

"You're scum. Your gang hurt Tori."

Lorenz's smile twisted. "I know. I ordered it."

Sofie felt like the floor fell away. She couldn't breathe or find her balance. "What?"

"It started years ago, when I was at university. I found a pretty victim. I watched the light leak from her eyes while I loved her." He shivered, clearly reliving his sick, twisted fantasy. "It was near-perfect, but she died too soon. I wasn't patient or experienced enough to dispose of her body well." He expelled a breath. "I was almost caught. It took me a long time to find the courage to indulge my passions again."

Sofie couldn't put all the pieces together. "Why? Why hurt people?" She couldn't understand.

"We all have skills, sweet Sofie. Mine is showing a woman the ultimate death, and the pleasure in it."

He was totally unhinged and made her want to vomit. "You didn't rape Tori."

"No, I had two of my men do it." He smiled. "I watched. And I fueled her fear and paranoia afterward."

Sofie felt a tear slide out of her eye and track down her cheek. "She trusted you, cared for you."

"She wasn't what I'd hoped she would be. I wish I'd been brave enough to take her life myself, but by then, I'd seen *you*." Lorenz stepped closer.

Sofie steeled herself.

"That first woman I released into death, she had beautiful hair just like yours. The color of a beautiful sunset."

"Well, you can't have me."

"You're mine." He leaped at her.

Sofie fell back and they hit the floor. They wrestled across the carpet, and he clamped his hands on her neck.

No! She scissored her legs and rolled. Lorenz cursed.

She scrambled onto her hands and knees. "Rome is coming. He'll tear you apart."

Lorenz's face twisted. "You should never have let that big brute touch you, Sofia."

Sofie shoved to her feet and edged toward the door. "I love it when he touches me."

Lorenz made an angry sound and charged. He slammed her into the wall, all the air rushing out of her.

She elbowed him, then stabbed her fingers into his eyes.

He yelped.

She scratched his face. "Rome's coming, and you're going down. Your Black Fox gang is going down too."

Lorenz made an enraged sound, like an angry animal.

"I've been gathering information on your gang for months," she spat. "I'll hand it over to the authorities, along with you, and your gang of criminals will be dismantled piece by piece."

"You know nothing." He advanced on her, his hair and jacket askew from their fight.

"I know a lot." She lifted her chin. "I learned more every time I stole back the jewelry your gang had taken."

His eyes widened. "*You're* Robin Hood."

Sofie smiled.

Lorenz's face twisted, a crazed edge flaring in his eyes. He sprang at her.

The elbow to her jaw had her seeing stars. They both gripped each other, staggered, and then he knocked her down. Her knees hit the floor hard.

He leaned over her, his hands clamping around her neck, fingers digging in.

Sofie coughed and struggled. It hurt so badly.

She thought of Tori.

She thought of Rome.

Dammit, she'd fight.

She punched Lorenz between the legs.

He let her go, and let out a horrible gurgle of sound.

With a sob, Sofie pushed to her feet and spun, cursing her skirts.

Lorenz grabbed a handful of her dress. She tried to wrench away and heard fabric rip.

Then she was sprinting.

She shoved out the door and ran through several rooms. *Where was the way out?* She sprinted through another door and came out on the mezzanine level.

She heard the sound of the gala below.

Find Rome. Get to Rome.

She ran, her dress flaring behind her.

"You're mine, Sofie," Lorenz gritted out behind her. "I'm going to kill you, here and now."

She heard his footsteps. He wasn't far behind.

Panting, she found herself hemmed in. At the railing, she looked through the gaps in the lattice, and saw people down below, resuming the party.

A hysterical sob built in her chest. She met Lorenz's gaze.

He was disheveled, blood at the corner of his mouth, and scratches from her nails down his face.

"No, you're not." Sofie glared at him. "I have everything to live for, and one of those things is seeing you pay for your crimes."

Lorenz shoved her and made an angry noise. Her hip smacked into the stone railing.

"Sofie!"

Rome's deep shout.

Relief flared in her. She turned her head and saw him sprinting down the mezzanine level toward her. Ace and Vander were right behind him.

Rome—big, powerful, his eyes blazing.

She smiled. "And there's the other thing I have to live for."

"He can't have you! No one can have you!"

She heard more shouts and looked the other way.

Saxon, Easton, and Rhys were running up the stairs from the other direction.

"It's over, Lorenz."

"No! *No.*"

He gave her a vicious shove.

With a cry, Sofie fell back and Lorenz's weight pushed her straight through the flimsy lattice. The wood cracked and she tipped over the railing.

No. For a second her heart stopped, then it raced with terror.

She fell through the air, and threw her arms out. Then a hand gripped her wrist, jerking her to a stop. She dangled in the air.

She looked up into Lorenz's strained face.

"You're mine, Sofie. Mine to kill."

CHAPTER TWENTY

When Rome saw Sofie fall over the edge, his brain shut down.

No. Fucking, no.

He wasn't losing her. She was sweetness and light. Love and laughter.

She was his to love, protect, and cherish. Even though she did a damn good job of protecting herself.

This asshole couldn't have her.

Rome leaped forward, and saw her dangling from the asshole's hand. Screams started down below.

"Back up or I'll drop her." The man's voice was strained.

"Fuck you." Rome focused solely on Sofie. He reached down and clamped a hand on her slim wrist, below where her stalker was holding her.

"I said back off!" With his other hand, the man pulled a small knife.

"Rome!" Sofie cried, her legs kicking and her dress flowing around her.

The asshole stabbed at Rome. He felt the prick of the blade on his arm, but blocked out the pain. Nothing would make him let go of Sofie.

"Vander," Rome growled.

Like a shadow, Vander appeared. He rammed a brutal punch into the man's kidneys.

The attacker cried out and let Sofie go. Rome took her full weight.

Vander followed through with a hard hit with the butt of his Glock to the back of the man's head. The guy crumpled.

Vander grabbed the back of the man's jacket and dragged him away.

Rome looked down at Sofie. "I've got you."

"I love you," she said. "This is bad timing, I know, but I wanted you to know."

There was an explosion of emotion in Rome's chest. "I love you too, beautiful."

Her brown eyes shimmered with tears. "You do? Oh, God."

"How about we talk more about this once you aren't dangling off the side of a balcony," he suggested.

He grabbed her with his other hand.

"You know, I'm actually pretty good at dangling off buildings."

Rome grunted. "You'll be retiring from that."

With a smooth jerk of his arms, he pulled her up and over the railing.

Below, the gala guests cheered.

Rome yanked her into his arms and sank to the floor.

"Fuck." He let out a shuddering breath. "When I couldn't find you... When I saw you go over the edge..."

She cupped his cheek. "I'm right here, Rome. Perfectly alive. I knew you'd come."

He shuddered.

"I knew you'd never give up. Like you never gave up with Lola. You were only a child, you did nothing wrong, Rome. The blame for what happened to her lies solely with her attacker. We can't live in fear. We have to live."

"I know, beautiful. Damn, Lola would have loved you."

Sofie shoved her ripped skirt aside, straddled him, and kissed the hell out of him.

Rome didn't care where they were, or that they had an audience. She was safe. He felt her pulse under his fingers.

He kissed her with all the love he felt until she moaned into his mouth.

"Well, looks like Rome has things under control."

Rome lifted his head and saw Zane Roth standing behind the Norcross men, grinning at them. There was amusement and relief on all the men's faces.

With a laugh, Sofie leaned against Rome's chest and he held her tight.

Vander dragged her attacker to his feet. "I'll get this waste of space to Hunt. We've got the others downstairs."

"His name is Lorenz Stalder," Sofie spat. "He's a rare book dealer and the head of the Black Fox gang."

"Antiquarian." Ace snapped his fingers. "That relates to rare and antique books."

"And I assume he restores the old book leather with

chemicals," Vander said. "Like the chemical we found on the notes."

Sofie gripped Rome. "He was Tori's boyfriend. He ordered her attack and stalked me."

"He'll get everything he deserves," Vander drawled.

Rome saw the bruising starting on Sofie's neck. He touched the marks gently. "I could just kill him right now."

Stalder froze. Rage welled in Rome and he glared at the man, imagining his revenge.

"Hey." Sofie's face filled his view. "No grisly murders today."

His rage softened as he took her in. She was so damn resilient.

Then she lifted her hand, and blinked at the blood on her fingers. Her eyes widened. "Rome?"

"He cut me a little. It's fine."

"You're bleeding! We need a doctor, a hospital—" She scrambled up.

Rome rose and swept her into his arms.

"You can't carry me, you're hurt—"

"Like hell. I'm carrying you out of here and not letting you go. Ever."

Her lips parted, her eyes swimming with emotion.

"*You* need the hospital," he said.

"No." She shook her head. "There will be people and reporters." Then she winced and touched her neck.

"Yes," he said.

"*No*. Get Ryder to come to the house. I want him to look at that cut of yours." She was using her princess voice.

"Anything else, Your Highness?"

"I want a hot bath, and for you to never let me go."

He hitched her higher. "That I can do."

Norcross Security whisked them out of the gala without stopping to talk to the curious onlookers or the gathering reporters outside.

Rome knew that Gia and the rest of the women would want to see Sofie, but getting her safe and checked over were the most important things.

As they were leaving, he caught Easton's gaze. "Can you get my mom and sister home?"

The oldest Norcross brother nodded. "Count on it."

"Wait!" Sofie cried. "I completely forgot about the Sapphire Wave tiara. I hid it."

The men all paused.

"You forgot about the million-dollar, historic tiara?" Rome said.

Her cheeks heated. "I was kind of busy."

Vander shook his head, a faint smile curving his lips. "Tell me where it is. I'll get it."

Sofie told him, then Rome slid into the back of the X6 and settled her in his lap.

She snuggled into him. "Right here."

He pressed his cheek to the top of her head. "Right here what?"

"This is where I feel safest. Where I belong."

He tightened his hold on her, realizing that it was nowhere near as tight as the hold this woman had on his heart.

SOFIE SAT STILL as Ryder lifted the ice pack off her neck.

"Well, that lovely skin will have some ugly bruises for a bit." The paramedic glanced at Rome. "You beat the asshole up?"

"Vander did," Rome replied.

Rome had shed his jacket and was standing in his bloodstained shirt. She'd watched Ryder clean and bandage the cut on his arm, which thankfully had been shallow.

She hated seeing the blood on his shirt.

"Sofie, take some painkillers before bed." Ryder closed his black bag. "But you're lucky. There's no other permanent damage to your neck or voice box."

Tonight the paramedic was wearing dark blue scrubs, with his muscular, tattooed arms on display. He'd come from the clinic where he donated his time.

"Thank you, Ryder."

"Don't mention it." He shook Rome's hand. "You both take it easy. You've earned it."

Sofie watched Rome show the paramedic out. When he returned, he scooped her off the stool.

"Rome, I can walk."

"Don't care. I'm carrying you."

He headed up the stairs and straight to her bathroom. When he stepped inside, she gasped.

"*This* is what you were doing when you disappeared earlier."

He set her down and she took in all the candles dotted around and the tub filled with warm, fragrant water.

His big hands reached for the zipper of her dress.

"Let's get you in." He pulled the dress off her, then she felt him stiffen. "Hell, Sofie."

She looked into the mirror. He was standing behind her, the candlelight flickering on his dark skin. She was wearing a tiny whisper of lace that cupped her breasts and gossamer panties in sapphire blue. He didn't seem to see her scrapes and bruises.

He ran a hand down her arm and she shivered.

"There it is." He dropped a kiss to her shoulder.

Oh. She was so turned on. Her muscles felt liquid, and she was slick between her thighs.

"I could have lost you today," he murmured.

"No. I told Lorenz that I'd fight with everything I had. I have so much to live for."

Rome opened the bustier and let it drop. She turned and undid the buttons on his shirt.

In the flickering candlelight, they undressed each other.

"So beautiful." He kissed her. "I can't believe you're mine."

"So hot and handsome." She touched his strong jaw. "I can't believe you're mine."

She still wasn't sure how they'd make this work—his job, her duties—but she wasn't worrying about that tonight.

Tonight was a celebration of life and love.

Lola and Tori had both had their chance to live stolen from them, but Rome and Sofie would live for all of them. They'd make every moment count.

When they were both naked, he lifted her and

stepped into the tub. He sank down, shifting her to straddle him.

Sofie smiled at the big, gorgeous hunk in the bath. "How often do you have a bath?"

His nose wrinkled. "Never."

She nipped his jaw, his lips. "Well, I like them, so expect to do it more often."

He cupped her breasts in his palms. "If you're with me, I think I can struggle through." His face turned serious. "I love you, Sofie. So much." He leaned forward and kissed her injured neck.

She arched her head back. He gently kissed every one of her bruises. Her insides turned to mush. No one had ever cherished her like Rome.

They took their time—slow kisses, long caresses, soft moans.

Finally she couldn't stand it anymore. She grabbed the condom he'd set out on the side of the tub earlier. She tore it open, then fumbled in the water to slide it on him.

"Fuck," he growled.

Sofie rose up, notched the head of his hard cock between her legs, and slowly sank down.

Their gazes stayed locked, staring into each other's eyes as he filled her.

"Sofie. My Sofie."

His big hands clenched on her ass.

"Rome. My Rome."

She moved faster, water splashing.

Soon they were kissing wildly, bodies straining. Then she felt a rush of pleasure, her muscles clenching.

"Oh, *Rome.*" She burst apart.

He swallowed her cries, then pushed her down.

"Sofie...*fuck*." He groaned through his own release.

Afterward, they were both breathing heavily, holding onto each other.

"I want to wake up with you every day," he said. "I don't want to only see you occasionally."

"I want that too."

"But I have a job here. One I like. One that I need."

She knew he wasn't talking about a financial need. His work filled a void inside him. She understood that.

"I know." She sucked in a breath. "And I have duties. Some of them international." She touched his cheek. "But I want to make this work, Rome. Whatever it takes."

He kissed her again. "Whatever it takes."

"Now, how about we get out of this bath and into bed?"

"Tired, Princess?"

"No." She slid her hand down his abs. "Not at all."

"I'M FINE, Mum. I promise you."

On the laptop screen, Sofie looked at her worried parents. Beside them was Caro, her face creased with concern.

Sofie sat in the kitchen, which was drenched with mid-morning light. She'd slept like a rock the night before, held in Rome's arms. He was around somewhere, with his phone glued to his ear.

Sofie met her best friend's gaze. "It was Lorenz all

along. He ran the Black Fox gang, he hurt Tori, and he was stalking me."

Caro cursed—using some very creative phrases in a few different languages.

Sofie's father raised a brow.

Caro flushed. "Your Highness, I'm sorry."

"Don't be sorry," Sofie's father said. "If not for years of royal protocol and fatherly instincts, I'd do the same."

"I'm not hurt," Sofie assured them.

"I can see the bruises, sweetie," her mother said. "I'd like a crack at Lorenz myself."

"He's in police custody and the Black Fox gang is in disarray. The San Francisco PD are working with Interpol to dismantle the gang's operations." Sofie felt a small kernel of warmth inside her, like a flower unfurling.

It was over.

She'd anonymously turned over all the information that she'd collected. San Francisco PD, via Hunt, had received a package from Robin Hood. Her stalker was behind bars and the Black Fox gang was done. The Sapphire Wave tiara was secure in the safe at Norcross Security.

"When are you coming home?" her mother demanded. "I want to hug you."

"Oh, well." Sofie pushed a strand of hair behind her ear. "The thing is—"

Caro leaned forward. There was glee on her face. "You met someone."

Sofie broke out in a grin. "I'm in love and ridiculously happy."

Her parents blinked.

"Mum, Papa, I'd like to move to San Francisco." She glanced around. "Actually, I'm thinking of buying this house that I've been renting." She met their startled gazes. "Rome is...amazing." Her smile widened as she thought of him. "He's big, strong, protective. He saw the real me from the first moment we met."

"Rome?" her father said. "Rome Nash? Your bodyguard from Norcross Security?"

Sofie pulled in a breath. "Yes."

Her father scowled. "This is highly improper. He has an excellent resume and I know he was a special forces soldier, but bodyguards do not get personally involved with the people they're protecting."

"Ooh," Caro said. "That's much better than a movie star."

Rome walked in and Sofia waved him over.

He stopped behind her, resting his hands on her shoulders and squeezed. He sat down beside her.

"I'm Rome Nash." His voice was its usual deep rumble.

On-screen, her mother's and Caro's mouths dropped open.

"Mr. Nash," her father said.

"Your Highness." Rome inclined his head.

"It is against protocol for a bodyguard to get personally involved with his charge, Mr. Nash."

"I'm aware of that. I struggled with it for a while." Rome squeezed Sofie's hand. "But I couldn't keep my distance from Sofie. I think I started falling for her from the first time I saw her."

She softened. "Rome."

"My God, our little girl is in love, Nicholas. It's right there on her face." Sofie's mother clasped her hands together, smiling.

"Prince Nicholas," Rome said, "the fact of the matter is, how I feel about Sofie makes me more protective of her. I'd fight the entire world to keep her safe."

Sofie leaned into him. Then she heard a sniffle and looked back at the screen. "Caro, are you crying?"

"No." Caro dashed away the tears on her cheeks. "I'm just so happy."

Rome gave a bemused shake of his head.

"Papa, Rome and I don't want to be living in different countries. I love San Francisco and I love his friends."

Her father shifted. "You have royal duties—"

Sofie opened her mouth.

Then her father held up a hand. "Which can be scaled back and altered."

Her pulse leaped and this time she squeezed Rome's fingers. "Thank you, Papa."

"As the new Caldovan ambassador to the Americas, you can take on the bulk of the North and South American duties."

Excitement whipped through her. "It would be my honor to do that. And I can expand my charity work here as well."

"And when you're required here in Europe—" her father's gaze moved to Rome "—I'm certain you'll have your own personal bodyguard to accompany you."

Rome nodded. "I'd like to be in charge of all Sofie's security."

The prince nodded. "Norcross Security does excellent work. I'll speak with Mr. Norcross about a special contract."

They talked some more, and her parents and Caro planned to come out to San Francisco to visit soon.

After the call ended, Sofie jumped to her feet and spun in a circle. "I'm *so* happy." She felt so light. She threw herself into Rome's arms.

He carried her to the couch, and sat down with her straddling him. She pressed her lips to his.

"*Mmm.*" Her man could really kiss. She shivered.

"There it is." He cupped her ass and things got heated. "Let's go upstairs."

She tugged at his shirt. She needed skin. "Here."

The doorbell rang.

"Damn." Frowning, Rome pulled out his phone and looked at the screen. He growled. "I'm surprised it took them this long."

"Who?"

"The gang's here to check on you." He cupped her cheek. "Later, we'll have time for the two of us."

She smiled and shimmied against the hard bulge beneath her, enjoying his low groan. "I'll be counting down."

Rome went and opened the front door.

Their friends poured in.

"We brought ribs for lunch," Gia called out. Saxon was holding several grocery bags.

"I've got beer." Vander cradled a box under one arm.

"We brought the wine," Harlow announced.

Haven smiled. "Rhys and I made salads. Okay, we bought salads from the store."

Rome's mom and sister entered. Lia winked. "I brought an appetite."

As Rome slid an arm around Sofie, the two women smiled at them, happiness in their eyes.

Friends. Love. Laughter.

Sofie looked up. Rome's green gaze was on her.

She was happy beyond words.

"Can you die from happiness?" she asked.

"Nope." He nipped her lips. "Buckle up, Princess, because there's lots more happiness ahead for you."

I hope you enjoyed Sofie and Rome's story!

Stay tuned for more Norcross Security stories coming later in 2021 (and yes, that includes Vander's story!)

Want to know more about the Billionaire Bachelors of New York? Then check out the first book in the **Billionaire Heists trilogy**, *Stealing from Mr. Rich* (Zane Roth's story). **Read on for a preview of the first chapter.**

Keen to learn more about photographer Dani Navarro Ward and her former Navy SEAL husband, Callum Ward? Then check out their story, *Uncharted*, in the **Treasure Hunter Security** series.

Don't miss out! For updates about new releases, free books, and other fun stuff, sign up for my VIP mailing list and get your *free box set* containing three action-packed romances.

Visit here to get started: www.annahackett.com

Would you like
a FREE BOX SET
of my books?

PREVIEW: STEALING FROM MR. RICH

Monroe

The old-fashioned Rosengrens safe was a beauty.

I carefully turned the combination dial, then pressed closer to the safe. The metal was cool under my fingertips. The safe wasn't pretty, but stout and secure. There was something to be said for solid security.

Rosengrens had started making safes in Sweden over

a hundred years ago. They were good at it. I listened to the pins, waiting for contact. Newer safes had internals made from lightweight materials to reduce sensory feedback, so I didn't get to use these skills very often.

Some people could play the piano, I could play a safe. The tiny vibration I was waiting for reached my fingertips, followed by the faintest click.

"I've gotcha, old girl." The Rosengrens had quite a few quirks, but my blood sang as I moved the dial again.

I heard a louder click and spun the handle.

The safe door swung open. Inside, I saw stacks of jewelry cases and wads of hundred-dollar bills. *Nice.*

Standing, I dusted my hands off on my jeans. "There you go, Mr. Goldstein."

"You are a doll, Monroe O'Connor. Thank you."

The older man, dressed neatly in pressed chinos and a blue shirt, grinned at me. He had coke-bottle glasses, wispy, white hair, and a wrinkled face.

I smiled at him. Mr. Goldstein was one of my favorite people. "I'll send you my bill."

His grin widened. "I don't know what I'd do without you."

I raised a brow. "You could stop forgetting your safe combination."

The wealthy old man called me every month or so to open his safe. Right now, we were standing in the home office of his expensive Park Avenue penthouse.

It was decorated in what I thought of as "rich, old man." There were heavy drapes, gold-framed artwork, lots of dark wood—including the built-in shelves around the safe—and a huge desk.

"Then I wouldn't get to see your pretty face," he said.

I smiled and patted his shoulder. "I'll see you next month, Mr. Goldstein." The poor man was lonely. His wife had died the year before, and his only son lived in Europe.

"Sure thing, Monroe. I'll have some of those donuts you like."

We headed for the front door and my chest tightened. I understood feeling lonely. "You could do with some new locks on your door. I mean, your building has top-notch security, but you can never be too careful. Pop by the shop if you want to talk locks."

He beamed at me and held the door open. "I might do that."

"Bye, Mr. Goldstein."

I headed down the plush hall to the elevator. Everything in the building screamed old money. I felt like an imposter just being in the building. Like I had "daughter of a criminal" stamped on my head.

Pulling out my cell phone, I pulled up my accounting app and entered Mr. Goldstein's callout. Next, I checked my messages.

Still nothing from Maguire.

Frowning, I bit my lip. That made it three days since I'd heard from my little brother. I shot him off a quick text.

"Text me back, Mag," I muttered.

The elevator opened and I stepped in, trying not to worry about Maguire. He was an adult, but I'd practically raised him. Most days it felt like I had a twenty-four-year-old kid.

The elevator slowed and stopped at another floor. An older, well-dressed couple entered. They eyed me and my well-worn jeans like I'd crawled out from under a rock.

I smiled. "Good morning."

Yeah, yeah, I'm not wearing designer duds, and my bank account doesn't have a gazillion zeros. You're so much better than me.

Ignoring them, I scrolled through Instagram. When we finally reached the lobby, the couple shot me another dubious look before they left. I strode out across the marble-lined space and rolled my eyes.

During my teens, I'd cared about what people thought. Everyone had known that my father was Terry O'Connor—expert thief, safecracker, and con man. I'd felt every repulsed look and sly smirk at high school.

Then I'd grown up, cultivated some thicker skin, and learned not to care. *Fuck 'em.* People who looked down on others for things outside their control were assholes.

I wrinkled my nose. Okay, it was easier said than done.

When I walked outside, the street was busy. I smiled, breathing in the scent of New York—car exhaust, burnt meat, and rotting trash. Besides, most people cared more about themselves. They judged you, left you bleeding, then forgot you in the blink of an eye.

I unlocked my bicycle, and pulled on my helmet, then set off down the street. I needed to get to the store. The ride wasn't long, but I spent every second worrying about Mag.

My brother had a knack for finding trouble. I sighed.

After a childhood, where both our mothers had taken off, and Da was in and out of jail, Mag was entitled to being a bit messed up. The O'Connors were a long way from the Brady Bunch.

I pulled up in front of my shop in Hell's Kitchen and stopped for a second.

I grinned. *All mine.*

Okay, I didn't own the building, but I owned the store. The sign above the shop said *Lady Locksmith.* The logo was lipstick red—a woman's hand with gorgeous red nails, holding a set of keys.

After I locked up my bike, I strode inside. A chime sounded.

God, I loved the place. It was filled with glossy, warm-wood shelves lined with displays of state-of-the-art locks and safes. A key-cutting machine sat at the back.

A blonde head popped up from behind a long, shiny counter.

"You're back," Sabrina said.

My best friend looked like a doll—small, petite, with a head of golden curls.

We'd met doing our business degrees at college, and had become fast friends. Sabrina had always wanted to be tall and sexy, but had to settle for small and cute. She was my manager, and was getting married in a month.

"Yeah, Mr. Goldstein forgot his safe code again," I said.

Sabrina snorted. "That old coot doesn't forget, he just likes looking at your ass."

"He's harmless. He's nice, and lonely. How's the team doing?"

Sabrina leaned forward, pulling out her tablet. I often wondered if she slept with it. "Liz is out back unpacking stock." Sabrina's nose wrinkled. "McRoberts overcharged us on the Schlage locks again."

"That prick." He was always trying to screw me over. "I'll call him."

"Paola, Kat, and Isabella are all out on jobs."

Excellent. Business was doing well. Lady Locksmith specialized in providing female locksmiths to all the single ladies of New York. They also advised on how to keep them safe—securing locks, doors, and windows.

I had a dream of one day seeing multiple Lady Locksmiths around the city. Hell, around every city. A girl could dream. Growing up, once I understood the damage my father did to other people, all I'd wanted was to be respectable. To earn my own way and add to the world, not take from it.

"Did you get that new article I sent you to post on the blog?" I asked.

Sabrina nodded. "It'll go live shortly, and then I'll post on Insta, as well."

When I had the time, I wrote articles on how women—single *and* married—should secure their homes. My latest was aimed at domestic-violence survivors, and helping them feel safe. I donated my time to Nightingale House, a local shelter that helped women leaving DV situations, and I installed locks for them, free of charge.

"We should start a podcast," Sabrina said.

I wrinkled my nose. "I don't have time to sit around recording stuff." I did my fair share of callouts for jobs, plus at night I had to stay on top of the business-side of the store.

"Fine, fine." Sabrina leaned against the counter and eyed my jeans. "Damn, I hate you for being tall, long, and gorgeous. You're going to look *way* too beautiful as my maid of honor." She waved a hand between us. "You're all tall, sleek, and dark-haired, and I'm...the opposite."

I had some distant Black Irish ancestor to thank for my pale skin and ink-black hair. Growing up, I wanted to be short, blonde, and tanned. I snorted. "Beauty comes in all different forms, Sabrina." I gripped her shoulders. "You are so damn pretty, and your fiancé happens to think you are the most beautiful woman in the world. Andrew is gaga over you."

Sabrina sighed happily. "He does and he is." A pause. "So, do you have a date for my wedding yet?" My bestie's voice turned breezy and casual.

Uh-oh. I froze. All the wedding prep had sent my normally easygoing best friend a bit crazy. And I knew very well not to trust that tone.

I edged toward my office. "Not yet."

Sabrina's blue eyes sparked. "It's only *four* weeks away, Monroe. The maid of honor can't come alone."

"I'll be busy helping you out—"

"Find a date, Monroe."

"I don't want to just pick anyone for your wedding—"

Sabrina stomped her foot. "Find someone, or I'll find someone for you."

I held up my hands. "Okay, okay." I headed for my office. "I'll—" My cell phone rang. *Yes.* "I've got a call. Got to go." I dove through the office door.

"I won't forget," Sabrina yelled. "I'll revoke your best-friend status, if I have to."

I closed the door on my bridezilla bestie and looked at the phone.

Maguire. Finally.

I stabbed the call button. "Where have you been?"

"We have your brother," a robotic voice said.

My blood ran cold. My chest felt like it had filled with concrete.

"If you want to keep him alive, you'll do exactly as I say."

Zane

God, this party was boring.

Zane Roth sipped his wine and glanced around the ballroom at the Mandarin Oriental. The party held the Who's Who of New York society, all dressed up in their glittering best. The ceiling shimmered with a sea of crystal lights, tall flower arrangements dominated the tables, and the wall of windows had a great view of the Manhattan skyline.

Everything was picture perfect...and boring.

If it wasn't for the charity auction, he wouldn't be dressed in his tuxedo and dodging annoying people.

"I'm so sick of these parties," he muttered.

A snort came from beside him.

One of his best friends, Maverick Rivera, sipped his wine. "You were voted New York's sexiest billionaire bachelor. You should be loving this shindig."

Mav had been one of his best friends since college. Like Zane, Maverick hadn't come from wealth. They'd both earned it the old-fashioned way. Zane loved numbers and money, and had made Wall Street his hunting ground. Mav was a geek, despite not looking like a stereotypical one. He'd grown up in a strong, Mexican-American family, and with his brown skin, broad shoulders, and the fact that he worked out a lot, no one would pick him for a tech billionaire.

But under the big body, the man was a computer geek to the bone.

"All the society mamas are giving you lots of speculative looks." Mav gave him a small grin.

"Shut it, Rivera."

"They're all dreaming of marrying their daughters off to billionaire Zane Roth, the finance King of Wall Street."

Zane glared. "You done?"

"Oh, I could go on."

"I seem to recall another article about the billionaire bachelors. All three of us." Zane tipped his glass at his friend. "They'll be coming for you, next."

Mav's smile dissolved, and he shrugged a broad shoulder. "I'll toss Kensington at them. He's pretty."

Liam Kensington was the third member of their trio. Unlike Zane and Mav, Liam had come from money, although he worked hard to avoid his bloodsucking family.

Zane saw a woman in a slinky, blue dress shoot him a welcoming smile.

He looked away.

When he'd made his first billion, he'd welcomed the attention. Especially the female attention. He'd bedded more than his fair share of gorgeous women.

Of late, nothing and no one caught his interest. Women all left him feeling numb.

Work. He thrived on that.

A part of him figured he'd never find a woman who made him feel the same way as his work.

"Speak of the devil," Mav said.

Zane looked up to see Liam Kensington striding toward them. With the lean body of a swimmer, clad in a perfectly tailored tuxedo, he looked every inch the billionaire. His gold hair complemented a face the ladies oohed over.

People tried to get his attention, but the real estate mogul ignored everyone.

He reached Zane and Mav, grabbed Zane's wine, and emptied it in two gulps.

"I hate this party. When can we leave?" Having spent his formative years in London, he had a posh British accent. Another thing the ladies loved. "I have a contract to work on, my fundraiser ball to plan, and things to catch up on after our trip to San Francisco."

The three of them had just returned from a business trip to the West Coast.

"Can't leave until the auction's done," Zane said.

Liam sighed. His handsome face often had him voted the best-looking billionaire bachelor.

"Buy up big," Zane said. "Proceeds go to the Boys and Girls Clubs."

"One of your pet charities," Liam said.

"Yeah." Zane's father had left when he was seven. His mom had worked hard to support them. She was his hero. He liked to give back to charities that supported kids growing up in tough circumstances.

He'd set his mom up in a gorgeous house Upstate that she loved. And he was here for her tonight.

"Don't bid on the Phillips-Morley necklace, though," he added. "It's mine."

The necklace had a huge, rectangular sapphire pendant surrounded by diamonds. It was the real-life necklace said to have inspired the necklace in the movie, *Titanic*. It had been given to a young woman, Kate Florence Phillips, by her lover, Henry Samuel Morley. The two had run away together and booked passage on the Titanic.

Unfortunately for poor Kate, Henry had drowned when the ship had sunk. She'd returned to England with the necklace and a baby in her belly.

Zane's mother had always loved the story and pored over pictures of the necklace. She'd told him the story of the lovers, over and over.

"It was a gift from a man to a woman he loved. She was a shop girl, and he owned the store, but they fell in love, even though society frowned on their love." She sighed. "That's true love, Zane. Devotion, loyalty, through the good times and the bad."

Everything Carol Roth had never known.

Of course, it turned out old Henry was much older

than his lover, and already married. But Zane didn't want to ruin the fairy tale for his mom.

Now, the Phillips-Morley necklace had turned up, and was being offered at auction. And Zane was going to get it for his mom. It was her birthday in a few months.

"Hey, is your fancy, new safe ready yet?" Zane asked Mav.

His friend nodded. "You're getting one of the first ones. I can have my team install it this week."

"Perfect." Mav's new Riv3000 was the latest in high-tech safes and said to be unbreakable. "I'll keep the necklace in it until my mom's birthday."

Someone called out Liam's name. With a sigh, their friend forced a smile. "Can't dodge this one. Simpson's an investor in my Brooklyn project. I'll be back."

"Need a refill?" Zane asked Mav.

"Sure."

Zane headed for the bar. He'd almost reached it when a manicured hand snagged his arm.

"Zane."

He looked down at the woman and barely swallowed his groan. "Allegra. You look lovely this evening."

She did. Allegra Montgomery's shimmery, silver dress hugged her slender figure, and her cloud of mahogany brown hair accented her beautiful face. As the only daughter of a wealthy New York family—her father was from *the* Montgomery family and her mother was a former Miss America—Allegra was well-bred and well-educated but also, as he'd discovered, spoiled and liked getting her way.

Her dark eyes bored into him. "I'm sorry things

ended badly for us the other month. I was..." Her voice lowered, and she stroked his forearm. "I miss you. I was hoping we could catch up again."

Zane arched a brow. They'd dated for a few weeks, shared a few dinners, and some decent sex. But Allegra liked being the center of attention, complained that he worked too much, and had constantly hounded him to take her on vacation. Preferably on a private jet to Tahiti or the Maldives.

When she'd asked him if it would be too much for him to give her a credit card of her own, for monthly expenses, Zane had exited stage left.

"I don't think so, Allegra. We aren't...compatible."

Her full lips turned into a pout. "I thought we were *very* compatible."

He cleared his throat. "I heard you moved on. With Chip Huffington."

Allegra waved a hand. "Oh, that's nothing serious."

And Chip was only a millionaire. Allegra would see that as a step down. In fact, Zane felt like every time she looked at him, he could almost see little dollar signs in her eyes.

He dredged up a smile. "I wish you all the best, Allegra. Good evening." He sidestepped her and made a beeline for the bar.

"What can I get you?" the bartender asked.

Wine wasn't going to cut it. It would probably be frowned on to ask for an entire bottle of Scotch. "Two glasses of Scotch, please. On the rocks. Do you have Macallan?"

"No, sorry, sir. Will Glenfiddich do?"

"Sure."

"Ladies and gentlemen," a voice said over the loudspeaker. The lights lowered. "I hope you're ready to spend big for a wonderful cause."

Carrying the drinks, Zane hurried back to Mav and Liam. He handed Mav a glass.

"Let's do this," Mav grumbled. "And next time, I'll make a generous online donation so I don't have to come to the party."

"Drinks at my place after I get the necklace," Zane said. "I have a very good bottle of Macallan."

Mav stilled. "How good?"

"Macallan 25. Single malt."

"I'm there," Liam said.

Mav lifted his chin.

Ahead, Zane watched the evening's host lift a black cloth off a pedestal. He stared at the necklace, the sapphire glittering under the lights.

There it was.

The sapphire was a deep, rich blue. Just like all the photos his mother had shown him.

"Get that damn necklace, Roth, and let's get out of here," Mav said.

Zane nodded. He'd get the necklace for the one woman in his life who rarely asked for anything, then escape the rest of the bloodsuckers and hang with his friends.

Billionaire Heists

PREVIEW: TEAM 52 AND THS

Want to learn more about the mysterious, covert *Team 52*? Check out the first book in the series, *Mission: Her Protection.*

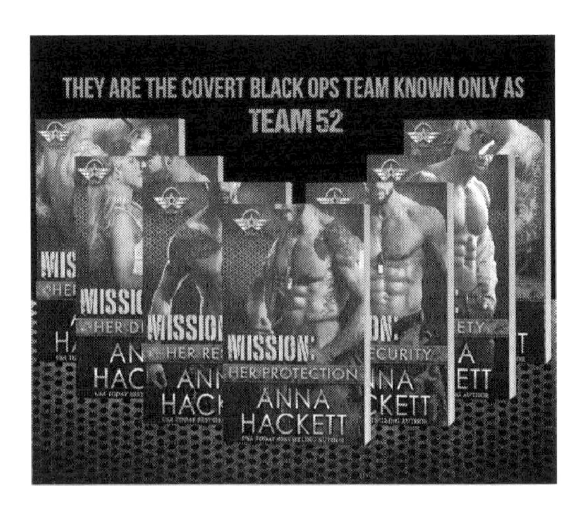

When Rowan's Arctic research team pulls a strange object out of the ice in Northern

Canada, things start to go wrong...very, very wrong. Rescued by a covert, black ops team, she finds herself in the powerful arms of a man with scary gold eyes. A man who vows to do everything and anything to protect her...

Dr. Rowan Schafer has learned it's best to do things herself and not depend on anyone else. Her cold, academic parents taught her that lesson. She loves the challenge of running a research base, until the day her scientists discover the object in a retreating glacier. Under attack, Rowan finds herself fighting to survive... until the mysterious Team 52 arrives.

Former special forces Marine Lachlan Hunter's military career ended in blood and screams, until he was recruited to lead a special team. A team tasked with a top-secret mission—to secure and safeguard pieces of powerful ancient technology. Married to his job, he's done too much and seen too much to risk inflicting his demons on a woman. But when his team arrives in the Arctic, he uncovers both an unexplained artifact, and a young girl from his past, now all grown up. A woman who ignites emotions inside him like never before.

But as Team 52 heads back to their base in Nevada, other hostile forces are after the artifact. Rowan finds herself under attack, and as the bullets fly, Lachlan vows to protect her at all costs. But in the face of danger like they've never seen before, will it be enough to keep her alive.

Team 52

Mission: Her Protection

Mission: Her Rescue

Mission: Her Security

Mission: Her Defense

Mission: Her Safety

Mission: Her Freedom

Mission: Her Shield

Also Available as Audiobooks!

Want to learn more about *Treasure Hunter Security*? Check out the first book in the series, *Undiscovered*, Declan Ward's action-packed story.

One former Navy SEAL. One dedicated archeologist. One secret map to a fabulous lost oasis.

Finding undiscovered treasures is always daring, dangerous, and deadly. Perfect for the men of Treasure Hunter Security. Former Navy SEAL Declan Ward is haunted by the demons of his past and throws everything he has into his security business—Treasure Hunter Security. Dangerous archeological digs – no problem. Daring expeditions – sure thing. Museum security for invaluable exhibits – easy. But on a simple dig in the Egyptian desert, he collides with a stubborn, smart archeologist, Dr. Layne Rush, and together they get swept into a deadly treasure hunt for a mythical lost oasis. When an evil from his past reappears, Declan vows to do anything to protect Layne.

Dr. Layne Rush is dedicated to building a successful career—a promise to the parents she lost far too young. But when her dig is plagued by strange accidents, targeted by a lethal black market antiquities ring, and artifacts are stolen, she is forced to turn to Treasure Hunter Security, and to the tough, sexy, and too-used-to-giving-orders Declan. Soon her organized dig morphs into a wild treasure hunt across the desert dunes.

Danger is hunting them every step of the way, and Layne and Declan must find a way to work together...to not only find the treasure but to survive.

Treasure Hunter Security

Undiscovered

Uncharted

Unexplored

Unfathomed

Untraveled
Unmapped
Unidentified
Undetected
Also Available as Audiobooks!

ALSO BY ANNA HACKETT

Norcross Security

The Investigator

The Troubleshooter

The Specialist

The Bodyguard

Billionaire Heists

Stealing from Mr. Rich

Blackmailing Mr. Bossman

Team 52

Mission: Her Protection

Mission: Her Rescue

Mission: Her Security

Mission: Her Defense

Mission: Her Safety

Mission: Her Freedom

Mission: Her Shield

Mission: Her Justice

Also Available as Audiobooks!

Treasure Hunter Security

Undiscovered

Uncharted

Unexplored

Unfathomed

Untraveled

Unmapped

Unidentified

Undetected

Also Available as Audiobooks!

Eon Warriors

Edge of Eon

Touch of Eon

Heart of Eon

Kiss of Eon

Mark of Eon

Claim of Eon

Storm of Eon

Soul of Eon

Also Available as Audiobooks!

Galactic Gladiators: House of Rone

Sentinel

Defender

Centurion

Paladin

Guard

Weapons Master

Also Available as Audiobooks!

Galactic Gladiators

Gladiator

Warrior

Hero

Protector

Champion

Barbarian

Beast

Rogue

Guardian

Cyborg

Imperator

Hunter

Also Available as Audiobooks!

Hell Squad

Marcus

Cruz

Gabe

Reed

Roth

Noah

Shaw

Holmes

Niko

Finn

Devlin

Theron

Hemi

Ash

Levi

Manu

Griff

Dom

Survivors

Tane

Also Available as Audiobooks!

The Anomaly Series

Time Thief

Mind Raider

Soul Stealer

Salvation

Anomaly Series Box Set

The Phoenix Adventures

Among Galactic Ruins

At Star's End

In the Devil's Nebula

On a Rogue Planet

Beneath a Trojan Moon

Beyond Galaxy's Edge

On a Cyborg Planet

Return to Dark Earth

On a Barbarian World

Lost in Barbarian Space

Through Uncharted Space

Crashed on an Ice World

Perma Series

Winter Fusion

A Galactic Holiday

Warriors of the Wind

Tempest

Storm & Seduction

Fury & Darkness

Standalone Titles

Savage Dragon

Hunter's Surrender

For more information visit www.annahackett.com

ABOUT THE AUTHOR

I'm a USA Today bestselling romance author who's passionate about ***fast-paced, emotion-filled*** contemporary and science fiction romance. I love writing about people overcoming unbeatable odds and achieving seemingly impossible goals. I like to believe it's possible for all of us to do the same.

I live in Australia with my own personal hero and two very busy, always-on-the-move sons.

For release dates, behind-the-scenes info, free books, and other fun stuff, sign up for the latest news here:

Website: www.annahackett.com

Printed in Great Britain
by Amazon

86439697R00176